BOys

by

Scott Semegran

MUTT PRESS

Austin

Second Edition

Mutt Press
Austin, Texas
http://www.muttpress.com
info@muttpress.com

ISBN 978-0692470114

Photo of Scott Semegran by Lori Hoadley
Cover Illustration by Andrew Leeper & Scott Semegran
Edited by Brandon R. Wood & Robyn Smith

Books by Scott Semegran:
Sammie & Budgie
Boys
The Spectacular Simon Burchwood
The Meteoric Rise of Simon Burchwood
Modicum
Mr. Grieves

Find Scott Semegran Online:
https://www.scottsemegran.com
https://www.goodreads.com/scottsemegran
https://www.twitter.com/scottsemegran
https://www.facebook.com/scottsemegran.writer
https://www.instagram.com/scott_semegran

For Lori

Table of Contents

The Great and Powerful, Brave Raideen

The little boy sat on the floor in his room surrounded by his toys--Micronauts action figures, Hot Wheels race cars, Star Wars action figures and vehicles, Evel Knievel doll and motor cycle, Shogun Warriors in various sizes, and a pile of Legos intermixed from various sets. His name was William. His mother called him Billy, just like his uncle who died ten years earlier in the Vietnam War was called, but he liked to be called William. More than anything, he liked to play in his room all by himself with all of his toys surrounding him on the floor. In his room, he was safe. He liked that.

He had a vivid imagination and enjoyed introducing the different toys to each other, intersecting their fictional worlds into one. The few times that other neighborhood children were allowed in his room, they had an issue with that, the fictional worlds colliding.

They all said to William, "Micronauts don't fight Star Wars people!"

"And why not?" William said.

"Because Micronauts aren't in the movie *Star Wars*, dummy!" they all said.

The other neighborhood children weren't allowed in his room after that. William spent most of his time after school in his room although he would occasionally venture into the back yard, a large grassy area with a tall oak tree in the back near the fence, a mostly completed treehouse perched up in its canopy. With two rooms to play in--one inside and one outside--his world seemed rather large; there wasn't much need to go anywhere else except for school. School, to him, was an evil place. He hated going to school.

William stood up one of his Shogun Warriors, the one called Brave Raideen (the tall one painted red and black with a bow and arrow and a crazy, silver mask that made him look like King Tut or something), and he said, "What are you going to do about that jerk Randy at school?" William made his voice as low and gravelly as possible to speak like what he thought Brave Raideen would sound like.

"I don't know," William said in his normal voice.

"You should do something to scare him *real good*," Brave Raideen said.

"Like what?" William said, curious.

"You should get the thing in your mommy's nightstand. That'll scare him *real good*!" said Brave Raideen, then laughing an evil laugh.

"Yeah!" William said, jumping to his feet. He tossed Brave Raideen to the side, opened his door, and ran down the hallway to his parents' room, his long, lanky arms swinging like those of a spider monkey. His mother heard him running and called out to him.

"Billy? What are you doing?"

"Nothing, mom!" he said, entering her bedroom and running around the queen-size bed to where her nightstand sat. He laid down on his stomach in front of the nightstand and reached under the bed. "Randy is going to be sorry he messed with *me*."

He wrapped his hand around the metal railing of the bed frame then slid his hand down the length of it until he found what he was looking for: a small key wedged between the mattress and the frame. He propped up on his knees and looked at the nightstand--a cheap Sears piece made of particle board to look like oak with various things of his mother's on top like a bottle of nail polish, a women's magazine, a lamp, an alarm clock, a remote control for the TV, a framed photo of William with his step-dad--then he slid the key into the keyhole above the handle of the nightstand drawer.

"I hope this still works," he said, whispering to himself, turning the key to the right, and then turning it to the left. The lock popped and he slid the drawer open. "Yes!"

Inside the drawer were three things: a Bible, a vibrator that looked more like a skinny curling iron than a sex toy, and a 25-caliber American Derringer pistol. That gun was considered a "lady gun" by firearms enthusiasts, but to William, it was James Bond's gun since it looked similar to the 9mm Walther pistol in the Bond movies. He picked up the gun and held it tightly, aiming at an imaginary target on the wall, picturing Randy's stupid face looking scared in his mind.

His mother called to him from the other side of the house and said, "Billy? Are you in my room?"

"Yes, mommy!" he said, putting the small pistol in the pocket of his shorts and closing the drawer. "I needed a tissue!" He locked the drawer and placed the key back where he found it then ran to his room.

"Please respect mommy's privacy and stay out of her room!"

"Yes, mommy! Sorry, mommy!"

Back in his room, he returned to his place on the floor and propped up Brave Raideen, restoring his majestic stance in the middle of the toy congregation.

"Did you get it?" said Brave Raideen, his voice as menacing as William could make it.

"Yes, I got *it*," William said. He pulled the gun out of his pocket and showed it to Brave Raideen.

"I have taught you well, young Shogun Warrior."

William smiled at Brave Raideen, pleased with himself.

***

William attended Crestridge Elementary School in Converse, Texas. He was in the second grade. Like most of his schoolmates, William lived in a nice, suburban neighborhood and he rode his Huffy bike to school almost every morning, unless it rained or was overly foggy. William didn't like fog. He worried the fog would eat him if he rode his bike into it. On the front of his bike, strapped to the handlebars, was a wire basket which he used to carry his lunchbox. The metal lunchbox had a cartoon image of Luke Skywalker and Princess Leia on the side--Luke wielding a lightsaber and Leia brandishing a blaster--while Darth Vader loomed over them from the sky. Inside the lunchbox was a peanut butter and jelly sandwich, a bag of Fritos, a Little Debbie cupcake, a Thermos of juice, and the 25-caliber American Derringer pistol. The gun rattled inside the lunchbox as it bounced up and down on the ride to school.

"I'm going to scare Randy *real good*," William said to himself as he briskly peddled his bike.

Later that day, while William stood in line for lunch, he knew he wanted to move the pistol from his lunchbox to his pocket so he could take it with him outside to recess, which immediately followed lunch. He asked his teacher, Ms. Brookshire, if he could use the bathroom before going into the cafeteria.

"Yes, you may William. Don't forget to wash your hands afterwards," she said.

"Yes, Ms. Brookshire," he said, then departed the line for the bathroom.

Inside, he locked the door to the last toilet stall, opened the lunchbox, and pulled out the small pistol. It's black, gunmetal shined brightly under the fluorescent lights in the bathroom, and he could see the muddled reflection of his face in its side, an unrecognizable, smeared facsimile of his face. He admired the pistol for a few seconds then slipped it into the front pocket of his Levi's Jeans. It fit snuggly in his small pocket. Again, he was pleased with himself then left the bathroom to rejoin his class for lunch. When he got back in line, he accidentally bumped into Darren, a plump kid with frizzy hair, freckles, and a sassy mouth.

"Hey, watch where you're going, you dufus!" Darren said, irritated, then shoved William with his elbow.

William didn't apologize. He put his hand in his pocket and held the pistol grip tight, thinking of the look he hoped to see on Randy's face when it was time to confront him on the playground after lunch.

***

Behind the school and beyond a long stretch of blacktop basketball courts, the playground equipment majestically stood in the sun, waiting for the children to come out for recess. The school bell rang loudly and a sea of kids poured out of the back doors of the school, flooding the playground with laughter and screams and chatter, red balls bouncing and flying, and teachers huddling to gossip. Everyone enjoyed the respite from the school routine--kids and teachers alike--except for William. He dreaded recess every day because of that jerk Randy. Instead of playing, William stood at the corner of the playground, peering across the blacktop, keeping an eye on Randy's whereabouts around the swing set or jungle gym. Randy was not in William's class but their classes shared a segment of recess together, a twenty minute period of torture. After scanning the entirety of the playground, William eventually found Randy on the opposite end, wearing his usual fascist uniform--blue striped t-shirt, brown corduroy pants, white tennis shoes, short-cropped hair--and shoving a girl to the ground. William slipped his hand in his pocket and gripped the pistol grip.

"I'll show you!" he said, stomping across the blacktop, his face red. "I'll show you *real good*."

William beelined for Randy, both hands in his pockets, his face searing with anger and resentment and hurt. Any kid in his path quickly moved out of it, looking at poor William with confusion since he was generally considered a sweet boy by all the students and teachers. Randy, too busy laughing at the crying girl on the ground, didn't notice William until he was right next to him, huffing and puffing and panting and sweating. He looked at William's red face and laughed.

"You eat a hot pepper or something?" he said, stepping over the girl toward William.

William just stood there, huffing and puffing, his hand gripping the pistol in his pocket tightly, thoughts rushing through his mind like scenes in a movie. The visions in his brain caught his attention and the scene in front of him blurred out of focus. He imagined blasting Randy in the gut with his pistol and felt satisfaction while watching him crumple to the ground, his arms wrapped around his midsection, writhing on the ground in agony. The daydream faded to black with explosions like fireworks in his eyes. The next thing he knew, he was on the ground, his back in some gravel, Randy on top of him thrashing him about, then Ms. Brookshire lifting Randy by his shirt collar, scolding his bad behavior.

"You are going to spend some time in the office, mister!" she said to Randy, a sour look on his face. "You go right now. I'll see you there in ten minutes."

She released his collar and he sulked off, kicking a rock innocently sitting on the blacktop. Ms. Brookshire knelt next to

William and helped him up. He dusted himself off, his face still red but red with embarrassment, not anger.

"Are you all right, sweet William?" she said.

"Yes, Ms. Brookshire," he said. He did his best to hold back the tears but his eyes sprung a leak.

"Don't you worry. I'll make sure they punish that rascal *real good*."

"Thanks, Ms. Brookshire."

She instructed her class to line up to go back inside. William got in the back of the line, embarrassed and dejected. As his class made its way inside, William watched Randy approach the door closest to the principal's office. William didn't know what was going to happen to Randy but whatever happened, he hoped it involved a paddling and a call to his parents. He slipped his hand in his pocket to make sure the pistol was still there and hadn't popped out during the ruckus. Feeling its cold, metal body gave him a sense of relief while he followed his classmates back inside the school.

***

After school and in the backyard of his home, William dragged Brave Raideen with one hand across the grass toward the tall oak tree with the treehouse up top. In his other hand was a wad of action figures--Han Solo, Spider-Man, Batman, a Micronaut missing his head and one leg--cinched at the wrists by a rubber band. When he reached the base of the tree, he set the wad of action figures on the grass and placed a dangling rope hanging from the tree around the neck of Brave Raideen. Up in the tree, a pulley attached to the treehouse waited for William's queue to work and so he pulled on the rope to lift up Brave Raideen. William wasn't strong enough to carry Brave Raideen with him up the wooden ladder attached to the side of the tree. After Brave Raideen reached the top, hanging stiffly in midair like a condemned criminal with a noose around his neck, William shoved Spider-Man (his favorite) in his pocket while the other action figures held on to the rubber band so he could climb the ladder to the treehouse. Once up and inside, he pulled Brave Raideen into the treehouse with an old wooden cane then released him from the noose. He was setting up his toys when his mother called for him.

"Billy?" she said, yelling from the back patio, her floral-patterned kitchen apron around her waist, her auburn hair in a tight bun at the back of her head. "Billy? Are you in the treehouse?!"

"Yes, mommy!" he said, calling back.

"Come in when it gets dark, please."

"Yes, mommy!"

The treehouse was a six-foot by six-foot wooden structure, mostly enclosed, and sparsely furnished inside--a two by eight wood plank was attached to the wall inside to function as a bench, a milk crate was turned upside down and used as a table, a throw rug that smelled like mildew and old dog lay under the milk crate, tying the room together. It wasn't much but to William, it was a boy's heaven. The doorway to the treehouse faced the back patio to his family's house and the window, the single portal on the opposite side of the treehouse, faced the wooded area behind William's house. The window's sill also served as a stage for William's dramatic reenactments of comic book or movie scenes, his action figures the pawns in his make-shift plays. He set Han Solo, Spider-Man, Batman, and the Micronaut on the window sill while Brave Raideen watched from the floor.

"Almost ready," William said.

Outside in the woods, some colored movement caught his eye. He reached under the milk crate for a pair of military binoculars--a wonderful present from his father last Christmas/Hanukkah--and he examined a tree in the distance with a strange blueish blob near its trunk. He discovered a face peeking at him, a face he was familiar with: Randy's face. Still wearing his blue-striped shirt, he peered around the tree at William's treehouse while William peered through his binoculars at Randy. And to his absolute, utter astonishment, Randy waved at him, a wilted gesture of surrender. William dropped the binoculars and rubbed his eyes. He couldn't believe what he was seeing. It was as if he was witnessing Darth Vader handing Princess Leia a bouquet of beautiful flowers as a peace offering, just plain weird. He picked up his binoculars and looked some more. Randy gestured if he could come over and William reluctantly nodded. He turned and sat on the floor, all his toys around him, and braced himself. 'What have I done?' he thought. 'What does Randy want?'

A few moments later, he heard the sound of someone scaling the tree. At the threshold of the doorway, the familiar short-cropped hair and blue eyes cautiously appeared, and then slowly the rest of Randy came in the treehouse, sitting on the floor and looking around curiously.

"Wow! This is so cool," he said. "I've seen this treehouse before but never inside. You're so lucky."

William smirked then looked up at the ceiling, an open space where the roof was unfinished, some leaves and branches poking through, and he sighed.

"Yeah, but Steve is too busy to finish. He works all the time. He's my step-dad."

"At least he does *something* for you. All my dad does is--" Randy said, then he started to cry. William was shocked at the sudden display of emotion from his bully. Randy turned his head to reveal a bruised spot on his jaw near his ear lobe. It was pretty clear, even to William, that he had been slugged and it looked like it really hurt.

Randy sniffled then wiped his nose on his short sleeve. "I just wanted to say I was sorry for shoving you at school today."

"It's OK," William said, embarrassed.

"No! It's not OK. I don't know why I did it. I guess I was tired of being bullied by my dad."

"Your dad?" William said, surprised.

"When the school called and told him what I had done to you, my dad got real mad. He said I was no good. It hurt so bad when he hit me that I knew I must have hurt you bad too. So I wanted to say I was sorry. Do you forgive me?"

"Ummm."

"No one made me come here and do it. I just feel bad is all."

"OK. I forgive you," William said, smiling.

"Yeah?!" Randy said, delighted.

"Yeah."

"The Secret Crestridge Handshake?" Randy said, extending his hand out to William. He was happy to finally be offered the opportunity to perform the secret ritual (which he knew by heart) with another student. I would tell you the choreographed steps to The Secret Crestridge Handshake but then it wouldn't be a secret anymore. The two friends completed the shake flawlessly and laughed. "We did it!"

"Yeah."

"What is that?" Randy said, pointing at Brave Raideen.

"That's Brave Raideen. He's a Shogun Warrior."

"Oh. Why is Han Solo standing next to Spider-Man?" Randy said, pointing at the window sill.

"I don't know. I like to make up new stories with all my toys," William said, sulking, waiting for a disapproving sneer from Randy.

"Oh! That's neat. Let's make up a new story together!"

Surprised, William smiled and handed Han Solo to Randy. They rearranged the toys together, setting the stage for a new story.

***

William's mother pulled the meat loaf from the oven, set it on the stove to cool, and then wiped her manicured hands on her apron. Her husband Steve, William's step-dad, would be home from work soon and he was almost always on-time--something William's natural father never was. They divorced when William was a baby and William spent some time in the summers with his natural father; the rest of the year he lived with his mother, Pam, and Steve (whom he called Steve, not Dad). Steve liked to eat as soon as he got home from work so he would have time to watch the evening news and deflate from his stressful day by drinking a cold Pearl Beer. Looking out the window, Pam realized it was getting dark and that William (or Billy, as she liked to call him) was still out back, playing in the treehouse. She hadn't heard him come back inside and decided to fetch her son. She turned off the oven and went outside.

On the patio, she could see William's head bobbing around in the treehouse. She was about to call his name when she noticed another head in there, leaving her bewildered.

'Does Billy have a *friend* up there?' she thought. He didn't mention to her about having anyone over. How could she have not noticed? She called to William and he appeared, standing in the doorway of the treehouse.

"Yes, mommy?" he said, calling back to her.

"Do you have someone up there with you?"

"Yes, mommy. My friend Randy from school."

"Randy?" she said, sorting through the list of names of kids she knew from the neighborhood or from the school. The name seemed very familiar to her but she couldn't place his face. "Does Randy need to go home? Or does he want to eat with us?" she said.

"I don't know. Let me ask him," he said, disappearing back into the treehouse.

She scratched her head and pondered some more. 'Randy? That name sounds so familiar,' she thought.

A moment later, William appeared in the doorway, this time with his friend Randy, whom his mother had never seen in person before although she had heard William describe the bullying he received from Randy many, many times before. Not putting two and two together at that very moment, she was pleased to see her son playing with another child.

"Randy wants to eat with us!" William said.

"OK, come inside then," she said, raising an approving thumb.

The two boys quickly huddled and discussed something that Pam couldn't hear. When they were done, they separated, gave each other a high five, put about a foot of space between each other, and then braced themselves to jump. Before Pam could scream for them to stop, immediately worried that they would hurt themselves, the two boys were airborne. They dropped to the ground, quick and heavy like two sacks of potatoes, and when they touched the Earth, a loud bang rang out--the discharge from the 25-caliber American Derringer pistol in his pocket--startling the slumbering birds in the woods behind their house, setting them in flight. Both boys crumpled to the ground. Randy quickly got up. William did not.

Pam ran to her son who was laying in the grass in a fetal position. She knew he wasn't dead because he was moving but a large blood stain covered the majority of his right thigh. He was bleeding profusely and, not having any foresight whatsoever that this would happen, she didn't know what to do.

"Oh my god!" she said, violently shaking. She knelt next to her son and picked him up, wrapping him in her apron. She quickly took him in the house while Randy followed her inside.

***

Pam stared at her apron while she waited for her son in the lobby of the emergency room. Randy sat quietly in a chair next to her, playing with a Rubik's Cube she had in her purse, something she kept with her in case William ever got bored. She stared at the blood on her apron and marveled at the sheer amount of it and how it changed the colors of the floors from white and yellow to a dingy, brownish maroon. After William was taken away by some nurses, Pam asked Randy how William came to have her pistol in his pocket, but Randy didn't know. She wasn't quite sure what to think of that and, mostly, she felt extreme anguish for what had happened to her son and couldn't help but think that it was all her fault. She had purchased the pistol for protection in the years between divorcing William's father and meeting Steve, when there wasn't a man around to protect them. Once she married Steve, she thought of getting rid of the pistol but never did, being swept up in the busyness of newfound love. All of this was lost on Randy who was immersed in the perplexed profundity of the Rubik's Cube. She placed her hand on his shoulder and said, "Are you thirsty?"

"No ma'am," he said, not looking at her, still twisting the colored cube diligently.

"Should I call your parents?"

"I don't remember my phone number."

"You don't know it?" she said, puzzled.

"Nope."

"Well, I'm sure they'll understand when I tell them what happened."

"I'll probably get in more trouble," he said, sniffing.

"Why? It wasn't your fault."

"I'm *always* in trouble."

Just then, a doctor entered the waiting room, standing in front of Pam and Randy, a couple of fingerprint-sized smears of blood on his shirt, a clipboard in his hand, and a stethoscope around his neck. His name tag said "Dr. Masala." Pam quickly stood up while Randy continued to play with the toy.

"Ma'am, your son is going to be fine. The bullet went straight through muscle and didn't hit any bone or tendons. William is very lucky," he said with a slight Indian accent.

Pam raised her hands to her mouth, sighing heavily.

"Thank god!" she said, holding back tears.

"Let me ask you a question. Why did your son have your pistol in the first place?"

Pam stood there, stricken by guilt and shame, and didn't know what to say. She didn't know how her son got a hold of the pistol so her mind was a black hole that she was looking into for answers but not finding any.

"To be very honest with you, I have no idea how he got it."

"Mmm hmm," he said incredulously. "And why didn't you keep it locked up?"

"It was locked up in my nightstand, I swear."

"Mmm hmm," he said, scribbling something on the paper on the clipboard. "Well, when these types of incidents occur, we are required to call family protective services. You will be getting a call from them in the next few days."

"Oh, OK," she said, perturbed.

"You can see your son now. Have a nice night," he said, then turned and walked back into the emergency room.

Pam looked at Randy and said, "Do you want to go see Billy with me?"

He looked up, confused. "Who is Billy?"

"I mean, William," she said, putting her hand out. Randy gave her the Rubik's Cube then followed her into the emergency room.

***

A few days later, William sat in the cafeteria at his school, scarfing down his lunch--a peanut butter and jelly sandwich, a bag of Fritos, a Little Debbie cupcake, and a Thermos of juice. He finished his lunch before all the other kids then sat at the end of the table, excited to go outside for recess. Sassy mouth Darren looked down at the brace around his leg, put there to keep his leg straight, and said, "How do you walk with that thing on?"

"I put one foot in front of the other," William said, smiling.

"Boy, you're a real genius. You know that?"

William didn't respond. He was too excited.

When the bell rang, William bolted outside as fast as he could with his gimp leg, heading straight for the playground. Waiting for him by the jungle gym was Randy who was wearing brown corduroy pants, white tennis shoes, and a red Spider-Man t-shirt. Behind Randy, a few feet away, stood his teacher Ms. Benedict. She watched William limp his way from the back of the school to Randy, who was patiently waiting for him. Concerned that Randy was going to start trouble, she decided to intervene. She stepped next to Randy and put her hand on his shoulder.

"There's not going to be any problems today, is there?"

"No, Ms. Benedict. We're the best of friends now," he said, smiling. "Really!"

"Well, that's great."

When William reached Randy, he put his hand out and they commenced giving each other The Secret Crestridge Handshake. Ms. Benedict was pleased seeing their little friendly ritual. Randy whispered something to William, and he agreed then limped to the other side of the jungle gym. He stepped on top of a short, cement wall, spread his legs into a stiff, heroic stance, raising one arm straight up, his finger pointing to the clouds. He indicated that he was ready.

"All right! Here I come!" Randy said.

"What is William doing over there?" said Ms. Benedict, shading her eyes with her hand, squinting.

"That's not William!" Randy said, scoffing. "That is the great and powerful, BRAVE RAIDEEN! Not even a bullet can keep down the Brave Raideen!"

"And who are you supposed to be?"

"I'm Spider-Man. Duh!"

Randy left Ms. Benedict behind to join his friend on the other side of the jungle gym.

Good Night, Jerk Face

My dreams were sturdy when I was young; they became more fragile as I got older. Summer of 1986. All I thought about was the car I hoped to get for my 16th birthday the following summer. That was all I thought about when I was 15, all day, all night. I thought I had a pretty good chance of getting the car I wanted too because I lived in a pretty good neighborhood and I thought my dad made pretty good money, and the majority of my friends got good cars for their 16th birthdays. The odds looked pretty good in my favor, at least. Plus, I made good grades. It seemed like a no-brainer to me. The car I wanted was a 1980 Mazda RX7. I really, really, really wanted that car, preferably a stick shift even though I didn't know how to drive stick shift, let alone drive a car.

Every summer since I could remember, I spent a couple of weeks at my grandparents' house in Moore, Oklahoma, probably to give my parents a break. During the drive from San Antonio, Texas to Moore, I read the classifieds of the *San Antonio Light* newspaper, scouring the used car section, looking for Mazda RX7's for sale, particularly 1980 models or ones that were close to that year like the '78 or '79, just not an '81 cause they were different. I found a few for sale with prices ranging from $4,000 - $6,000. That seemed like a pretty good deal to me even though I had no idea really what a good deal was for a car. I was only 15. I didn't know shit.

"What are you looking for?" my mom said. She was somewhat thin with auburn, short cropped hair, kind hazel eyes, and had lightly freckled pale skin. She gripped the steering wheel of her Toyota Camry confidently and sat up straight, ready to bear the heavy burden of the long, boring drive to Oklahoma.

"The car I want for my 16th birthday," I said.

"What makes you think you'll get a car for your 16th birthday?"

"Isn't that what you get when you turn 16?"

"Sure, some kids get a car for their 16th birthday. What kind of car do you want?"

"A 1980 Mazda RX7. Stick shift. Silver."

"Ha! A sports car?"

"Do you think dad will get me one?"

"I don't know. You'll have to ask him."

"What do you think he'll say?"

"Trying to guess what your dad will say at any given moment is impossible. You'll just have to call him and ask him. OK?"

"OK."

I read the few ads for used RX7's over and over, imagining what they might look like, thinking that they were probably all like new, lightly used, hardly dirty. I imagined myself in one, driving it to school, impressing the shit out of girls, making my friends jealous, and stuff like that. It was a damn, good daydream.

The drive to Moore seemed to take an eternity.

***

My mom only stayed one night in Moore. The next morning after we arrived, we sat down for breakfast with my grandparents. My mom wanted a good meal before she started the drive back to San Antonio, a drive that took seven hours or so, depending on if she stopped to pee or not. She seemed to be in a hurry to leave. I was distracted. All I could think about was the car I wanted.

My grandparents were both well-worn and travel-weary, both reaching their 70s without experiencing too many life-threatening diseases or personal fiascos that would leave scars like most of their contemporaries had. My grandfather moved his hunched-over frame with the grace of a cowboy shuffling a two-step, his elderly chuckle filling the room with joy, his snappy demeanor always punctuating his interactions with dirty jokes or whacky riddles. My grandmother was as thin as a stalk of wheat, her left hand gripping a highball glass of scotch on the rocks, her right hand pinching a Virginia Slims 120 cigarette with an ash two inches long. They asked a million questions about everything except for what I was really thinking about. My grandfather noticed my unusual behavior.

"What cha thinking about, son?" he said.

"Cars."

"Oh yeah, which car?"

"He wants a car for his 16th birthday," my mom said.

"Which car?" he said, a smile slithering across his face, his arm around my shoulders.

"A Mazda RX7."

"Ooo! Those look fun. And with rotary engines, too."

"Yeah. Rotary," I said, uneasy like, not sure what he was talking about.

"Must be expensive," he said.

"Not if it's used."

"True. It'll be cheaper than new."

My mom was completely uninterested in this conversation but my grandfather liked cars, liked working on cars. He was curious, at least. My mom finished her breakfast, grabbed her stuff, kissed me goodbye, and was out the door as fast as she could go. I didn't get a chance to tell her to butter my dad up about getting me a car for my 16th birthday.

My grandfather placed his hand on my shoulder as I watched her drive off. He squeezed my shoulder gently.

"Are you sure you want a Japanese car? How do you feel about Fords?"

***

I had a thing for sugary cereals. I could eat almost an entire box in one sitting. Fruit Loops, Lucky Charms, Smurf Berry Crunch--practically any cereal except for the bran varieties--I could scarf down bowl after bowl. My grandparents knew this about me. When I got up for breakfast, I discovered dozens of boxes of cereal, waiting on the kitchen counter. My grandparents didn't eat cereal so I knew it was all for me. They preferred to eat eggs, bacon, toast, the eggs coated with salt and pepper, the toast covered with margarine, the bacon burnt to a blackened crisp. I grabbed two boxes of cereal--it didn't matter which ones--and sat down at the table. I commenced to scarfing them down. My grandmother cackled as she watched me.

"Good thing we went to the store before you got here," she said.

"Mmm hmm," I said.

"Do you want any orange juice?"

"Uhh uhh," I said, shaking my head.

My grandfather shuffled into the breakfast room from the kitchen, the morning paper in his hand. He sat down at the breakfast table, pulling the plastic wrapper off the rolled up newspaper, then unraveling the paper on the table. I watched him, with my mouth full of half-chewed cereal, spreading the sections across the table. He liked reading the newspaper during breakfast.

"Why do you have to cover the whole goddamn table?" my grandmother said.

"There's a lot of sections in here, dear," he said.

"That newspaper is dirty. We eat here."

"Well, I *know* we eat here. It's a breakfast table, isn't it?"

"Yes, it's a breakfast table, not a *reading the newspaper* table."

"Well, for Christ's sakes, I didn't know you had such an aversion to the morning paper."

"Well, I didn't either until I watched you spread the filthy thing all over the table."

They went on like this for ten minutes. I continued to scarf down my cereal. My grandfather turned through the different sections of the newspaper, looking for the editorial section, to the displeasure of my grandmother. He liked to read the editorial articles and comment about them aloud to whoever was around. It made him feel invested in the community, I guess, to speak about these civic matters, even though he didn't do much else about them. He found the classified section, lifted it up in front of him, spread it open, and ruffled the pages.

"Look here, my boy. Let's see if there are any Mazda RX7's for sale here in Moore. You know, for fun!"

I set my spoon in the bowl and chewed the remainder of what was in my mouth. He turned the pages, scanned them, turned some more. He blurted out car maker names in alphabetical order: Audi, BMW, Buick, Cadillac, blah blah blah. The suspense was getting to me. It irritated my grandmother.

"You're not buying him a car," she said.

"I know that, dear," he said.

"Then what are you looking for?"

"Because I'm curious, dear."

"Curious about what?"

"How much they... Mazda!"

"You're gonna get his hopes up."

"Oh, stop it. Mazda, Mazda... here. 1979 Mazda RX7. Used. Automatic. Blue. Needs work. $4,100."

"$4,100?!" she said, shocked, like it was an insane amount of money.

"Does it have a stick shift?" I said.

"Nope. It says automatic," he said.

"Oh."

"Here's another. 1980 Mazda RX7. Used. Silver. 5 speed. Excellent shape. $5,999."

"5,999?!" my grandmother said.

"That's what it says, dear," my grandfather said.

"Does it have stick shift?" I said.

"That's what it says, my boy." He looked over at me, a big grin stretched across his face. Pretty quick, the grin turned downward and a look of concern appeared on his wrinkly face. "You know, you need to talk to your dad first about this. Otherwise, it's all pie in the sky."

A feeling of disappointment sunk in my stomach.

"I know," I said.

"I'd love to help you look for Mazdas but it would be like looking through a fashion magazine thinking you're going to get a date. That's not a good thing to do, is it?"

"No," I said.

"Why don't you give your dad a call today and ask him about it?"

"OK."

"That's my boy."

I poured some more cereal in my bowl and started another round. This time, it was Count Chocula. I was still hungry.

***

I sat in my room by myself, on the floor, the newspaper spread out in front of me, the used car section open wide. There seemed to be the same amount of RX7's for sale in Moore as back home, a few in the same price range, $4,000 - $6,000, more or less. I felt a sense of relief for some reason, like an affirmation that my hope to own this car was achievable, because my research would reveal the same thing to my father. I believed my father liked that I did research, looked into things, absorbed some information from various sources, at least tried to be informed. I was still scared to call him, though. I worried that he would say no. He was a dream-crusher. He could be a real sour-puss when he wanted to be, particularly with me. I looked at the rotary phone and sensed my father's dark cloud form in the room. It seeped through the phone line and hung over my head, heavy, dreadful.

I stared at the phone for an hour. Then another hour.

After a deep breath, I picked up the phone and dialed my father's work phone number, the rotary dial grinding back and forth, the numbers clicking in the handset. The line rang and rang. He finally answered.

"Colonel Bennigan," he said.

"Dad? It's me."

"Hello son. What can I do for you?"

"Well, I've been thinking."

"Yes?"

"Ummm..."

"Make it quick. I'm very busy."

"Well..."

"Oh, for Christ's sake," he said. I heard a bang on the other end of the line, like the handset was dropped or tossed or whacked, and some grumbling. "Excuse me, Sam. Can you call back when you have a clear idea of what you are trying to ask?"

"Dad, I know what I want to ask. Next summer, I will be 16."

"Yes?"

"And I was hoping I could talk to you about the kind of car I'm going to get, when I turn 16."

"You're not getting a car for your birthday."

"But..."

"If you want a car, then I suggest you save your money. Get a job. Make lots of money. Save for a car and the cost of owning that car. There's gas. Oil changes. Maintenance. Auto insurance. My god, the auto insurance! Owning a car is a big deal, a huge expense. Are you prepared to pay for these things?"

"No. Where do I get a job?"

"I have no idea. You think you're so smart. If you're so smart, then you can find a job. Are your grandparents feeding you?"

"Yes."

"Good. See you when you get back." He hung up the phone.

I put the handset on the cradle, wadded up the newspaper into a huge crumpled ball, and threw it in a trash can in the corner of the room.

***

I spent the remainder of my time at my grandparents' house formulating a plan for finding a job and a couple of weeks later, I was back in San Antonio. My grandfather advised that I scour the want ads when I got back and I did just that. The want ads were mostly a place for potential salesmen, it seemed to me, and I didn't want to be a salesman. I heard that a lot of kids my age had jobs in restaurants or fast food places but I didn't see ads for jobs at those types of places in the newspaper. I asked my mom where I should look and she suggested I look in the phone book for listings under restaurants. I did that. They were in alphabetical order so I looked for the businesses that were on the road in front of my neighborhood: Blanca Road. I called them one by one and asked the same question when someone answered.

"Are you hiring?" I said.

"No," the mysterious voices all said.

San Antonio was a pretty big city and there were a lot of restaurant listings. When I eventually got to the "D" listings, I came across a Greek restaurant that I had never seen before. It was called Demitri's Greek Restaurant. I tried to imagine where it was on Blanca Road or what the front of it looked like. I couldn't for the life of me imagine it. I called anyway.

"Are you hiring?" I said, gripping the handset tightly.

"What?" a lady said. "Hold on." The phone crackled, a hand over the mouthpiece muffling the sound. I could still hear her yelling a question though, asking if they were hiring or something. The muffling went away. "Yes, we're hiring."

"Really?!"

"I said yes, didn't I?"

"Oh OK. What do I need to do?"

"Are you 16?" she said.

"Yes," I said. I lied. I wasn't 16.

"Then come here and fill out an application. We'll see what happens."

"OK. Thanks!"

She hung up the phone. I jumped up, tossing the phone handset, landing in a triumphant pose, hands stretched to the sky, feet planted to the earth spread wide, a big grin on my face. I called to my mother and explained the good news. She seemed pleased at my enthusiasm.

"Would you like for me to drive you down there?" she said.

"Yes, please," I said.

"OK, then brush your hair, brush your teeth, and put on clean clothes."

I ran to my room to get ready. I was ready in five minutes.

***

I had no idea what I was going to be doing for my first stint as an employed person. Being that I was a young kid, the possibility that I could be doing something meaningful or important seemed plausible in my mind, although the reality was that "meaningful or important" were relative to my experience in the world outside of my parents' home. I was in for an awakening.

"What position are they hiring?" my mom said.

"I don't know."

"Aren't you curious?"

"Yes."

"Why didn't you ask then?"

"I don't know."

"Hmmm. You don't know what you are getting yourself into?"

"No."

"I didn't think so."

I sat quietly in my mother's Toyota Camry, the cold, conditioned air enveloping my body, some Top 40 music playing on the radio, Lionel Ritchie or something. I watched the different businesses as we passed by, wondering if they were hiring too, and what it would be like to work there: a convenience store, a sandwich shop, a dry cleaner, a paint store. We also passed my high school, Abraham Lincoln High School. Since it was summer time, it was closed. The parking lot was empty except for one car, a bright red Ford Mustang, somewhat new, with shiny alloy rims and glossy trim, freshly coated with Armor All. A boy I recognized from school stood next to it, leaning in a cool fashion against it, smoking a cigarette by himself. I didn't know his name but I sure did recognize him. He looked cool as fuck. I watched him smoke and he watched me gawk at him until I couldn't see him anymore. I daydreamed about owning a Mazda RX7 and challenging him to a drag race. I daydreamed about our race the rest of the way to the restaurant.

When we arrived, I recognized the strip mall. We had passed it a hundred times but I didn't ever remember shopping there or parking there before. We went around to the back end of the strip mall and my mom parked in a spot directly in front of the entrance of the restaurant. I had never been inside before and had no idea what to expect or what the interior even looked like. I didn't even know who I was supposed to talk to. My mother handed me a ballpoint pen and my identification card for being a military brat. The photo of me on the card was really embarrassing. I looked like a complete dumb ass.

"Do you want me to go inside with you?" she asked.

"No. I'll be fine."

"OK. Well, call me when you're ready for me to pick you up. OK?"

"OK."

She kissed me on the cheek and I got out of the car. She peeled the car out like the wine at home was sitting on the couch unsupervised. Once her car was gone, I went inside.

The restaurant was sparsely furnished and split into two areas. The first area had a couple of tables with checkerboard tablecloths, a beverage area with a soda fountain, a tea dispenser, and a water dispenser. There was also a counter where you ordered your meals with a huge menu on the wall behind it with an open-air kitchen, a grill, deep-fryer, cutting area, prep area, a lean-in cooler, and a beer / wine cooler. The second area was a dining room that was up two steps and separated from the other area by a low wall. In the dining area were a dozen tables, four tops with checkerboard tablecloths, salt and pepper shakers, and a large white candle on each. There was a painting or two of some Greek landscapes--pastures, the Parthenon, and shit like that--and that was about it. It was pretty minimal. I would find out later that this minimalism was useful for parties or wedding receptions held at the restaurant since Greeks liked to toss dishes around and break them when they were celebrating and getting drunk on wine or ouzo.

After standing around for a minute or two like a dumbass, I was greeted by a woman who was petite with curly dark brown hair, short on top and longer in the back. She wore dirty white jeans and a blue Polo shirt with the name of the restaurant on it: Demitri's Greek Restaurant. The jeans and the polo shirt looked like they had been submerged in olive oil then washed then repeated like that over and over. She had a nice smile but looked very tired, as if she had been working 21 days straight without a day off. She extended her hand to me.

"Hi! My name is Desmona. My brother owns the restaurant but I help him run it. You here to apply for work?"

"Yes, but how do you know that?"

"You have a pen in one hand and an ID card in the other and you don't look like a customer. Am I right?"

"Yes."

"Tell you what. Demitri is busy unclogging a toilet but all employees get one free meal with every shift. Do you want to eat something while you wait?"

I looked at the menu and my eyes glazed over. I had never eaten Greek food before and everything on the menu might as well have been from another planet. I had no idea what any of it was or what it might even taste like. I stared at the menu like an aborigine whose eyes were peeled at the sky, watching a jumbo jet tear through the clouds, stunned.

"I guess you haven't had Greek food before," she said, shaking her head. "I'll get you a gyro. If you like that then you'll be on the right foot. Sound good?" I nodded. "Have a seat over there and fill out the application. I'll get it for you."

I sat down and she quickly brought over a piece of paper, dropped it on the table, then went back into the kitchen to make my meal. Before I could even finish filling out the contact information section, she was back at the table with my food. In a red basket lined with red and white checkered tissue paper was a large gyro sandwich, hand cut fries, and one dolma. It was the most divine smelling food I had encountered in weeks.

"Enjoy! Demitri said he'd be out in a minute," she said then vanished to the back of the restaurant through a door in the kitchen.

I examined my food and took a big whiff. The gyro sandwich was the size of a massive burrito, meat and onions and tomatoes and tzatziki sauce spilling out the front of it. I took one bite of the Mediterranean sandwich and immediately fell in love. What had I been missing all my life so far? My taste buds exploded and I worked on that sandwich like a riding mower taking down an overgrown lawn. I must have been a real sight to see because Demitri was laughing up a storm when I noticed him for the first time, standing next to me, all five feet of him, his hands on his hips, laughing and laughing. He didn't look much different than his sister Desmona, about the same height, similar curly hair but cropped shorter in the back, same dirty white jeans and a blue Polo shirt.

"I love watching people eat my food for the first time. It's like a food baptism," he said, extending his hand to me. "I'm Demitri and this is my restaurant." He saw that I was holding my sandwich with a tight, saucy grip. He put his hand in the front pocket of his jeans. "Nevermind. Well, finish up your meal and meet me in the back so we can get started."

"Don't you want me to fill out the application?" I said, my mouth still half-full of food.

"You want to work, don't you?" I nodded. "Good. We'll finish the paperwork later. Let's go!"

He clapped his hands then vanished to the back of the restaurant.

***

In the back was a storage room, a walk-in cooler, a few prep tables, and a dishwashing station complete with a massive, stainless steel sink and attached dishwasher. It was mostly pretty clean but in slight disarray. There were some shipping boxes to be unpacked and some bussing bins filled with dirty dishes to be unloaded. Demitri seemed very proud of his restaurant. He stood there in a manly stance, his fists firmly pressed into his hips, like a short Superman prepared to take flight. I wasn't all that impressed but what did I know? I didn't know shit.

"So, this is where some of the magic happens. You'll be doing a lot of work back here, washing dishes, cutting fries, unpacking shipments from Greece."

"Your food is from Greece?" I said.

"Most of the ingredients are from Greece. I have family over there. They send me the good stuff, mostly, for cheap. It's not authentic Greek food unless it's from Greece, right?"

That seemed like a reasonable statement to me so I didn't say anything. Demitri had a look about him that reminded me of the actor Tom Selleck, mainly because he had a big, black, bushy moustache and curly dark hair in a similar hair style, but Demitri was barely five foot one and he smelled like olive oil instead of tanning oil.

"All right, kid. Be careful of the water coming out the faucet because it's hot. And when I mean hot, it's hot enough to melt dried tzatziki sauce off the plates so be careful. Got it?" he said, pointing a finger into my chest.

"Got it," I said.

"Follow me."

We walked to the back of the storage room to a door that lead out into a hallway where the one restroom was for the diners, the hallway then lead back out to the dining area. But we didn't go out to the dining area. Demitri used his foot to prop open the door to the co-ed bathroom. The smell of a messy turd wafted out.

"The bathroom is usually very clean except this old man came in here after eating a large Greek salad and three servings of baklava. He was in here an hour and blew a gasket. I like to keep it clean in here... for the ladies. I need you to clean this up before the dinner rush. Got it?"

"Got it," I said.

"Follow me."

We went back into the storage room and stepped in front of a table with three very large tins on it. The tins must have been four or five gallon containers. They looked like humongous tuna fish containers without labels. Demitri slowly turned one around, looking for something.

"These came in today. Feta cheese. I need you to open these, take the cheese out, put the cheese in a plastic bin, pour some of the brine in, and cover the bins with Saran Wrap. Got it?"

"Got it," I said.

"Good. Here's a can opener to open these. Please don't cut yourself. Got it?" he said, pointing a finger into my chest. He really liked to do that, point and poke me, even though I was taller than he was. Then he left me alone.

I examined the can opener and didn't recognize its shape from the ones my mother had in our kitchen at home. In fact, it looked more like an antique scalpel that you would see in an old movie than a can opener. I gripped it tightly in my hand and turned one of the large tins around, examining it. There were some indentations on the top that seemed like a logical place to open it so I placed the sharp tip of the can opener there and pressed firmly, trying to puncture the top of the tin. Instead, the impenetrable top rejected the opener and my hand crumpled. The can opener pierced my skin and blood gushed from it, deep crimson red. It dripped on the metal table. I called for Demitri but he didn't respond.

The next thing I knew, I saw black.

***

I opened my eyes and Demitri and Desmona were wrapping my hand with something, like a towel or a rag, and I was sitting at the front of the restaurant. I was out of it and I didn't really understand what was going on. I could see that they were talking to me but I didn't understand what they were saying. I was lightheaded and groggy. To my surprise, my mother appeared in front of me and helped me stand up. She hung my good arm around her shoulders and helped me walk to the car. As she opened the door and helped me sit down, I heard her consoling Demitri and Desmona and they seemed concerned about me. She put the seatbelt on me, rolled the window down, and closed the door. As she went around the car to get in, Demitri leaned on the car door, looking in.

"Don't worry kid, you got the job. You seem like a good kid even though I asked you not to cut yourself. Go home and get better and I'll see you in a few days. I gave your mom your schedule," he said, a big smile on his face, his bushy moustache sitting above his white teeth like a furry hat. I could tell he felt sorry for me though. He slapped the car roof and my mother drove off.

As we went, I looked in the side mirror and saw him waving at us. I heard him call out, "Good night, jerk face!"

My mom looked at me, puzzled, and said, "He must not speak very good English."

We drove home.

***

The next day, I was sitting in my room, the auto classifieds sprawled out in front of me on the floor. I looked for the elusive 1980 Mazda RX7. I held a marker in my left hand because my right was wrapped in ace bandage and gauze, still tender and sore from the cut. I usually wrote with my right hand but my left was good enough to circle ads with a marker. I read the listings under the Mazda section carefully, listed in chronological order from newest year to oldest, and I heard an enthusiastic auctioneer in my head, calling them out with a speedy, Redneck accent. It made reading the ads much more enjoyable that way to me. I then was interrupted by a knock at my door.

"Come in."

"Your mother wanted me to give you this," my dad said, poking his head in. He handed me a pill and a glass of water. "It's a painkiller."

My dad was short and stalky and kind of pudgy in a way a bull dog can be those things except he didn't have a loveable side. He was all business all the time, no fun.

"Thanks," I said, gulping the pill down with water.

"What are you looking at?"

"Huh?"

"There, in the paper," he said, pointing. "What are you looking at in the paper?"

"I'm reading the classifieds. For cars."

"I'm not giving you a car for your 16th birthday," he said, staring at me.

"Uh, OK."

"You'll need to save up for a car yourself."

"I know. That's why I got a job."

"If you keep cutting yourself on the job, pretty soon you won't have a job. Shape up."

"OK."

He left my room and closed the door behind him. I stared at the door for a moment, making sure he wasn't going to come back in. He didn't.

I looked down at the paper and the auctioneer continued his chant in my head: *I have a 1979 Mazda RX-7 in very good condition. Let's start the bidding at $3,900. You, there, in the pink shorts, $3,900! How about $4,000? Who will give me $4,000? The little fella, there, good-looking kid, $4,000! Now how about $4,100? Who will give me $4,100?*

***

The water that shot out of the sink hose was scalding hot. Demitri was not kidding when he said the water was hot enough to melt dried tzatziki sauce off the plates and silverware. Tzatziki sauce, a combination of yogurt mixed with cucumbers, garlic, salt, olive oil, and other wonderful ingredients to make a divine sandwich dressing, although delicious served cold and fresh, turned to cement when exposed to air too long. It was a dishwasher's nightmare. I blasted the plates with the hot water to get that shit off but when it didn't work, I had a scraper to use, like a windshield ice scraper but smaller. Washing dishes and bussing tables in a restaurant was an eye-opening experience for me as a young man. I didn't have to work at Demitri's for long to realize that people were pigs, absolutely disgusting slobs. Not only was the tzatziki sauce difficult to get off plates, imagine getting that shit off walls or window blinds. Ugh.

That was the majority of my work, washing dishes and bussing tables, although I also was asked to clean the restrooms, take orders, cook food, and prep ingredients. Every once and a while, I was also asked to be a taste-tester. I liked that job the most although it was pretty infrequent. Demitri had family members doing all kinds of things for him, cousins doing bookkeeping, his aunt doing his taxes, his sister managing the place, and so on and so forth. But one of his secret ingredients for success was his mother, who gave him most of his recipes and who also baked his baklava, which if you didn't know, is the most amazing dessert in the world--a rich, sweet pastry made of layers of filo filled with chopped nuts and sweetened with honey. Hers was to DIE for and I'm not kidding. She would bake a tray of it at her home then bring it in to the restaurant and sit the tray in the back area on the prep table behind where I washed the dishes. Every time she put the tray down, she would tap me on the shoulder and when I looked at her and the baklava, she would wag her finger in my face as if to say, 'Don't touch!' And every time she left, I always took a piece for myself to eat when no one was looking. That was the one thing that made washing dishes somewhat bearable: amazing baklava. I'd shove the entire piece in my mouth and enjoy it while I blasted dried tzatziki off dinner plates.

A few days after my hand healed up, I was back at Demitri's, a rubber glove covering my wounded hand, washing dishes, bussing tables, and cleaning the bathroom. As I said, it didn't take me long to realize just how messy people were when eating out in a restaurant. I found all kinds of disgusting things, food smashed on the walls and under the tables, boogers and gum stuck under everything, tampons and wads of paper towels jammed in the toilet, urine in the bathroom sinks, turds smeared on the bathroom walls, and more too disgusting to talk about. It was a goddamn nightmare, if I say so myself. Demitri took it all in stride though.

"As long as they're paying me for their meals, I look the other way for everything else--mostly," he would say to me.

"What would make you not look away?" I asked one time.

"Well, maybe murder..." Then he laughed so hard that I knew even murder could be overlooked for a price. "Now, go bus table seven. They just left."

Table seven was occupied by a young family, a man, his wife, and a little baby; the man and the woman not much older than 18, the little baby a demon spawn. The parents looked like they had survived a horrific event, their hair matted down, their clothes in tatters, their eyes weary and their shoulders slumped. As they ate quietly, their baby destroyed everything it could get its little paws on, the salt and pepper shakers dismantled and emptied, napkins wadded and torn, sugar packets ripped and tossed, straws bent and jammed into crevices, food smashed on the table, and water flung on the floor. When they were done eating, they scooped up their baby and quietly left. Demitri laughed at me as I stood over their disastrous remains, table seven turned into a miniature representation of the city dump. It took me a good twenty minutes just to pick up the food and trash and another ten minutes wiping and cleaning the chairs, table, walls, and floor. The only thing worth salvaging was part of the *San Antonio Express-News*--the other city paper--and the only section that wasn't drenched in tzatziki sauce and olive oil: the classifieds. I folded it and placed it under my arm for safekeeping.

When my shift was over, it was late in the evening and my mother wouldn't be coming to pick me up for about an hour so I ordered my free meal and sat at a small two-top by myself. I had fallen in love with their gyro sandwich and fries and looked forward to eating my free sandwich almost as much as receiving my paycheck. As I ate, I read through the classified section from the newspaper I saved from table seven. With a ball point pen, I marked each Mazda RX-7 that looked interesting or promising even though I had absolutely *no way* of buying it. But to me, it was like keeping my dream alive, my dream of owning that car, when I looked in the classifieds. Demitri watched me from the kitchen and eventually came over to my table. He cocked his head to the side and tried to make out what I was doing. He read some of the listings out loud.

"1979 Mazda RX-7, red/black int, 5 spd, factory sunroof, clean, fun sports car to drive, cold A/C," he said, slowly and deliberately. "You looking to buy a car?"

"Yes."

"And you want one of those little sports cars?"

"Yeah."

"So you can get special lady in it?" he said, snickering. He slapped my shoulder pretty hard.

"Maybe," I said, rubbing my shoulder.

"Is that why you wanted to work here, to save money for a little sports car?"

"Yes."

"You know, it really doesn't matter what kind of car you have as long as you have a car that runs with an air conditioner that works. That's all you need."

"But I like this car."

"Sure. It's nice. When I go out on dates, I take the delivery truck, the one out front."

"You pick up dates in the delivery truck?" I said, horrified.

"Yes, the delivery truck. It has cold A/C and a cassette deck. Super nice!"

I didn't know what to say because it was so weird to me but I smiled anyway, a forced smile like when an old lady calls you hot or good-lookin' or something. Demitri was very impressed with himself.

"You have a driver license, kid?" he said.

"Yes," I said. I lied.

"Good, I may need you to deliver food some time, just so you know. You can drive stick shift?"

"Yes," I said. I lied again.

"Good. I'll let you know. Good luck finding a sports car," he said, then walked behind the counter. "I have to dump some frying oil out back. I'm leaving right after so I guess I'll say goodbye to you. Good night, jerk face!"

He laughed really hard then disappeared to the back.

***

After I worked at Demitri's for a few weeks, my parents began to drop me off in quicker, more hurried fashions. At first, they parked right in front of the restaurant in a parking space, hugged me, told me they'd see me after my shift, and waited for me to go inside. Then they stopped parking in a space and just pulled up front to let me out, no more hug. Then they stopped at the entrance of the parking lot to let me out of the car and quickly turned around to exit the lot. It got so hurried that they were slowing down to a crawl and practically shoving me out of the car. Although I appreciated them taking me to work since it was six or seven miles from our house, I couldn't help but feel like I was a burden to them in some way. Asking me to get out of the car at the side of a busy street was a pretty good hint that they were trying to get back home as soon as possible, without concern if I made it inside of my work or not. One evening, after getting out of my father's pickup truck and watching him tear off, I decided to checkout some of the other stores in the strip mall. Demitri's was at the far end of the mall so I made my way under the overhang and perused the front of each shop, looking in the windows, checking out what and who were inside. There was a jewelry store, a nail salon, and insurance salesman--all the standard strip mall crap.

One of the stores was a dancing apparel store called Capezio. They sold clothes for tap dancers and ballerinas and shit like that. As I walked in front of the store window, I saw a girl inside that I knew, a pretty girl from school, a really beautiful thing. Her name was Kirsty and she was in my math class. She was also on the dance squad at school and apparently into tap dancing since she was looking at some tap shoes. All I can say was that every time I looked at her, she crushed me, just swathed my heart with ooey, gooey, teenage emotional lustiness. Her smile was like a million stars twinkling in the night sky and my heart was the moon. I knew her well enough and had spoken to her a half dozen times so that when she saw me, she waved and motioned for me to wait where I was, to not move. I froze in place, nervous. She burst out of the store, her arms open wide, and hugged me. She smelled like strawberries and cream and laundry detergent, a delicious combination.

"Sam! What are you doing here?"

"I'm walking to work."

"You work at Capezio?" she said, puzzled.

"Oh, no no. I work at Demitri's," I said, pointing to the restaurant. "Over there. I bus tables, wash dishes, and things like that."

"Oh! That's cool. You saving for college?"

"No, a car."

"Cool!" She placed her hands behind her back and twisted one foot nervously around on the cement sidewalk, then her mother rapped on the window, waving at her to go back inside. Her mother's hand-waving embarrassed her. "Oh God! She's so annoying," she said, rolling her eyes.

"Yeah," I said.

"Well, when you buy your car, will you take me for a ride?"

"Yeah," I said, turning red in the face.

"Great! See ya, Sam!"

She went back into Capezio and I walked to Demitri's so I could start my shift. The ooey, gooey, teenage emotional lustiness returned and put a skip in my step. When I got to the front door, Demitri was sweeping off the walkway outside the restaurant. He had a big grin on his face.

"Pretty, pretty girl," he said, sweeping in a way that looked like he was mimicking a waltz, like Mickey Mouse in that movie where the broom sticks came alive and danced around.

"Yeah," I said.

"You take her on a date?"

"Not yet."

"I'll let you borrow the delivery truck for your date if you need a car."

I almost told him by accident that I didn't have a driver license but I stopped myself from talking. I went inside and started bussing tables instead.

***

Later that night, the restaurant was busy as hell. We were packed, every table was full, and there was a line out the door waiting to order. It was nuts. I had been bussing tables and washing dishes pretty much nonstop for a few hours straight and it didn't seem to be letting up. The kitchen was going bonkers, cooking everything on the menu. Demitri seemed to relish it, the unexpected influx of paying customers. He wasn't very good at predicting when this type of rush was going to happen but when it did, he loved it. He ran around like a madman, cooking, taking orders, cleaning, restocking, everything. He was a one-man show which wasn't good for the rest of us working for him. When he saw a cook wasn't cooking fast enough, he would shove him aside and take over. When he saw that other tables were dirty while I was bussing, he would take the bus tub out of my hands and bus tables. He was crazy. Now that I'm older, I get what he was doing; he wanted to succeed. But back then, I thought he was just crazy.

At one point in the evening--and I don't even remember when--I was in the back washing dishes and Demitri came rushing back there, his eyes open wide with panic, the calligraphy of veins in the whites of his eyes flaring brightly, and he screamed at me.

"Sam! Sam! I need you to deliver some food! Come up front now!"

Panic immediately set in. I did NOT know how to drive. I didn't even have a driver license. I didn't know what to do but I went up front anyway. I didn't want to get yelled at by my diminutive, freaked-out boss. Demitri shoved some plastic to-go containers in paper sacks, shuffling receipts, writing things down. He looked at me, frantic.

"I have five orders I need you to deliver, most of them to the neighborhood right behind this mall. I'll load the truck but you got to go. OK?!" I nodded. "Come on! And don't worry," he barked to the waiting customers. "We have plenty of delicious Greek food for all of you!"

He handed a bag to me and grabbed the other four bags, all cinched at the top. We weaved through the customers waiting to order and went out the front door, Demitri's arms flailing, the to-go bags swinging wildly. He opened the passenger door of the truck and tossed them in, grabbed my bag and tossed it in too. He handed me the keys and a piece of paper, a serious, grave look on his face.

"Can you drive stick-shift?" he said, looking me straight in the eyes.

"Yes," I said. I lied.

"Good. Reverse is to the right and down. Got it?"

"Yes," I said. I didn't understand what that meant.

"Four of the deliveries are right back there, behind the trees." He pointed to a row of trees behind the mall. "The last one is farther up Castle Hills." He handed me the keys to the truck. "Go!"

He ran back inside the busy restaurant. I opened the driver side door and got in the truck. The seat seemed low and narrow and the stick shift was a long stick that protruded up from the floor board with a replica of the Parthenon as the shift knob. There wasn't even a shifting pattern on the top of the Parthenon, only its ancient visage molded in plastic. And just as he claimed, there was a super nice cassette deck and knobs for A/C on the dash, a pretty nice setup. I didn't know what to do so I sat there for a moment, wondering if my lies had gotten me in a tough spot. Pretty soon, I saw Demitri's red face in the window of the restaurant, glaring at me. In a matter of seconds, he was back outside standing next to the truck. I rolled down the window with the manual turning crank.

"What's the problem?!" he said.

"I don't know how--"

"The clutch needs to be in all the way to start it," he said, pointing to my left foot. "I forgot to tell you that. Push the clutch." I pushed it to the floor with my foot. "Now crank it!" I put the key in the ignition and turned it. The truck started. "Now go!" he said, running back inside the restaurant.

The truck was parked in such a way that I could ease forward if I turned the wheel to the left. I didn't have to back out of a spot, thank goodness. First, I pressed on the gas and the engine revved wildly so I let off the gas. Then I slowly eased up on the clutch and I felt the truck want to go. I pushed the clutch back in and took a huge, deep breath. Knowing what I know now about driving a stick-shift, the truck must have already been in first gear because during the next hour, I never *ever* moved the stick-shifter. I didn't even think about it. I just kept both hands on the wheel, slowly eased off the clutch, and pressed on the gas pedal when I needed to. The truck eased forward and I slowly drove the truck toward the exit at the back of the parking lot. When I felt I needed to brake the truck, I slammed the brake pedal with my right foot, screeching the truck to an abrupt stop. Since the clutch was out, the car would die, choking back to sleep. I repeated as Demitri commanded, putting the clutch in then cranking the ignition and it would start again. Like a mortally wounded tortoise, the truck eased forward slowly then lurched again to a complete stop. It was frustrating and totally embarrassing but I didn't know what else to do. I wasn't going back to tell Demitri I lied to him about knowing how to drive stick-shift.

Little did the truck know that for the next hour it would be put through a torturous, grueling workout of its transmission that it had never, ever experienced before in its trusty life. A delivery journey that should have taken ten to fifteen minutes at the most took over an hour. A noxious fume of burnt lubricant and oil wafted into the truck and singed my nose hairs while a plume of grey smoke surrounded the poor truck as it started and stopped. My neck ached from all the whipping around it had to endure, slight whiplash. My poor excuse for driving must have been a strange sight in the quiet neighborhood.

When I reached the first house, the driver-side front tire lurched over the curb onto the lawn while I tried to park. The truck belched itself to sleep. I grabbed their bags of delivery food and ran to the door, knocking furiously. A pudgy, old man dressed in a loose bathrobe--can of Pabst Blue Ribbon in one hand, a Pall Mall cigarette in the other hand, his thin, white hair sticking up like a cockatiel crest--opened the door. He looked over my shoulder quizzically at the horrid parking job on display in his front lawn.

"Sorry I parked in your grass," I said, looking back at the truck, white smoke rising from under the hood, the smell of burnt rubber in the air.

"Keep the change," the old man said, taking his food then slamming the door in my face.

The next delivery was maybe a quarter mile away, at the most, and it took me a good fifteen minutes to coerce the poor truck to get me there. No matter what I tried to do, no matter what gentle motion I attempted to shuffle between my feet, the truck would not cooperate with me. Like a raging bull within the death throes of a bull fight, I battled the beast to submit but its obstinance and pride got the best of me. I felt like the truck was about to explode when I reached the second house. I was able to keep the tires off the lawn this time. When I lifted my foot off the clutch, the truck violently lurched forward then died.

I ran to the door with their delivery. Again, I furiously knocked on the door. I knew I was taking entirely too long to deliver their food. A tiny old lady opened the door--a margarita in one hand, a Virginia Slims 120 cigarette in the other, wearing a loose fitting mumu with the gaudiest floral pattern I had ever seen adorned on an article of clothing--and she gazed over my shoulder at the smoking delivery vehicle in the street.

"You're not Demitri," she said, puzzled.

"No ma'am. I'm Sam. I work for Demitri," I said, running my fingers through my hair, attempting to fix myself up.

"Oh, that's too bad. I always look forward to Demitri visiting me. He usually comes inside and chats with me."

"Really?"

"Yes, and if I'm lucky, he'll give me a nice foot rub."

"Oh... well. I'm kinda too busy for--"

"Did you forget the baklava?"

"I don't think so." I handed her the delivery bags and she handed me a $20 bill. I patted my pockets but I knew I didn't have any change.

"Keep it," she said. "You really look like you need it." She smiled at me with her stained dentures and bright pink lips then winked at me and closed the door. I couldn't get the image out of my mind of Demitri rubbing her wrinkly, knotty feet, a pervy grin peeking out from under his bushy moustache.

Back in the truck, I read the delivery instructions, mapping in my mind the next destination, when I realized that there were no more bags in the truck to deliver. I stared at the passenger seat for ten, maybe fifteen seconds, as if I stared hard enough they would reappear, but they didn't. I then looked on the floor board, behind the seat, out the back window at the truck bed to see if they magically moved from inside the cab to the outside of the cab without my knowledge. The bags weren't there either. I must have inadvertently given the rest of the food to the old man with the cockatiel hair and the old lady with the floral mumu. A part of me was disappointed in myself for messing up my first delivery assignment, but another part of me was relieved that I could go back to the restaurant and resume my normal duties of washing dishes and bussing tables. I only hoped I could make it back to the restaurant with the truck in one piece.

When I got back from the long, torturous ride, I parked the truck the best I could at the farthest point in the parking lot from the restaurant. I was surprised it made it back, seriously. As I walked to the front door of Demitri's, I looked back at the truck, smoke rising to the night sky, the smell of oily, singed motor components in the air. I knew I broke it but I wasn't going to admit it to anyone. I decided to just pretend everything went well. Inside, the long line of hungry patrons dissipated and so had Demitri's furious pace. He stood next to his sister behind the counter while she took the last of the dinner rush orders. He was counting stacks of cash, a big grin on his face, a happy tune hummed under his breath. He saw me come in and winked at me.

"There's my boy! How did it go?"

"Fine," I said, making a beeline to the back.

"You have some money for me?"

"Yeah," I said, pulling the bills from my pocket and tossing them on the counter. I dashed to the back as quick as I could.

"Wait! There should be more money," he said.

I didn't reply. I put on my apron and washed dishes.

***

Most nights, when I wasn't at work, I was at home. And most of those nights, I thought about owning a 1980 Mazda RX-7. Or, if I couldn't find an '80, then I would have been OK with a '78 or a '79, just not an '81 because they were different, and I didn't want one of those. My dad would bring the newspaper back home from work where he took it to read while on a coffee break or in the crapper, or wherever he was when he wanted to read the newspaper. I would pull out the auto classified section and take it into my room so I could scour through it, marking listings that sounded close to what I wanted with a colored marker, usually green, my favorite color. Also, if I had a few extra dollars on me, I would buy a copy of *Auto Trader* and scour that magazine for ads too, but they usually seemed to have a crappier selection of cars. I wasn't sure why that was, but they rarely had many listings for Mazda RX-7's. They mostly listed American cars like Chevys and Fords and Buicks and shit like that but I looked anyway, just in case.

On the floor in my room, I laid sprawled out on my stomach, the newspaper and *Auto Trader* magazine spread out in front of me, a series of colored markers next to me, different colors for different marking emphasis, green usually meaning "YES!" and the other colors meaning lesser versions of "yes" or "ok." I listened to Scritti Politti while I scribbled on the pages. My dad knocked on the door and popped his head in, giving me a sour look.

"I've been knocking on your door for 30 seconds," he said, his lips twisting into a disappointed pretzel.

"Sorry," I said. "I didn't hear you."

"Sure, sorry. Don't you have homework?"

"It's summer, dad."

"Right. I need to talk to you for a moment, OK?"

He entered my room and found an uncluttered spot at the corner of my bed to sit down. I pushed the newspaper aside and sat up, crossing my legs. He seemed a little excited, which was very unusual for him. His demeanor was usually either sour or bitter so anything other than those two emotional states was strange for the rest of us in the family. A crooked smirk appeared on his face.

"I have a coworker who has an elderly mother selling her car. It has extremely low miles and is in excellent shape, like new really. She only drove it to church or the hair salon a couple of times a month. It's practically new!"

"What kind of car is it?"

"A 1977 Toyota Corona. It's brown."

"A Toyota Corolla?" I said, worried.

"No, it's called a Corona. I hadn't heard of it either but that's what it's called."

"Oh."

"Oh? Is that all you have to say? This is a good deal and a great used car."

"But I was hoping to save my money for a Mazda RX--"

"You're not getting a Mazda RX-7. I'm buying this car. It's too good a deal to pass up. They only want $2,000. Heck of a price!" He stood up and put his hands on his hips. "I'll let you know when I'm going to pick it up and I'll transfer the money you've earned from the restaurant into my account when I need it."

He stepped over the newspaper and left my room. I sat there for a moment, an image of the car I wanted still lingering around in my brain, looking down at the ads in the newspaper and the scribbles and the lines I had drawn into a colorful constellation of circles and arrows and exclamation points and stars. I got back down on the floor, laid on my stomach, grabbed a marker, and looked for more ads of Mazda RX-7s.

***

The next shift I had after the "delivery incident," I called in sick. I was worried that Demitri was going to be mad at me for messing up the delivery truck. I was also worried he knew I lied about knowing how to drive. When I called in, his sister Desmona answered. I told her I was sick and that I wasn't coming in.

"OK. I'll tell Demitri," she said and hung up the phone.

A few hours later, Demitri called me at home.

"You OK?" he said. I could hear his moustache rustling against the headset. He sounded concerned yet upbeat and a little anxious.

"Yeah."

"You're not going to die, are you?"

"No."

"Good because you're one of my best employees. I need you. Got it?"

"Yeah."

"Good. Get some rest and I'll see you tomorrow night."

"OK."

"Good night, jerk face!" He hung up the phone.

I wondered if he had even driven the delivery truck since the other night. I certainly destroyed the transmission on that thing. In fact, I was pretty certain I caused catastrophic damage to it. Although, come to think of it, I wasn't absolutely sure. I was just a dumb kid. Anyway, he didn't sound angry on the phone so I decided to go to work the next night, like he wanted.

My mother gave me a lift to work the next evening. As we passed by my high school, I looked for the boy with the bright red Mustang but he wasn't parked there. Nobody was in the parking lot I recognized except a security guard sitting in a parked golf cart. A wispy sigh seeped out of my mouth as I looked out the window at the school. My mother placed her hand on my shoulder.

"You all right, sweetie?" she said.

"Yeah."

"You don't sound OK. You're not sick, are you?"

"I'll be fine."

"Are you looking forward to getting your new car? Your dad tells me it's in really good shape."

"Yeah."

"Sheesh. Don't get too excited, Wordy McTalkative," she said, sarcastically.

"I was really hoping to get an RX-7."

"Not that again," she said, lifting her hand off my shoulder. She peered out of her window. "Jesus. You've got a one-track mind."

I didn't speak the rest of the way to work. She pulled up to the curb at the shopping center, I got out, and she sped away, her Toyota Camry leaving a plume of dust, smoke, and gravel hanging in the air. As I walked toward the restaurant, I looked around for the delivery truck. I didn't see it anywhere. The worry I had the night before made a dramatic return, a feeling in my stomach like a hunk of cement tossed in a placid pond, and I was certain I was going to get fired. Or worse, yelled at by Demitri then having him call my parents. Ugh. After I entered, I headed straight for the back and immediately began washing dishes. Demitri didn't come around for a long while and I couldn't figure out why. Eventually, after worrying about it through five loads of dirty dishes, Desmona came into the back, bringing more dirty dishes from the dining area.

"Hi Sam," she said, setting the dish tub next to the sink and turning around to walk away.

"Is Demitri here?!" I said, blurting it out like a game show contestant beating the buzzer to end a big-money round. I took a deep breath when I realized just how stupid I sounded.

"No, he's out, doing a few things. But I know he wants to talk to you, about something important. He told me to tell you that."

"What about?" I said, nervous.

"How do I know? I'm not Demitri."

"He didn't say what about?"

"No. Now, get back to work." She left.

Her comment made me even more nervous. He knew. And I knew he knew that I didn't know how to drive and that I fucked up his delivery truck. The dread weighed on me, a lot, so rather than seek out Demitri, I just skirted around the perimeter of restaurant business. I stayed in the back mostly, but when I had to come out to bus tables, I walked along the walls of the dining area, like a ninja except carrying a bus tub and wearing an apron, trying not to be seen. I wasn't very good at it though. Demitri found me rather quickly.

"Sam, I need you outside. It's important," he said when he found me, a heavy hand on my shoulder, a serious tone in his voice.

"Is something wrong?"

"I don't know," he said, confused. "You tell me?"

"Ummm."

"Just come with me, please."

I followed Demitri through the dining area, through the front door, and outside in front of the restaurant.

"You wait here," he said, running off around the side of the building.

I didn't know what to think and expected the worst. It was bad enough that I knew I wasn't getting the car I wanted but to lose my job as well would have been too much. What would be next? My parents getting a divorce?! Jesus.

As I stood there waiting for Demitri to do God knows what, I heard a rumbling sound, not too different from the sound of some kind of drag racing car, a deep, gurgling, mechanical roar from behind the building. I could feel the rumbling through the concrete under my feet and as it got stronger and more forceful, Demitri appeared from around the building driving a monster-sized, white pickup truck so large that it was comical. It was huge and loud and ridiculous. In the driver seat of the massive off-road truck, Demitri appeared diminutive in size, small like a toddler sitting on a phone book trying to look out the best he could. He rolled down the driver side window and unfurled a magnetized sign that he stuck to the outside of the door. It read, "Demitri's Greek Food DELIVERS! Call 49G-REEK!" After reading the sign, I looked up at him, hanging out the window with a big shit-eating grin on his face. He looked like a kid getting ready to unleash the fury of impatient hands on Christmas morning presents. He turned off the engine, opened the door, and jumped down. He firmly placed his hand on my shoulder, as he liked to do.

"Sam, my boy, this is our new delivery truck. What do you think?"

"What happened to the other truck?" I said, meek and worried.

"I don't know. Something was wrong with it but that's not your fault. It was old and rundown and... well, it was time for something new. This truck will pay for itself as *advertising*! It makes a statement." He placed his hands on his hips in his masculine, super hero pose.

"You can't miss it," I said, a little happier, relieved.

"Exactly, my boy! And you, YOU are my new delivery driver."

"What? Me?!"

"Yes, you. I need to increase revenue. The restaurant is too small to fill with more customers. I must get my food to the people who want delicious Greek food but don't want to wait in our long lines. What do you think?"

"It makes sense."

"Good," he said, squeezing my shoulder tighter, leaning in. "Do you accept this promotion?"

"Yeah."

"OK. Go wash up and take that dirty apron off. You have deliveries to make."

He slapped me on the back and gave me a little shove. I ran to the back area of the restaurant, washed my hands and face, yanked off my apron, tossed it to the floor, and ran back out front. Demitri handed me the key to the monster truck--well, it wasn't really a monster truck in the literal sense but it was massive nonetheless--and told me he'd bring out the deliveries. I climbed up into the beast and sat in the cushy driver seat. The steering wheel was wrapped with a fuzzy cover, black like the rest of the interior of the white truck. I adjusted the seat and the rearview mirror, wiggling my posterior to make myself more comfortable for only my second outing in an automobile. Crazy to think but true. Demitri soon came back out with a single to-go bag in his hand. He smiled as he looked up at me in that giant, gaudy, delivery / advertising truck.

"Just one to-go order for now. More will come later, I'm sure. This order is for Ms. Cazamine who lives right back there. She's the old lady who--"

"I don't have to give her a foot rub, do I?"

"No, my boy. No foot rub," he said, smiling. "Now, take your time. Get used to driving this thing. It's your new office! Ready?"

"Yeah."

"Turn it on."

I turned the key and the engine roared to life, smoke billowing from out back, the chassis shaking, and some loose paneling inside rattling. It possessed power that I had never experienced before. I felt its power through the seat right through my testicles. It was divine. I closed the driver-side door, waved to Demitri, pulled the column shifter, put the truck in "D," and slowly drove off. I immediately found it easier to drive without the manual shifter and I paid extra attention to not punch the gas too hard. I really didn't need to. Once I lifted my foot off the brake, it accelerated itself.

I slowly pulled out of the parking lot and navigated the truck to the neighborhood behind the restaurant. The sound of the truck must have been to that quiet neighborhood like when the Japanese first were aware of Godzilla in the distance, the ominous, rumbling noise from behind the mountains, or beyond the horizon scaring the soy beans out of the unsuspecting civilians, never having heard that sound before. The few kids still running around and playing kickball or dodgeball or whatever ball game they were playing in the dimly lit late evening ran for the curbs and looked on, their mouths agape, their eyes wide, at the massive white truck with a caricature of Demitri on its side rumbling through their sleepy neighborhood. Some of the kids even dared to toss empty soda cans into the bed of the truck but none of them were able to hit the target. I waved at them like a fireman driving through his precinct in a shiny, fire truck.

When I arrived at Ms. Cazamine's house, I paid extra attention to not run over the curb or park in her lawn again. I killed the beastly truck and jumped down from the cab with the to-go food in my hand. After I rang the doorbell, I experienced a little déjà vu when she answered the door. There she was--a margarita in one hand, a Virginia Slims 120 cigarette in the other, wearing the same loose fitting, god-awful mumu she had on before--with a big, nicotine-stained, toothy smile on her face. I knew exactly what she was thinking: foot rub.

"You're not Demitri," she said, bitter disappointment in her voice.

"No ma'am. I'm Sam. I work for Demitri."

"Oh, that's too bad. I always look forward to Demitri visiting me. He usually comes inside and chats with me."

"I know. Here's your food," I said. She gave me a $20 bill.

"Keep the change," she said, taking the food, a little frown on her face as she closed the door. I didn't care. I ran back to the truck, opened the door, and hopped in the cab.

I felt a euphoria that I hadn't experienced in a very long time, a feeling of joy and adventurousness, a feeling that was more like an inner voice that told me to enjoy myself, have fun, go wild. I heard Demitri's voice in my brain insisting to take my time. When I started the truck, I decided to go somewhere first before heading back to the restaurant. I decided, right then and there, to go see that girl Kirsty, my math classmate, my crush. She didn't live too far away and I didn't think it would take too long to pay her a visit.

I started the truck. It roared to life and I drove it north on Blanca Road, past my high school, past the other small businesses I daydreamed about working at, past my parents' neighborhood to Kirsty's neighborhood, Lincoln Estates. When I turned in, the squirrels and grackles scattered in several directions, making way for the monster truck and its underage driver. I drove down a few blocks and turned on a street I remembered my school bus turning on before, a street I was pretty sure was her street. After passing a few houses, I found the one I thought was hers and I parked in front. The rumble of the truck set off some motion detectors on the house, flood lights sparked to life to illuminate the driveway. I killed the engine, hopped out of the cab, pulled the magnetic Demitri's Greek Food sign off the side of the truck, and tossed it in the bed. I made my way up the walkway to the front door. A pair of hazel-green eyes peeked through the beveled glass of the front door. When I rang the doorbell, the door quickly opened. It was her, my crush, Kirsty.

"Hey!" she said, nervous and a little confused. "What are you doing here?"

"I thought you lived here."

"Obviously!" she said, rolling her eyes, snickering. "That's funny."

"Yeah."

"Did you need something?" she asked, cocking her head slightly, looking at me then over my shoulder at the huge truck in front of her house. "Is that yours?"

"Yeah," I said. I lied.

"Pretty cool. Must be nice having your own truck."

"Yeah. It's cool."

"Cool," she said, extending her right foot forward, then swirling it around as if she was writing a note in cursive on the door threshold.

"Want to go for a ride with me?" I asked. Then her mom started yelling something from deep inside the house. "It won't take long."

"A friend is at the door mom! I got it!" she said, yelling back at her mother. "She's sooo annoying." She rolled her eyes.

"Sorry if I came without asking."

"No, it's OK. I promise. I just have a lot of homework to do. Can I get a rain check?"

"Yeah."

"Was that the kind of car you really wanted to buy with the money you made from your job?"

"No, I wanted something else, actually."

"Well, I don't care what kind of car you have as long as you take me for a ride. Deal?"

"Deal," I said. I could feel my face getting flushed.

"I gotta go. See you at school." She smiled before closing the door.

I walked back to the truck, hopped in the cab, and drove that beast back to Demitri's.

***

Fall of 1987. All I thought about was my girl Kirsty. That was all I thought about when I was 16, all day, all night. We talked about eloping to California because she wanted to be a movie star. I wanted to be an artist so I thought that was a pretty OK idea. We both were ready to leave home and we made plans while driving around in my 1977 Toyota Corona, a car I partially paid for with money I made working at Demitri's Greek Food. I didn't work at Demitri's anymore but I still would go there every once and a while and eat a gyro sandwich with my girl. She didn't care much for Greek food but I didn't care about that. I loved her anyway.

We made crazy plans, together, all the time talking about what we would do and where we would go. When we were in my little shitty car, we were in our own world. We listened to the Pet Shop Boys and drove around all night, the cold, conditioned air blowing from the dash vents, *West End Girls* playing on the cassette deck, the two of us dreaming of living in California, Los Angeles or maybe San Francisco, anywhere but San Antonio, Texas.

The Discarded Feast

1. Dinner from the G.D.A.M.

We sat across from each other in the small living room of my small apartment, on the floor around my beat-up coffee table, piles of coins and dollar bills on top, two tall boys of beer on ratty paper coasters from the restaurant there too, counting our tips. It was not a good night for tips but the quantity of coins and bills looked deceiving in their unorganized state, looked like we had a lot more money than we actually had. We enjoyed the optical illusion, briefly. We smiled as we pushed the piles of coins and bills around in front of us then raised our cans of beer to toast.

"To Pasta Warehouse," I said.

"To Pasta Warehouse!" my friend Alfonso said.

"Cheers!"

"No, say it the Mexican way. When you toast, say 'Salud!'"

"SALUD!"

We touched our cans together then gulped the cheap beers, crushing the cans when we were through, tossing the cans to the side on the floor, returning to organize the coins and bills, hoping to make rent. We were an odd looking pair of friends. I was lanky and short and white. Alfonso was massive and tall and Hispanic. But what we lacked in commonality of outward appearance was made up by similar character traits of kindness, empathy, and extreme loyalty. We were good young men and good friends to each other.

"You count yours. I'll count mine. Let's see what we got," I said.

"All right," Alfonso said.

We each counted our loot, stacking coins by type, stacking wadded dollar bills, slowly but surely. When everything was accounted for, we looked at each other unenthusiastically.

"Wha cha got?" I said.

"$19.43." Alfonso said. "Wha choo got?"

"$21.25. I win!"

We both laughed a hearty laugh, one filled with exuberance as well as relief. It couldn't get much worse.

"You *are* the winner. Of what, I really don't know. Want another beer?" Alfonso said.

"We're out."

"The GODDAMN has more tall boys for 99 cents. I think they're still open."

"Let's go!"

We left my apartment and hurried down the indoor hallway toward the building exit. My apartment building was old and kinda rundown and a little neglected and the floors squeaked and cracked as we ran down the hall, a loud racket that was annoying to all the tenants of the building. We knew this and shooshed each other as we changed gears to a speed-walk. All we could think about was more beer.

SALUD!

Outside, we careened through the parking lot, walking briskly. The apartment complex--probably built in the early 1970s from the cheapest building materials possible--was nestled in some hills covered in live oaks and the asphalt covering the parking lot rolled and humped and curved its way to the main street. We sped-walk with purpose: beer.

"Are you worried that we don't have the rent?" Alfonso said.

"Nah. If I need to, I will call my folks for help. Don't worry about it. OK?"

"OK."

"Or we can just pickup extra shifts."

"Another eight hours for another $20 in tips?"

"Yep."

"Lame."

"I know."

The convenience store was on the corner across the street from my complex: The G.D.A.M. Or, as we called it, The GODDAMN. The G.D.A.M. actually stood for something along the lines of Gerald's Deli and Asian Market considering the owner's name was Gerald and he was Asian and he sold Asian stuff as well as sandwiches. But to us, it was The GODDAMN. That's where we bought our beer, cigarettes, and cat food, and sometimes dinner. A couple of bucks went a long way at The GODDAMN.

Inside, the owner Gerald sat behind the counter, surrounded by display after display of scratch-off lottery tickets and penis enlargement pills and energy drinks and condoms and candy bars and, well, you name it. Gerald knew us and always greeted us when we came in his store late at night.

"Hal-oh, my friends!" he said.

"Wazzup, Gerald!" Alfonso said.

"Got Miller on special. In the ice."

"Thanks Gerald."

We dug in the trough of ice, pulling out two tall boys of Miller beer. 99 cents each.

"We should probably get Mr. Whiskers some dinner too," I said.

We perused the pet food aisle and grabbed a can of cat food. 50 cents each. Back at the counter, we placed the beer and cat food on it for Gerald to see. He had a sly grin on his face like one of the creatures in the cantina from the movie *Star Wars*. The skin on his face was smooth and pale except around his eyes, where crow's feet--pointed and jagged like arrowheads--revealed the wisdom buried deep in his skull. He was an amiable dude except there was something about him that let you know he'd be ready if the shit ever went down. It wasn't exactly the best part of town, for sure.

"I got Marlboro on special. Buy two, get two free. Want some?" he said.

"Yep." I said.

"Beer and cat food? Looks like a party night," he said, cackling afterwards, stuffing our purchase in a brown paper sack--a cartoon of his face emblazoned on the side.

"Yeah, it's party time," Alfonso said, sarcastically.

"Oh friends, life is *hard* but beer always make it better. Enjoy! See you tomorrow." He slid the brown paper sack across the counter to us.

We smiled and waved goodbye and walked out of The GODDAMN and crossed the empty street. To our right, the city skyline of Austin, Texas, stretched above the street in the distance, glowing with a mix of fluorescent and phosphorescent and neon lights, a few skyscrapers poking the night sky, wispy clouds slithering behind them. Just a mile or so away, it seemed to us like thousands of miles.

"I wish we could go out tonight, have some drinks, meet some chicks, get our dance on. Something. Anything, except sit at home doing nothing," Alfonso said.

"Yeah," I said.

Back in my apartment, we plopped down around the coffee table, opened our beers, took some swigs, and I opened the can of cat food, the sound of the lid bending and crackling and popping open, called to the cat, who appeared instantly, meowing and purring and nuzzling and flustered. Alfonso got a kick out of my cat's crazed behavior.

"Ha ha! Look at Mr. Whiskers. He's psycho!" he said.

"Poor little dude," I said. "I forgot to feed him this morning and we were gone for over 12 hours."

I set the can of cat food on the carpet and Mr. Whiskers devoured it in a matter of seconds. He purred contentedly, rubbed his kitty face along my leg, rubbed his kitty butt along Alfonso's leg, then jumped on the couch to give himself a bath.

"He's good."

"He's lucky to have you as an owner," Alfonso said. "I'm lucky to have you as a roommate, Seff. I don't know what I would have done if you didn't help me out."

"No worries, buddy."

"As soon as I save up some money, I'll get my own place," he said, looking down with what I could only discern was shame.

"Don't worry about it, stay as long as you want."

"Are you sure?"

"I'm sure. It's kind of nice having a roommate, actually. Mr. Whiskers likes it too, another hand to scratch him."

"Cool."

"Cool."

"We gotta get some better shifts at the P.W. Why do they give all the good shifts to the females?"

"Cause they're hot!"

"True. True. But we gotta get some more cash. You need to talk to Laura Ann about switching or picking up some of the shifts the females got."

"Why do I need to talk to Laura Ann?"

"Cause she *likes* you."

"No, she doesn't. She's way, WAY out of my league. WAY OUT!"

"Nah, I've seen her checking you out. She likes you."

"No, she doesn't. Quit saying that and getting my hopes up."

"It's true. You should talk to her, pick up some good shifts and help a brother out. Do it!"

"OK, I'll talk to her tomorrow."

"Do it now."

"But I don't have her number."

"I do," Alfonso said, a sly grin stretching across his face. "I got her digits."

"How do you have her digits?"

"That's none of your goddamn business, I just do. A pimp has to have his hooker's digits!"

We cackled uncontrollably, rolling over on the floor, beer flying here and there, Mr. Whiskers bolting out of the living room for a safer hangout.

"Seriously, though. She digs you. I can tell," Alfonso said.

"Sure."

"Whatever. What time's your shift in the A.M.?"

"I got the 10 which means I have to be there at 9:30. When's yours?"

"10:30. I'll just ride with you and hang out before my shift. Cool?"

"Yeah, cool."

"Want to watch *I'm Gonna Git You Sucka*?"

"Duh."

We turned on the tiny TV, which was hooked to a massive stereo system with large speakers, one of the few things held over from my previous life of comfort from upper middle-class privilege in San Antonio, Texas, a life that seemed like an eternity before our current life of slight desperation, basically a few missteps away from destitute poverty. We barely had enough to live on and were quite a ways from making the rent. But, we still had a couple of weeks before rent was due and we had each other and sometimes that's all you need to survive, sometimes that's all you need to hold off reality a little bit, to make things more bearable. That and something to laugh about.

SALUD!

2. The Trolley: The Assignment of Doom

Pasta Warehouse was a massive, corporate restaurant that sat in a primo spot in downtown Austin, about ten blocks south of the Capitol Building, one block west of Congress Avenue, and a couple miles away from where we lived, my crappy apartment just south of Town Lake. Originally, in the 1920s, the building it occupied was a downtown trolley station, but sometime in the 1980s, it became a family-friendly Italian restaurant. There were several other Pasta Warehouses in Texas, in similar downtown locations, in the other big cities across the State--Dallas, Houston, San Antonio, and we had visited all of them for some reason on excursions to those cities--but they didn't seem quite as fun to work at as the one in Austin. Alfonso and me usually rode to work together in one car so we could share the burden of paying to park, an unfortunate side effect of working downtown, and usually, without fail, got ready for work on the ride there while listening to old school rap--tying our neck ties, combing our hair, checking our teeth, looking for pens for for aprons, and rapping. We particularly liked to rap along with Chuck D to some nasty Public Enemy beats, the best pre-game routine if there ever was one for restaurant servers.

Since there wasn't a lot of inexpensive parking downtown and most parking lots around the restaurant cost $7 or $8 minimum per day, the hunt for a metered spot was very competitive and cutthroat. It was much more lucrative for a server to spend $2 or $3 on metered parking than $8 for a parking lot space, especially since the opportunity to be cut from our shift after two hours was always possible, usually the case actually. So, while I drove, Alfonso was on the lookout for a metered spot near the P.W.

"See anything?" I said.

"Not yet," Alfonso said. "Want a quick smoke?"

"Sure. Light me one."

Alfonso placed two cigarettes in his mouth and lit both simultaneously, giving one to me and keeping the other for himself. We inhaled and exhaled in unison, filling the car with smoke, as we continued to look for a spot. Then one appeared.

"There!" Alfonso said, pointing to his right, barking at me, bouncing in his seat. "See that spot?! Over there!"

"I see it!"

The spot was on the other side of the intersection as I waited behind a couple of cars at a stop sign. It was in a place on the one-way street that wasn't easily accessible from our current position so we were going to have to cross the intersection, turn right up an alley, make another right down another alley, then make a right so I could parallel park in the spot.

"We're not going to make it," Alfonso said.

"I'll get it," I said, determined.

"Wanna bet?"

"Shit yeah! Bet what?"

"Our dinner."

"Deal!"

When it was our turn at the stop sign, I barreled through the intersection, the spot still vacant as we passed it, hope in my heart as I turned right in an alley, more hope welling up to my throat as I turned right down another, crazed excitement as I turned on the street, then screeching to a skid-marked halt at the now-occupied parking space. Someone beat us to it.

"Shit!" Alfonso said.

"Fuck me," I said, looking at who stole our parking space. "Oh shit."

A beautiful brunette was sitting in the car in our metered spot. She applied lipstick to her plump lips looking in the visor mirror, her chocolate brown hair pulled back in a long, messy ponytail, her white blouse starched nicely with the top two buttons undone. She looked at me and Alfonso and winked.

"Laura Ann," Alfonso said.

"Yep. Lucky."

It took us another ten minutes to find a parking space, one that wasn't as close as the one Laura Ann stole from us, one that was a few blocks away. We ran to the P.W.--flicking our cigarette butts away, tying our aprons on as we ran, tightening our ties, slicking back our hair as we walked up the ramp--then walked in the entrance.

Inside, the P.W. was dark and musty and loud and bustling and filled with antique furniture and old gas station signs and gumball machines and ancient license plates from several states. The style the corporation was going for was antique / junkyard chic (boy, did they sure nail the junkyard part). A podium greeted people as they came in and one of our managers, Paula, was standing behind it, marking and scribbling on a diagram of the interior of the restaurant, writing names over groupings of circles and squares that represented table sections, telling a few servers lingering around the number of the section they were being assigned for their shift, groans and mumbles replying to her. She was attractive in the teenage MILF sense--still slender with long, straight, dirty blonde hair, sparkling blue eyes, a small straight nose, mild smoker's breath, and a baby bump on her belly that was barely noticeable. Laura Ann was there as well as a few other dipshits, most of whom were hungover, high, or just tired.

"Don't get too excited people. Make the best of what you have. Laura Ann?"

"Yes?" she said.

"Section 12."

"Thanks!" she said, smiling profusely, her assignment being one of the "better" sections.

"Alfonso?"

"Yes?" he said.

"Section 14."

"Sweet!" he said, happy with his assignment.

"Seff?"

"Yes?" I said.

"The Trolley."

"Great," I said, sarcastically, defeated.

Alfonso chuckled in a way that a big brother chuckles at a little brother's misfortune, knowing that I was going through something that would build character, or some stupid shit like that. The Trolley was an actual trolley car that sat in the middle of the restaurant with tables inside and, mostly, it was the refuge of families with little kids and babies, an eventual disaster of tossed spaghetti, chucked bread, and ripped up sugar packets. Parents with very young children usually didn't tip too well making working The Trolley a lot of work for little payoff. It was the assignment of necessity, being the hallmark decorative piece of the establishment, as well as the assignment of doom.

"I'll make it up to you tomorrow," Paula said.

"Sure you will."

"Now, go roll some silver. Help get ready."

"OK."

Me, Alfonso, Laura Ann, and the other dipshits meandered through the dining area back to the kitchen, a monstrous space with 30 foot ceilings and stations for salad, homemade bread, silverware, plates, soda, as well as a long prep area in front of the cooking line for the expeditor, the one responsible for communicating between the servers and the cooking staff. The new arrivals scattered among the stations, a dipshit on bread, another dipshit on silver, me and Alfonso manning the soda station. We emptied the stacks of clean drinking glasses from the dishwasher racks and stacked them above the soda fountain with the enthusiasm of punk rock kids going to bible school.

"The Trolley? Really?!" I said.

"Sorry, my man," Alfonso said.

"This shift is already shot. I might as well go home."

"Maybe this is the day, the golden day. You never know. You might make some good tips."

"Yeah, right."

"You're such a sour puss."

"Fuck off."

Paula the Assistant Manager scurried into the kitchen, slightly frantic, clipboard in hand, looking around the kitchen, squinting and searching. Her eyes locked on us. She stepped up behind us, placing her hands on our shoulders, leaning in between us.

"So, can you boys work a double today?"

"What?" Alfonso said.

"Two servers quit last night and I just found out. I need you guys to cover. Will you?" I could smell her perfume. It smelled nice to me, not too strong.

"Yeah, I guess," I said, still moping.

"Tell you what. If you work doubles then I'll give you the primo sections tonight. How's that?"

Me and Alfonso looked at each other, smiling a bit, a little hope in the upturned corners of my homie's mouth. We nodded.

"Great!" she said. "I'll assign your stations now for tonight."

We watched her scurry off, her clipboard in one hand, her other hand over her belly where I knew a baby was sleeping. We shook our heads in disbelief.

"Another double?" I said.

"Another one," Alfonso said.

We continued to stack drinking glasses.

***

One of the few perks of working at Pasta Warehouse was special employee pricing for food. All employees received 50% off of the cost of food as well as unfettered access to the salad bar and homemade bread. With this in mind, a server could practically get a feast for a few dollars. For instance, a basic order of spaghetti with tomato sauce was $7.99 and it came with all-you-can-eat salad and bread. So for under $4, a server could get that dinner plate plus grab a to-go bag and plastic container and load the bag with loaves of bread and the container with a mound of salad. It was an extraordinary amount of food for a few bucks. If there were any perks at all for a server, then this was it.

Section 14 was a bust for Alfonso and the Trolley was even worse of a nightmare for me than I had even joked about. My customers were all families with extremely agitated and unruly infants and toddlers who didn't think the Trolley was as fun and exciting as their parents promised. They commenced to trash and destroy the inside of the Trolley with the determination and ferocity of feral chimpanzees in the heat of an African summer, ripping and pounding and flinging every condiment, fork, dining accessory, crayon, and placemat in every which way they could, not even the free ice cream cup could placate them. Alfonso's section, though all more decent and peaceful than the Trolley patrons, were angry as well, mostly because the restaurant was full and the food took just too long to come out. Hungry people, in general, are angry people. It's a fact.

So, tired and defeated, the only thing we were looking forward to, besides not talking to another customer that night, was the massive amount of discounted food we were going to take home with us and shove down our tired, poor faces.

SALUD!

We stood at the computer in the kitchen, the one for ordering food, placing our own food orders instead of orders for angry, unappreciative customers, giddy as we touched the screen, knowing our small reward for a shitty night was soon coming covered in some type of tomato sauce.

"Have you done all your side work?" Alfonso said.

"Most of it."

"Want to have a quick smoke?"

"Yeah."

We gathered our things, slid them in our aprons, and headed through the kitchen toward the back exit, passing the others busy with their side work, rolling silverware, collecting dirty dishes, stacking cups and trays, sweeping the floors, past Warren, an obnoxious mooch if there ever was one. Warren was considerably older than us, plumper, messier, slightly undone, and always, ALWAYS, out of cigarettes or ball-point pens. He noticed where we were going.

"Hey, HEY! You guys going for a smoke?" Warren said, abandoning his side work.

We nodded, sheepishly.

"Can I come too? Hey, can I bum a smoke?" he said.

Alfonso motioned for him to come along, raising his index finger to his lips, winking that he should keep quiet, and not be so goddamn obnoxious. Warren giggled quietly and followed us to the back.

Outside behind the restaurant, an empty alley stretched along the length of the back of the building, and we sat on the edge of a walkway that perched four feet or so above the ground, a landing area for deliveries coming and going or garbage hauling or temporary storage or whatever. A large, stinky dumpster sat toward one end of the alley, Paula's parked car sat toward the other end, and not much else sat in between. Alfonso stuck three cigarettes in his mouth, unhinged a clinky, brass Zippo with a flick of his wrist and a snap of his fingers, and lit them all at once, like a nicotine-crazed ninja. He handed one smoke to me and the other to the obnoxious mooch.

"Thanks," Warren said. "I owe you."

"You owe me dozens," Alfonso said, annoyed.

"I know, I know. How did you guys do?"

"Horrid," I said.

"I'm worried we won't make rent," Alfonso said.

"Ah, man," Warren said, a shit-eating grin sliding across his face. "I made a hundy. Not bad for a couple hours of work."

We peered at him, super annoyed, ribbons of smoke curling and twisting around our heavy heads, disbelief sinking our stomachs. We just couldn't believe it.

"You owe my 25 cents for that smoke, then," Alfonso said, holding out his hand, squinting his eyes, forceful. "I barely made $20 and here you are mooching my smokes."

"All right, all right." Warren handed him a quarter. "Didn't mean to gloat. Just saying. I got lucky. Had a couple of nice tables, gave me big, fat tips. Don't know what else to tell ya. I usually get stuck with the section for the geezers, old and stinky geezers who are cheap and demanding and deaf. That's what I usually get. You know what I mean?"

"I like old folks, you asshole," Alfonso said.

"Yeah. Do you talk about your grandma like that?" I said, playfully shoving Warren.

"My grandma's dead," Warren said, inhaling the last of his smoke then flicking the butt across the alley, its cherry shattering into a million sparks, falling to the ground like orange falling stars. "And yeah, she was cheap, demanding, and deaf." He jumped up and disappeared back inside the restaurant.

We sat there quietly for a minute, inhaling our smoke, exhaling the stress from our souls, enjoying the silence around us, and the city noises muffled in the distance.

"I miss my grandma," Alfonso said.

"Yeah," I said.

"*Mi abuela* sure could cook. Her menudo was the shit!"

"I bet."

A loud bang interrupted our serene moment, the metal back door of the building swinging fast and hard into the brick wall, wobbling and shaking on its hinges, a squeaky plastic cart bouncing over the threshold, pushed by one of the cooks. We looked back, caught off guard by the loud noise, eyes-wide like owls staring at the moon, and watched as Levonne--a hefty black man that seemed almost as wide as he was tall, a neck as robust as a ham, arms like tree trunks, his nappy afro making the hair net bulge in weird places--pushed the plastic cart out the door and passed them, not saying a word. The cart was stacked tall with aluminum trays that looked very similar to the trays used for lasagna, chicken parmigiana, meatballs in marinara, raviolis, and the rest of pasta entrees served to the restaurant patrons, a dozen trays at least, wobbling uncontrollably as he shoved the cart toward the end of the walkway where the dumpster sat, its top open like a hippo sitting in a zoo pool with his mouth wide, waiting for food pellets from children. He parked the plastic cart as close as he could to the edge of the walkway, right next to the dumpster, and tossed the steaming aluminum trays into the trash, one by one, unapologetically, forcefully, quickly. When the last one hit the inside of the dumpster--the sounds echoing through the alley, grackles flying toward the stars or roofs of other buildings--Levonne wiped his hands on his apron and pushed the plastic cart back toward them. He skipped a little as he walked, a little joy in his step that we never saw in his face while he worked. It was strange to see.

"Your food is up," he said. "Get it quick cause the kitchen is closed. I'm going home."

We jumped up and followed him back in. We would be going home soon too.

3. Tears in Beers and Shit like That

I slid the key into the dead bolt of the door to my apartment, turned the door knob, and in we went, to-go containers from the P.W. in our hands, smiles on our faces when we saw Mr. Whiskers waiting for us by the door. He always waited for me by the door. He was a good cat.

"Hey buddy!" said I, leaning down to scratch his head. He purred loudly. "I bet you're hungry."

I turned the lights on and we made our way to the coffee table, setting our food on it, plopping on the floor, our dining area. Alfonso noticed a gang of slaughtered roaches on the floor next to the couch, still twitching, almost dead, flopping on the carpet. Mr. Whiskers pounced on them, jabbed at them for the last time, then promptly ignored them. He lost interest for some reason.

This was a typical haul for Mr. Whiskers. When he was on the prowl, he liked to crouch low to the floor, digging his claws into the carpet, his tail slithering side-to-side like a snake easing through a forest, his eyes narrowing into focus, his whiskers spreading out, stiff, quivering, waiting for bugs. The roaches made their way from the sliding patio door to under my couch and my dutiful cat would watch them, the bugs tip-toeing around dust bunnies and cigarette lighters and waded up hamburger wrappers and sticky bent straws. My apartment complex was surrounded by oak and cedar trees, straddling creek beds that fed Town Lake a couple of blocks away, making fertile ground for bugs and rats and mice and snakes. To say my complex was infested with vermin was almost a stretch (almost) but it was not unusual for roaches to make their way daily under the sliding door from the rotting wooden deck behind my apartment, and that was where Mr. Whiskers would lay, crouched on the hearth of the fireplace next to the back door, his eyes aimed at the bottom of the door where the sliding rails were, looking for tasty bugs, waiting to pounce on them and rip their legs off. He was an effective insect exterminator. The roaches under the couch attempted to make it to the kitchen like starving idiots. Mr. Whiskers wound up his hind legs, sprang into action, jabbing his front right leg under the couch, and pulled the roaches out, his claws ripping the roaches open in one swift motion. As the roaches flip-flopped on the carpet, Mr. Whiskers licked himself clean, setting his paw on the roaches whenever they bounced around too erratically, keeping them in check until their demise. He would leave the bugs to die, alone, in the middle of the living room--or actually, Alfonso's temporary bedroom--as a symbol of his love to me and my new roommate. Fucking gross.

"Looks like Mr. Whiskers was going to have a snack," Alfonso said, opening his container of food, a large pile of lasagna inside still steaming.

"Yeah, we were gone a long time today. Good thing I brought you some food, little buddy," I said, pulling a wad of aluminum foil from my container, unwrapping it, then setting it on the carpet. Some chunks of baked fish were in it and my cat devoured his dinner as quickly as he could. I pet him as he ate. "Good work with the bugs, too. Keep it up!"

"He could at least finish the job he started. One roach is still moving."

Mr. Whiskers walked away, leaving the room, the bugs, and us behind. Me and Alfonso enjoyed our warm food--the only food in the whole place, our only meal of the entire day--after another long day and very little money to show for it, a routine we were both getting tired of. Alfonso folded his empty apron, wrapping the string-tie around it, and set it on the coffee table. Outside, the sound of click-clacking began to echo in our cranny called a patio, large drops of rain hitting the wood planks of the deck, at first a few at a time, then quickly a torrential down pour, loud like pebble stones falling from the sky, bouncing off the wood and crashing into the glass sliding door. Then thunder crashed loudly, shaking the floor, car alarm sirens erupting from the parking lot, dogs barking. I leaned back against the couch (a black, orange, and green-striped pull-out couch I bought for $150 at a second-hand store a few months before), pulling a box of cigarettes from my pants pocket, lighting a smoke with Alfonso's brass Zippo lighter, sucking the cigarette to life, blowing a huge plume of smoke into the living room air. Alfonso leaned back from his food and repeated the same ritual. We sat together, in our silence, except for the sound of the rain hitting the deck, the rhythmic pummeling, menacing and soothing at the same time.

"Would you have a problem if I stayed here for a little while longer?" Alfonso said, hesitantly.

"Stay as long as you need," I said, enjoying my cigarette.

"Are you sure? You keep saying that but I feel bad about it."

"You shouldn't. Shit happens."

"True. True." He sucked on his cigarette and exhaled slowly, like an ancient dragon getting ready to slumber after a long day of torching villages.

"When do you want to go to San Marcos and get some of your things?" I said.

San Marcos was where Alfonso went to school, at Southwest Texas State University--which used to be called Southwest Texas State Teachers College a long time ago--the alma mater of Lyndon Baines Johnson, the 36th President of the United States. Johnson famously bragged that he was kicked out of Southwest Texas State and Alfonso sometimes inferred the same fate happened to him, although the truth was much tamer. He just didn't have the money to finish college; it was that simple. His parents wouldn't help him pay for school and, for whatever reason, he couldn't get a school loan. That shit happens too. He was stranded in an apartment he couldn't pay for in a town with not many jobs, which led him to Austin and the P.W.

"Hmmm. Maybe next Monday or Tuesday. That's when we're off next, right?"

"I think so. Sounds good."

"I'll pay for gas."

"OK," I said, pleased at the offer from him to pay for gas, a precious and scarce commodity in my life.

"I wish I knew what was wrong with my car."

"Yeah."

"It's been a good car for so long. Weird that it won't start."

"We could work on it instead of going to San Marcos," I said, taking a drag from my cigarette.

"No, I really need some of my stuff from my apartment. My lease will be up soon and if I don't go get some things, they'll padlock the door and toss my stuff."

"Shit."

"Yeah, fucking bullshit."

"When is your lease up?"

"The end of the month," he said, running his fingers across his tired scalp, the weariness in his bones showing. "You go off to college, you get a decent place and some help from your folks, then they get tired of helping you and set you free, then the shit hits the fan. I never thought I'd be in this spot, broke, no money for rent, one semester away from graduating. It sucks."

"Yeah." He was speaking the truth. Preach, brother.

"And I'm up to my eyeballs in debt and shit. I don't know what I'm going to do. I can't get a decent job without a degree but I can't graduate without a place to stay so I got this stupid job at P.W. to help pay the rent but I can't pay the rent because I'm not making shit. And now I'm stranded here in Austin cause my car won't start."

"Sounds like a country song!"

We both burst into laughter at the absurdity of it all, our miserable circumstance, our life rolling along in a clichéd fashion, just like a honky-tonk sing-a-long, tears in beers and shit like that.

"Yeah, it does," Alfonso said. "My life is like a goddamn country song. Great. That was *not* what I was aspiring to do."

"I was lucky my folks paid for my college so I don't have any student loans but I couldn't get a decent job after I graduated. All I found were minimum-wage office jobs. I had a hard time paying rent on minimum-wage. I thought waiting tables might be a better gig," I said, sitting back against the couch, smoking some more.

"Boy, were you wrong!"

We laughed some more, smoked some more, ate some more, played with the cat some more, and forgot about our shitty life some more, at least for a few minutes.

"Some days, I make good money," I said.

"Most days, I don't," Alfonso said. "I miss being at home sometimes."

"No worries when you're a kid, right? No bills, no responsibilities, no laundry."

"When I was a senior in high school, I couldn't wait to move away from home. I was itching to go! As soon as I could go, I went." He thrust his hand into the air like a jet plane taking off into the sky. "But now that I've been away for a few years, I miss home. I miss my mom, my family, my home. I never thought I'd say that."

"Yeah."

"I miss my mom's cooking, my abuela's cooking too. Now that the holidays are coming up, I'm sure I'll be thinking about it more, missing home more."

"Yeah, this is my first time being away from home during the holidays. I have to work every day except Christmas and I'm not even sure I'll have the time to go home on Christmas Day either."

"We'll probably have to work doubles the day before and the day after too," he said, sighing, releasing the disappointment in his heart.

"Probably."

"What did we get ourselves into?"

"I don't know. If you're still here, then you can help me put up my tree and decorate it."

"Yeah?"

"Yeah."

We smoked some more as Mr. Whiskers sashayed around the living room, his eyes on the roaches, a couple with twitching legs still, rain drops pummeling the wood deck outside. A bright flash of light lit up the sliding doors followed by a loud clap of lightning, shaking the apartment building roughly, catching Mr. Whiskers off-guard. He dashed out of the living room into my bedroom, probably diving under my bed, to wait for the giant rain monster outside to go away.

4. The Dusty Dessert Tray and the Saddest Place in the Building

Paula the Assistant Manager discussed the reservations for the evening with Dan the General Manager at the podium in the front of the P.W. before every shift, both pointing to the table-diagram like lost explorers looking at a worn, ancient map, mentioning names of servers then huffing and puffing, some eye rolling then some nodding. The servers always stood around in a disorderly bunch--mumbling to each other about what they might do after work, a house party here, an apartment get-together there, cheap beer to drink, bags of Mexican shwag to smoke--the usual pre-shift chit-chat. Dan the G.M. was a hulking mess whose build suggested he may have played football in high school or college, but gave up physical tackling for corporate maneuvering while maintaining the same caloric intake of a young athlete. His short-sleeved, button-down, light blue shirt sagged out of the back of his dark blue trousers and it struggled to remain buttoned at the front, his stomach giving all the buttons and his belt a real test of endurance. Dan the G.M. didn't speak much to the servers, either. He left that job mostly to Paula the A.M.--her sweet demeanor better suited for persuading the mostly younger and unmotivated wait staff to accept their poor assignments with a smile and a promise for a better assignment the next shift. Paula seemed to be a dutiful assistant manager, her hopes of one day assuming the position of general manager were worn on her sleeves, as Dan would one day move on to another newly opened Pasta Warehouse in another bustling city like Baltimore or Detroit or St. Louis or Shitsville or New Craptown.

SALUD!

Dan and Paula always agreed on their plan of attack for the evening dinner rush with a nod, he patted her on the shoulder every time, and retreated to his office without fail. Dan really was an enigma to the rest of the staff. Paula would glance at us--a routinely wilted smile on her face, a red marker in her hand, a single silver barrette in her long, straight, light brown hair. It must have been hard always making promises she couldn't keep but this night seemed more promising to us than usual. There was an electric buzz in the air outside the restaurant when we walked up and the hunt for a parking space was even more difficult than the previous few night shifts. Something must have been happening in downtown Austin, though we weren't sure what it could be. It just felt different, the air, the atmosphere, the city life.

Me and Alfonso were assigned sections 12 and 14 (the good sections) and our hopes of a better evening were high. The hungry patrons flowed to our sections first and filled them up quickly. Sometimes, just sometimes, if the stars aligned properly and the mood of the wait staff ebbed and flowed in empathetic unison with the hunger of the patrons, then the inside of the restaurant could twirl and swirl like ballroom dancers drifting effortlessly in a paisley pattern of a dinner waltz. This particular evening, as luck would have it, we all danced the dance.

After a few hours of diligent work, me and Alfonso took a break at the tea station between our sections, our arms folded across our chests, big smiles on our faces, a good amount of tip money in our aprons, and the satisfaction of knowing that sometimes, just sometimes, the P.W. could provide a living wage (well, almost). Our sections were still bustling but our last customers were slowing down, their stomachs full from eating too much pasta and wine and complimentary bread. Alfonso nudged me with his elbow, patting the rectangular bulge in his shirt pocket where his cigarette pack was nestled, a wink of the eye suggesting that we should take a congratulatory smoke break.

"Do you think we should roll out the dessert cart before we step out back?" I said.

"Nah. My customers are full and I made enough tips anyway."

"You sure?"

"Yeah."

"I'm gonna roll it out anyway to my customers. It's been a great night so far!"

I walked around the partition behind the tea station where the dessert cart normally was parked but it wasn't there. I peeked around the partition at Alfonso.

"Hey! Where is it?" I said.

Alfonso shrugged. I took my place back next to my friend.

"Maybe Paula is vacuuming the dust off the desserts," Alfonso said. We both giggled. The desserts presented on the cart were plastic imitations--a frugal decision made by the corporate office to save some money and to keep the sample desserts from being consumed by hungry servers and bussers or from being prodded by the tiny fingers of curious children--and were susceptible to blankets of dust or spiders looking for a new home.

Alfonso motioned for me to follow him and I did. As we weaved our way around the perimeter of the dining room, good ol' obnoxious Warren noticed our quick exit, knowing exactly what that meant, and he abandoned his customers--some of which were waiting for refills of iced tea or water, some of which wanted a chance to glance at the dusty dessert tray--and he followed us on our way to a smoke break. Laura Ann saw us all as well, and even though she didn't smoke cigarettes, took the opportunity to enjoy a quick break from her busy night, envying the smokers moxy to just *take a break* whenever the need arose. The four of us escaped without Paula the A.M. or Dan the G.M. noticing.

Behind the restaurant in the alley, we perched on the edge of the landing area, our feet dangling side to side, while Warren and Laura Ann jumped down to the street. Alfonso set three smokes in his mouth and lit them in a dramatic fashion with his brass Zippo lighter, then handed one of the lit cigarettes to me and another one to that mooch Warren. He offered a smoke to Laura Ann but she refused demurely, a little shake of her head then a shy upturn of the corner of her mouth, even blushed a bit. Plumes of smoke suddenly reached for the sky.

"Thanks for the smoke," Warren said.

"Yeah, yeah," Alfonso said, taking a huge pull from his smoke then exhaling through his nose, his dragon-like appearance impressing the shit out of the rest of us. "You make another hundy, Mr. Mooch?"

"Yeah, as a matter of fact, I did. What a good night!"

"Good for you, money bags," Alfonso said, rolling his eyes. He turned to Laura Ann, standing there with her hands in her back pockets, looking cute as hell. "What about you? You do all right tonight?"

"Pretty good," she said, caught off guard, turning her attention to the night sky.

"What about you, buddy?" Alfonso said, nudging me with his elbow.

"I made a hundy."

"No shit!" Alfonso said, clapping his hands together, sending a thunderous echo through the alley. "That's great. I'm glad it was a fruitful night. The tips have been kinda sparse lately."

"Nah, things have been all right. I'm getting by pretty well," Warren said, a weasely smirk sliding across his greasy mug. Laura Ann rolled her eyes. Alfonso noticed.

"What about you, pretty girl?" Alfonso said. "Has the money been all right for *you* lately?"

"It could be better," she said, her eyes shifting from the sky to me then back to the sky. "I've been working a lot of doubles. It seems like more work than it's worth but I need the money."

"Oh yeah?" Alfonso said, nudging me with his elbow again, physically demanding I pay attention to Laura Ann. I smiled at her, setting my hot smoke down to my side, being more present.

"Student loans," she said. We all groaned. As we grumbled collectively, Laura Ann turned away, looking toward the end of the alley, leaning as if to get a better look at something. She turned back to us, perplexed. "Do you see that at the end of the alley?"

We all peered that way toward the end of the alley. Down there, past the dumpster, near the corner, standing in the shadows was a shabby figure wearing a burly coat, a sock cap, and rumpled boots. It was not uncommon to see people in the alleyway but it was a little ominous, nonetheless.

"Just a bum," Warren said, sucking the life out of his smoke then flicking the butt to the ground. Laura Ann rolled her eyes again. She was pretty good at rolling her eyes.

"You're a bum," she said, sarcastically. Warren stuck his tongue out at her.

The back door to the restaurant suddenly slammed against the brick wall hard, startling the four of us. Levonne, the humongously squat head cook at the P.W., pushed a squeaky plastic cart through the door, walked past us all, not saying a word. The cart was stacked high with aluminum trays. We watched him push the squeaky cart to the other end of the landing area, as close to the dumpster as possible. One by one, he tossed the aluminum trays into the dumpster, the bum across the alley watching closely, the loud boom of the trays hitting the metal sides of the dumpster, echoing thunderously throughout the alleyway. The loud ruckus destroyed the serenity of our break and Warren and Laura Ann ran back inside the restaurant, leaving me and Alfonso there to finish our cigarettes alone. I eyed the bum, then Levonne, then looked at Alfonso.

"It's weird watching an obviously hungry man watch Levonne throw away a lot of food."

"He'll probably go dumpster diving when Levonne goes back inside," Alfonso said, snuffing out the last of his smoke.

"You think?"

"Yeah."

I snuffed out my smoke too. We were ready to go back in, straightening our aprons and our starched shirts so we were more presentable to our customers, watching Levonne toss more food into the dumpster while the bum watched, motionless, his stomach probably grumbling with anticipation of the dumpster dive for the discarded feast. The grackles fluttered to the top of the adjacent buildings with each subsequent thunder clap from the dumpster, waiting for Levonne to leave along with the bum so they could dumpster dive themselves without humans around. When the cook was finished discarding the trays, he pushed the squeaky cart back toward us then stopped. He peered at us, his yellowed eyes weary and watery, red veins glowing, their course crisscrossing around his chocolate, brown iris.

"Why doesn't the restaurant give that food to a homeless shelter instead of throwing it away?" I said, curiously.

"Huh?" Levonne said, putting his hands on his hips.

"Or give it away to the bums back here?"

"We ain't givin' away no food to bums," Levonne said, definitively, like a boxer declaring he was going to kill his opponent.

"Oh," I said, sheepishly.

"The company gets a tax ride off on food we don't sell. You think they just gonna give it away without no ride off?" Levonne said, his voice booming louder than the sound of the trays hitting the dumpster, louder than Zeus barking down at the lowly humans of Earth, and louder than Chuck D demanding the suckers watch Channel Zero.

"No, I guess not," I said.

"It would be worffless if weez just gave it away. Why do you think I carry around this clipboard wit me?" he said, reaching to the plastic cart, picking up a clipboard with a ball point pen attached to it. "I'zz keep track of what I toss for the ride off."

Me and Alfonso looked at each other, a little confused. We were ready to get back to our tables to close them out. We began to make our way back into the building before Levonne stopped us, raising his hands in front of us. He glared at us.

"When you go back in, the boss man wants to see you," he said, looking at Alfonso.

"What?!" Alfonso said, confused, his hulking frame towering over Levonne's wide, tank-like body.

"The G.M. needs to see you, I sez!"

"OK."

"If ya niggas is bored, then you'z can help poor Levonne dump all this here leffovers and shit."

"That's OK," I said.

"That's what I thought! Ya punks," Levonne said, cackling to himself. He thought that was pretty goddamn funny.

***

Dan the G.M. kept his office as tidy as a junk man kept his junk yard. Piles of three-ring binders containing outdated training manuals and kitchen procedures and stacks of papers with sensitive employee data and employment applications and vendor invoices lined the perimeter of the office on the floor, precariously stacked in a way that could easily be destroyed by a gust of wind or an accidental nudge from an unsuspecting employee. The mass of the clutter seemed to weigh down on him, crushing his soul slowly and deliberately. He sat at his desk, hunched over--his face in his hands, a pencil perched on his right ear--and he appeared to be sobbing when we came in. But he wasn't sobbing; that's just how he was, almost always on the brink of a meltdown. It was kind of sad.

Me and Alfonso stood at the office door, peeking in, standing there quietly, watching Dan the G.M. run his fingers through his thin hair, exhaling loudly, sighs of heavy depression. Alfonso knocked gently on the door frame and the G.M. waved at us to come in. We sat down in front of the desk, looking at some framed pictures and documents on the wall: a photo of Stevie Ray Vaughn, a Bachelor's Degree in Business from the University of Texas at Austin, a photo of the 360 bridge stretching over Lake Austin, some Dilbert cartoons, a dry-erase board with grids of employee schedules, and other unrecognizable things. An array of small black and white security televisions, dusty and staticky, revealed the deepest, darkest corners, nooks, and crannies of the restaurant--including the storeroom, the alley, the side street, and the basement. The office was literally the saddest place in the building, depressing in its oppressive, cluster-fuck, messy state of affairs. We sat in tightly wound balls, making sure not to touch or disrupt anything, and waited to be spoken to.

"So," Dan the G.M. said, then exhaling a long, stinking breath that seemed to deflate him. His breath smelled like death. "I have a favor to ask one of you or both of you, either way." We looked at each other, surprised. Dan the G.M. did not look at us as he continued. He seemed to be staring through the top of his desk. "Here at the Pasta Warehouse, we pride ourselves in helping the community when asked, and we have some special customers that we go out of our way to help because we can. Do you boys think that you would be willing to help some of our special customers?"

We looked at each other again, surprised at the unexpected request from our very impersonal boss.

"Sure, what do you want us to do?" Alfonso said. I looked at him with stink eyes, annoyed that he said 'us' and not 'me.'

"We have some elderly customers who love our meals but have a difficult time coming to our restaurant, so we deliver meals to them. And since we've had quite a few employees suddenly quit, I've been in a bind finding some newer employees to perform this duty. I've been delivering the meals myself lately but as you can see--" He raised his hand and presented the piles of papers to me and Alfonso like a game show hostess, a thin smile on his face, the furrow in his brow digging deep into his skull. He really looked really, really stressed out. "I've been a little busy lately."

"I can see that," I said, Alfonso shoving me in the ribs with his elbow. I rubbed the tender spot in my side, my feelings hurt as well.

"One of you interested? Hell, the both of you can go if you want. The more that go, the better the service."

"Sure," we both said, in unison.

"Good to hear. All I need for you to do is, when you come in tomorrow for the lunch shift, clock in at regular wages instead of server wages, and Levonne will have the meals packaged for you, with the address and some instructions attached. It'll already be paid for and a tip will be given to you at the residence. Any questions?" We shook our heads. "Good. I appreciate your help. Now, one of you grab a mop. A toddler just barfed up her spaghetti in the ladies room."

5. The Delivery or How to Work but Not Actually Work

I parked my dusty, gold 1989 Honda Civic in the alley behind the restaurant while Alfonso jumped out of the car, hopped up onto the landing area, then swung the rickety metal back door open--the crash into the brick wall almost sending it off the hinges--and disappeared inside the P.W. It seemed to me like a good time for a smoke break, so I too hopped out of my little piece-of-shit, Japanese car and leaned on its side, unsheathing a cigarette from my pocket and lighting it with deliberate coolness, knowing that there was a possibility *someone* may be watching me, even though nobody was around. The car continued to run, farting out wisps of exhaust and smoke, occasionally sputtering. I inhaled deeply, looking at the clear blue sky, watching some grackles flutter from building rooftop to rooftop. I looked around for the bum from the day before--curious if he came back to the same spot, wondered if he did some dumpster diving for food--but I didn't see him anywhere. I decided to pop the trunk to my car and be ready for Alfonso when he came back out.

The metal back door swung back open, the rattle from hitting the brick wall echoing throughout the alley, and Alfonso emerged, holding a few plastic bags filled with to-go trays of food, stacked tall and cinched at the top, dangling from his hands as he trotted out the door, a big smile on his face. He hopped down from the landing, winked at me, and placed the food in the trunk.

"Is that all?" I said.

"A few more things coming," Alfonso said.

Levonne emerged from the building soon after, a few more to-go bags in tow, and he handed them down to us.

"You got the directions?" he said.

"Yeppers," Alfonso said, tapping me on the shoulder, tilting his head toward the car, indicating it was time to jam.

"Later fools," Levonne said. "The Boss Man says to be back for the dinner shift." Then he hobbled back into the P.W. like some prehistoric monster retreating to its cold cave.

We hopped into my ride, turned up the radio, and were off to deliver the hot meals to our special customer. I barreled down the alley and weaved around a parking lot, turned a hard right onto Third Street, lifting the dusty car onto two wheels briefly before slamming back down onto the street, me and my homie whooping and hollering and rapping along with A Tribe Called Quest to the *Scenario*, weaving through traffic then turning left onto Guadalupe Street. We reveled in the change of routine from our usual day at work, watching the P.W. fade away behind us and Town Lake's body of water spread around us as we crossed over the South First Bridge, heading toward the south side of town. My apartment complex was close by and I thought about Mr. Whiskers and what mischief he was up to, sitting in the apartment by himself, cleaning himself or hunting for bugs or napping or spontaneously hallucinating, as cats are prone to do. 'What an exciting thing to happen without having to find a tab of LSD from a dealer in the wrong part of town at three in the morning,' I thought to himself.

SALUD!

As we headed south past Auditorium Shores, past the joggers on the trail with their dogs or girlfriends or their loneliness, past The Palmer Auditorium, past Sandy's Hamburgers, we soon passed my apartment, ignoring the urge to go home, plop on the couch, and smoke a bowl.

"Home sweet home!" I said, pointing.

"What do you think Mr. Whiskers is doing right now?" Alfonso said.

"Who knows. Licking his balls, maybe."

"Sounds nice."

"It does, doesn't it?"

Alfonso was the navigator and he attempted to read the directions to the special customer's house--holding the crumpled piece of paper in front of him, trying to decipher the written directions without his glasses because he was just too cool to be bothered with wearing his glasses sometimes--although it would still be difficult to read even with his glasses on because Levonne's handwriting resembled a kindergartener's handwriting. He called out the bits of information he could decode and I compiled them with my own knowledge of the neighborhood, planning my next turn accordingly, and once I knew I was near the Bouldin area, I turned right into the hood, slowing down to a crawl, turning the rap music off, rolling down my window, and watching for kids or pets in the street.

"We're close," I said, my eyes glancing left and right for surprise pedestrians.

"I've never been around here," Alfonso said.

"It's a quiet little neighborhood."

"Do you know where we're going?"

"Yeah, kinda, but we'll just have to park at the first spot I find so we can walk. Not much parking around here, not even for the residents," I said, scanning both sides of the street for an empty space between the V.W. vans, late model American cars, and Volvo sedans. A tiny space appeared and I exploded with excitement. "There!"

I parallel parked my Civic (like a champ) and we hopped out, popped the trunk, and gathered up our delivery. The food was still quite hot and I could feel the heat from inside the to-go bags. Alfonso offered me a cigarette as we began to walk.

"Question: what would you do if you won the lottery?" Alfonso said, sucking his smoke.

"The lottery, huh? How much are we talking about?"

"Well, the last big lottery jackpot was $6.5 million so let's round down and say $6 million. We don't want to be too greedy."

"Hmmm, what would I do with $6 million?"

"Yep, let's say we're at The GODDAMN and we bought some tall boys and some cat food and some Hamburger Helper but without the hamburger and you bought a quick pick and we went home and the next day you were reading the paper--"

"We don't get the paper!" I said, laughing up a storm at the ridiculous idea of wasting our precious money on buying a *newspaper*.

"Hey! This is my fantasy. Let me live it. So, you're reading the paper while sipping a cup of hot tea." We giggled some more. Preposterous! "And you check your numbers and discover that you won $6 million. What would be the first thing you do?"

"Goddamn, that's a LOT of money."

"Bet your britches, it is. A shitload of money."

We walked down the middle of the street, parked cars up and down both sides, no sidewalks in this old neighborhood, just lawns stretching to the curbs. Dogs barked from backyards, cats and squirrels raced. It was the kind of old neighborhood where the residence enjoyed their yards and each other. I just seemed to know where I was going--although I had no idea--and Alfonso just followed me.

"I imagine I would give most of it to my family and friends, maybe some to charity. That's an insane amount of money, really," I said.

"You wouldn't buy a new car?" Alfonso said.

"What's wrong with my car?!"

"Uh, it's kind of a hoopty," he said, punctuated with a *pshaw*.

"It gets us to work, doesn't it?"

"Yeah, I guess."

"I'm cool with my car."

"So, what you're saying is that if you won an insane amount of money, you'd give most of it away to friends like me and to your family who doesn't talk to you much or help you?"

"That's right."

"Weird."

"Oh yeah? What would you do with $6 million?" I looked at my friend, who was looking the other way, sucking on his smoke, contemplating something, accounting for his imaginary winnings.

"Probably the same as you. Give it away, except I'd buy a nice ass ride. Something pimp!"

"Word," I said. "What's the house number?"

Alfonso pulled Levonne's wadded instructions from his back pocket and read the house number.

"134," he said.

"We're close. Must be a little ways up on the left."

As we continued up the street, a calmness settled down around us, the barking dogs from earlier seemed more distant, giving way to a serene dance of June bugs, grasshoppers, and dragon flies in the front lawn of house 134: our destination. We walked across the well-kempt grass in front of the small cottage-style house, the front porch jam-packed with potted succulents, flowers, and cacti, organized meticulously, every one carefully in its place. The little house was in immaculate shape, lovingly cared for by its owner or someone, the paint fresh, the siding and roof pretty new, the windows clean and shiny. We admired it for a bit, looking around the yard, watching the dancing bugs over the green sea of St. Augustine grass blades. Alfonso nudged me to notify the owner and he looked for a doorbell. He found one to the right of the door, a colorful Rastafarian plate around the doorbell button. The plate was a bright red, green, and yellow, shaped like a silhouette of a Rasta's head--the button in the middle like it was the Rasta's nose--with two words embossed at the top of the plate. It said, 'One Love.' I pushed the Rasta's nose and the doorbell jingled a reggae tune inside the house. We could hear light footsteps inside coming toward us, the creak of the pier and beam foundation squeaking with each footstep. The front door opened, revealing a small, elderly woman with a sweet smile, teeth bright like pearls reflecting in the sun, long silver hair pulled back in a ponytail, her body diminutive and slim and her skin a translucent, milky white, wearing a brightly colored dress. She looked at us, smiling, even a small-fry like me a giant next to her.

"Good day," she said. Me and Alfonso nodded. "Please come in."

She opened the door wider, motioning for us to enter, and without hesitation, we did.

6. A Most Miraculous Trip

We tip-toed around the little, old lady, being careful not to accidentally trip over her and crush her, giving her room to waddle and maneuver. She giggled at our over-eager attempts at politeness, knowing full-well that we wouldn't hurt her on purpose (I was certain she could tell). She closed the door behind us and motioned for us to follow her.

"Please, if you may, bring the food into the kitchen. It's this way," she said.

We watched her slowly shuffle toward where we assumed the kitchen would be and took the opportunity to marvel at the parlor room we found ourselves in, as meticulous inside the house as it was outside, filled with a bohemian combination of antique furniture, music memorabilia photos and knick knacks, brightly colored accessories, burly Asian rugs, with a Victorian tea set here, a Japanese sake set there. Reggae music played from a small set of speakers perched on a window sill, a dub track that was slow and low and hypnotic and very soothing. I nudged Alfonso in his gut and the unexpected poke prompted him to rub his tummy, the circular motion of his hands around his mid-section accompanied by a giggle and a booty shake. We soon headed for the kitchen through a door at the back of the parlor room.

In the kitchen, the little, old lady stood on a stepping stool and leaned over a stove, turning a knob to light the oven, stepping down from the stool and motioning for us to come closer.

"Can you put the food in the oven?" she said, bowing down before us, sliding the stool away from the oven.

Alfonso stepped forward, leaned over, opened the oven door, and placed the trays of food he was carrying inside. He turned to me and took the bags I was carrying, opened them, and placed the food in the oven as well. This pleased the little, old lady. She waddled up to Alfonso and patted him on the back, gently and lovingly.

"Please, sit with me and have a drink. Would you?" she said.

We looked at each other, caught off-guard by her friendly request. At the end of the kitchen, a round table sat in a breakfast area in front of a very large picture-frame window overlooking the lush backyard--four chairs around the table, a bottle of rum and a few small glasses in the middle of the table top, and what appeared to be an ashtray and a lighter. Alfonso looked at his watch and I shrugged as if to say, 'Fuck it.' The proposition sounded much, much better than going back to the P.W. to work or going home to sit around my coffee table without a bottle of rum on it or any warm food in our oven. We nodded to each other then sat at the table. The little, old lady waddled after us.

"My name is Sarah. And you?" she said, sitting at the table then pouring some rum for us, then some for herself.

"Alfonso," he said.

"Seff," I said.

"Nice to meet you both," she said. She raised her small glass. "To good health. Toast with me. Cheers!"

"Cheers!" we said. Our three glasses clinked in mid-air and we drank our rum together.

SALUD!

"It was a surprise seeing your two kind faces. Another man has been delivering my food the last few weeks and he seems kind of dour, nice nonetheless, but still dour."

"That must be our boss man, Dan," I said.

"Yeah, he's the G.M. He runs the restaurant," Alfonso said.

"I see," Sarah said. "I hope he is a good boss to you, then." We said nothing, trying to sip the last drops of rum from our glasses, imagining sour-puss Dan the G.M. delivering this sweet, old lady's food with as much enthusiasm as trying to push out a constipated turd. The little, old lady offered us more rum and we accepted, then poured some in our glasses. "Did you both grow up in Austin?"

The rum began swerving through our veins and a warm, fuzzy feeling enveloped our bodies, that feeling that comes from downing straight alcohol midday without much food in the stomach. We looked at each other and laughed. Up until that point, nobody seemed to care about us enough to ask anything beyond what kind of salad dressing was available for the dinner salad or what kind of sauce was best on spaghetti or if there was any more free bread or if glasses could be refilled with tea. It was a nice change.

"I'm from Rosenberg," Alfonso said, his eyes fixated on the ashtray, a shiny cigarette laying in the glass dish--upon closer inspection--was not a cigarette at all, but a smoking device painted to look like a cigarette: a one hitter. "Do you mind if I smoke a cigarette?"

"Not at all. I didn't know young people smoked anymore. I'll join you in a bit. So, Rosenberg? That's near Houston. Am I right?"

"Yes, ma'am," he said, lighting a cigarette and looking at me, then rolling his eye in such a way to get me to look at what he discovered in the ashtray, but I wouldn't look. It seemed rude. "It's about 20 minutes outside of Houston."

"And you?" she said, smiling at me. "Are you from Rosenberg as well?"

"No, I grew up in San Antonio. I moved to Austin to go to college, fell in love with this town, and made it my home. I tried to find a real job after I graduated from college but couldn't. I guess that's how I ended up at the Pasta Warehouse. I thought making tips must be better than making minimum wage. Boy, was I wrong." We laughed a forced laugh, the type that comes after someone tells an uncomfortable truth, a truth with a little sadness behind it, and it bears the weight of complacency.

"Life can be funny that way. Sometimes, things turn out differently than you expect. Nothing wrong with that, though. That's just the way life is."

"Are you from Austin?" I said.

"Yes, pretty much. When I was a girl, my family lived near Georgetown. My daddy was an electrician. My mama was a school teacher. I have strong memories of wanting a big family, wanting a bunch of brothers and sisters to play with, but my parents only had me. And since I was an only child, I was also a lonely child. My parents worked so much that I always felt alone." Sarah picked up the one hitter and tapped it on the edge of the glass ashtray, a little ash sprinkling out, the high-pitched clink of metal on glass, a sound I immediately recognized. I stared in disbelief at the little, old lady with a one hitter in her hand and I gave a wide-eyed look to Alfonso. He rolled his eyes back at me, annoyed. "I learned at a young age that if I didn't get what I wanted then I had to go look for it. I knew I wanted to see the world so I moved to the big city, Austin, Texas."

She reached behind her and opened a drawer to a small table, pulling out a small, glass mason jar with three, bright green marijuana buds in it, tiny glistening tricomes reflecting in the sun light. She opened the jar and took a pinch from one of the buds, then crammed the pinch into the end of the one hitter. She offered it to us. Alfonso quickly accepted. He placed the one hitter to his lips and lit it with his Zippo lighter. As soon as the smoke hit his lungs, he coughed roughly, smoke pouring out of every orifice in his head. He passed the one hitter and Zippo to me and I took a more cautious hit than my overzealous friend. When I was through, I gave the one hitter to Sarah, who tapped it on the ashtray again, took another small pinch from her stash, loaded the pipe, and took a small drag herself. She didn't cough or explain herself; most stoners didn't when they realized they were in the midst of their own. A serene smile slid across her face as she continued.

"I was accepted to attend the University of Texas at Austin and I thought that would be a great starting point to get out and see the world. I moved into a Co-op and quickly realized just how different college life was going to be from the small town life I was used to. The friends I made there were so kind and loving. The seeds of the Hippie Movement were being sewn then in the early 60s and I was exposed to it right away at the Co-op. There was a lot of drinking and smoking and singing and sharing. It was an electric place to live."

"Oh, man. When I went to U.T., I spent a lot of time at those Co-ops," I said, leaning back in my chair, resting my arms behind my heavy head, a big smile on my face. "The best parties were at the Co-ops."

"So, we're both Longhorns, then?" Sarah said.

"Hook 'em," I said.

"Hook 'em," she said, raising her hand in the sign of the horns. "Anyway, as much fun as it was, I really wanted to see the world more than anything and I spent most of my free time when I wasn't doing my chores for the Co-op or smoking grass with my roommates looking into opportunities to travel and the most affordable way to do it, it seemed, was to volunteer."

"You mean, like join the Peace Corps or something?" Alfonso said, lighting himself a cigarette and pouring the three of us some more rum.

"Sure. That was an opportunity but there were many more opportunities as well. The world was becoming a smaller place and it seemed the United States wanted to be the leader. If you wanted to volunteer your time and see the world, then some charity was willing to let you do it. So I took the first opportunity I could during my first summer break from college and I never looked back."

"What did your parents think of you wanting to leave the country?" I said.

"You know, they were typical small town folk so the idea of leaving the country was a little scary to them. Asking their advice or opinion about it wouldn't have done me much good since I already knew they would say not to go. But I wanted to go. I wanted to see the world. I didn't want to just find a job in Georgetown and work or just stay on campus and study. Also, I didn't ask my parents for any money so my desire to see the world wasn't a burden on them. I found a volunteer opportunity in Haiti and I accepted it. The first time I ever flew in a plane to another country was for that trip. It was a miraculous flight."

We settled into a relaxed slump in our chairs, the THC coursing through our veins, the rum settling nicely in our guts, Sarah's story projecting in our minds. As she continued, a movement in the backyard caught my eyes and I gazed out to the picturesque yard, a dance of june bugs, grasshoppers, and dragon flies swirling around just outside the window. In combination with the slow dub tune playing softly from the front of the house, it was a mesmerizing sight to see.

"I just stared out the window the entire flight," she said, a sparkle in her eye as she reminisced. "The world was just so beautiful to my young eyes. When we landed in Haiti, my volunteer work started right away. I was sent there to help a charity whose sole purpose was vaccinating children from polio and it really was a wonderful opportunity for me. The people and especially the children of Haiti were so beautifully sweet and kind. I worked during the day in a renovated building in Port-au-Prince that once was a pool hall and at night, I was free to do what I pleased. I would find ways to go to the beach, catch a bus or ride a bicycle, and I would walk late into the night, looking at the stars, listening to the ocean crash onto the beach, and eating fruit for dinner. It was wonderful."

"Sounds amazing," I said.

"It really was. I heard rumors that things in Haiti weren't too great for its people and that there was an undercurrent of terror created by the government under Papa Doc but I never experienced or witnessed any of that. My days were consumed by smiling faces of the Haitian children and night walking on the beach. Before I knew it, the entire summer had passed by and it was almost time for me to go home. A few nights before I was supposed to fly back home to Austin, I was walking on the beach and I had a realization that it wasn't my time to go back home, I still had more traveling to do and more things to see. I decided that night that I was not going to get on the plane back to the United States."

"Oh shit! What did you do?" Alfonso said, sitting up in his chair, astonished with Sarah's younger self's moxie. "Sorry, excuse my language, sorry."

"That is perfectly fine, young man," she said, a proud smile on her face. "My confidence as a young woman grew immensely that summer and I really knew what I wanted. I knew that I wasn't ready to go home just quite yet."

"What did you do?" I said, sitting up in my chair.

"One of my supervisors was this phenomenal woman named Jane. She was tall and beautiful and regal and from Massachusetts and she had this way about her that was just very confident and strong. She spoke in a way that reminded me of Jackie Kennedy but since I was a girl from a small town in Texas, I imagined most people from back East spoke like this, and maybe they did. I approached her about staying in Haiti longer and she said there wasn't any way I could stay in Haiti. The political climate just wasn't right for me to do that, particularly by myself. The charity was closing up and most of the staff were going back to the United States. I asked her if she was going back to the United States and she said no. She said she was traveling on to Jamaica to join another charity group for more vaccination work. I begged her to let me go with her, to continue my travels with her, and at first, she said absolutely not. After I begged some more, I think she realized something about me that made her change her mind, maybe she knew I was a hard worker and the kids we encountered liked me. She basically told me that if I could make do in a moment's notice with how events would unfold, if I could 'go with the flow,' as they say nowadays, then she would help me get to Jamaica. I graciously accepted her help."

***

"Are you boys hungry? I'm famished!" Sarah said, standing up then brushing out the bunched up material at the front of her dress, then brushing out her dress again because that's what stoners do for good measure. We looked at each other, astonished at her generosity, and astonished some more at the adventurousness she seemed to exhibit as a young woman and the fun she seemed to want to still have as an old woman. She made her way around the table then toward the oven where the food was waiting. "Come on, I know you have the munchies."

We laughed. We *did* have the munchies. Sarah pulled the warm meals out from the oven then grabbed some dishes from the cabinets, setting them neatly on the counter, opening the to-go containers, steam rising from the hot food inside.

"I usually order extra food because I always have a guest or two in the house, friends, neighbors. You know? I like to share," she said. She divvied up the food equally on three plates, lasagna, spaghetti with marinara sauce, penne pasta with fettuccini alfredo sauce, warm bread, a nice lunch, nicer than we were used to. We had served this food to hundreds of customers over the last few months but we had never had this food served to us in this way. I was overcome with her generosity and kindness, to the point where a lump formed in my throat, rendering me speechless.

"You two look like you saw a ghost," she said, cackling at the idea of that, patting Alfonso on the back, then me. "I bet you boys haven't seen your mamas or your grandmamas in a long while. True?" We nodded in unison, a little ashamed. "Now you boys go ahead and start eating. I have to feed my animals lunch too. Then I'll continue my story."

***

"I had everything I owned in a shoulder bag and I accompanied Jane in a taxi to the air field where our plane was waiting to take her, I mean us, to Jamaica. She told me that since she didn't have a ticket for me that she was going to have to use her powers of persuasion, something she rarely did but since she already told me yes and we were on our way, it was going to have to work. She told me that no matter what happened that if we found ourselves in a jam, to go to the men piloting the plane, look them straight in the eyes, and give them a look of desperation and helplessness. She told me, 'Every man will help a damsel in distress. I guarantee it.'"

We listened intently, shoving food in our dry mouths, our eyes fixed on Sarah. She continued.

"We got out of the taxi at the air field and there was a plane waiting for us, one of those prop planes with two propellers, one on each wing. Jane motioned for me to follow her and I did. There was a small group of folks waiting to board the small plane, maybe 8 or 9 people. The plane looked like it could hold a dozen passengers at the most. We joined the group and Jane introduced me to them as her assistant and that was it. With the exception of a few who couldn't believe the fortune Jane came across to receive an assistant with such limited funding from the charity, I was now Jane's assistant, just like that."

"Whoa! That's crazy. They just believed it?" I said.

"Yes," Sarah said. "Why wouldn't they? Jane was a very well respected woman."

"Suckers!" Alfonso said. We all laughed.

"Anyway, when it was time to board the plane, Jane approached the pilot and immediately told him that I was her new assistant and that room was going to have to be made for me on the plane. The pilot looked flushed and exasperated, knowing full well that there wasn't going to be room for an additional person on this plane, but Jane was determined. She gently grabbed both his lapels with the tips of her fingers, locked her eyes onto his for a moment, then pulled him close. She whispered something in his ear and a smile slid across his face, a look similar to when an injured patient succumbs to the calming effect of a morphine drip. He nodded and smiled some more, leaned forward in a slight bow, then hopped on the plane, making some type of adjustments at the rear of the cabin, then hopped back out. He motioned for the passengers to board the plane but his eyes were fixed on Jane, like a malnourished lion gazing at a plump antelope grazing in a field. When it was my turn to board, he told me to go straight to the back of the plane and I did. Instead of a normal seat, which were all taken, my seat was a wooden plank that folded down from the cabin wall, a place for a flight attendant, if there ever was one. Instead of a seatbelt, my form of safety was a piece of chain, bolted to the wall on each side of the folding wooden chair, and instead of a buckle, a metal clip. I sat on the plank apprehensively. It didn't look very safe but Jane gave me an assured glance and a smile so I clipped my safety chain around my waist and pretty soon, we were flying to Jamaica."

"That is amazing," I said, sliding my empty drinking glass toward Alfonso, tilting my head as if to say, 'fill 'er up.' Alfonso acknowledged and filled up my glass as well as his own and Sarah's with more rum. She continued.

"Amazing indeed, what women can do if they put their minds to it. I was so young, I didn't have a care in the world. The flight took four or five hours and was pretty uneventful. I watched the turquoise water of the Caribbean underneath us, occasionally seeing a cargo ship being chased by dolphins. It was such an amazing thing to see for a girl from Texas. When we landed in Jamaica, I literally had no idea what I was going to do or where I was going to stay. But Jane had assured me she'd help me, so I had faith she would, and she did. I tagged along with her to the headquarters of the charity she was working for and she convinced them that I was her assistant and that whatever accommodations she had then I would just stay with her. They agreed without any questions. That's how it seemed to work in those countries with those charities; no one ever seemed to question anything, especially with Jane. The charity had a room for Jane at a nearby hotel and I stayed there with her, sleeping on a couch while she slept on the bed. Back in Haiti, I never spoke much with Jane on a personal level, but that first night, we stayed up late into the night, telling each other our hopes and dreams. She wanted to change the world and hoped it would eventually be through politics. I told her that I wanted to see and experience the world. We were like two school girls, giggling and chatting all night long."

"She must have been a very nice lady, that Jane," Alfonso said. "I've never met anyone who would do something like that for me."

"Shit, me neither," I said. "Most people seem to treat me like shit and I have no idea why."

"Ain't that the truth," Alfonso said. "Well, you don't buddy. You're my homie."

I held out my fist and Alfonso tapped it with his fist.

"Well, I was fortunate," Sarah said. "Obviously, Jane had a charitable heart, a charitable soul. I was lucky, I guess. That next morning, I went with her to the charity and we were assigned our duties. It was very similar work to what we were doing in Haiti, inoculating children from disease, but at night, things were different than in Haiti. I would walk around Kingston and catch the sights and sounds of Jamaica, which at the time, was a vital place for music. Ska and early reggae music was very popular in Jamaica and you could hear the music everywhere you went. It really was mesmerizing, hypnotic. I fell in love with the music and culture of Jamaica. I began to explore Kingston and I made new friends. They would take me to places to eat, clubs to listen to music, to interesting people's houses for parties. It was an amazing time for me. And that's when I met Robert."

***

"Would you boys like some pie?"

We looked at each other, amazed at our continued fortune that afternoon. It had been a very long while since we had been doted on by anyone, especially a grandmotherly woman offering pie. It was a nice feeling.

"We would never turn down pie, ma'am," Alfonso said.

"He's right. That would be rude," I said.

Sarah opened her refrigerator and pulled out a glass pie dish, a mountain of fluffy sweetness at the top of it, and brought it over to the table. She sat it between us as we sat there, speechless, our mouths wide and drooling. We adjusted ourselves in our chairs, sitting up attentively, preparing to fill our stomachs with sweet, delicious joy.

"Homemade lemon meringue pie," Sarah said. She smiled at her masterpiece, its appearance straight out of a cooking magazine, perfect light brown peaks of meringue, jutting up from the marshmallowy base, inviting us to indulge ourselves in a way that was almost shameful. "I'm not keeping you, am I?"

"Oh no... no, no, no, no, no, you are not keeping us," Alfonso said, holding his fork, licking his lips.

"Because if you need to get back to work, I would certainly understand."

"No, ma'am. We don't need to get back," I said. "I mean, we are at work. We're working right now. You know? We are delivering your meal to you." I nudged Alfonso with my elbow then winked.

"Right. We delivered your meal to you and we set your meal up for you. Then we served it to you," he said.

"We pride ourselves in delivering great service to our customers," I said.

"That's right. And we wouldn't be satisfied unless you were satisfied."

"And now, we are accepting a gratuity from you," I said. Me and Alfonso giggled and snickered like little kids. Sarah smiled at our mischievousness. She turned the pie a quarter turn, then another quarter turn, looking for the perfect place to slice first, then raised both hands to her face, surprised.

"Oh! I almost forgot," she said, turning back to the kitchen and walking to the counter. She leaned over the counter, pulling a coffee pot toward her. She adjusted the machine, making sure it was straight and in order, patting the top, then turned it on. "You can't have pie without coffee."

Alfonso and I looked at each other, the corners of both our mouths turning upwards. I leaned toward my roommate, my homie, my best friend.

"We lucked out today," I said, whispering. Alfonso nodded.

Sarah brought three coffee mugs to the table and sat them down. She placed her hands on our shoulders, giving a tender squeeze.

"The coffee will be ready in ten minutes. Now, where was I?"

***

"He was a beautiful young man. His father was white and his mother was black and the two of them created a man whose skin was the color of a macchiato, a creamy light tan, and his hair was as black as night, shaggy and wild. I met Robert in a tiny café one morning while waiting for a cup of coffee to take to work. He was filled with passion for music and pride for his country and when I asked him where he worked, he said he was a musician and that he was on his way to a recording studio to play guitar and sing. He asked me to tag along with him but I couldn't. I had to work. So he asked me to meet him after I got off work and, for whatever reason, I agreed. He gave me an address and I told him I'd meet him at seven o'clock."

"You weren't afraid?" Alfonso said. "I mean, you didn't know him at all."

"Oh, no. I wasn't afraid. He had the kindest smile I had ever seen. Do you want to see? I have a photo of him in the other room."

We nodded and she got up and fetched a framed photo from the parlor room. When she came back, she sat the framed photo down on the table and Alfonso and I looked at the photo of a young Sarah standing next to the man she was describing, her arms around him and one of his arms draped across her shoulders. He was tall and lanky and it seemed his skin was the color of a macchiato but it was hard to tell since it was a black and white photo. She had a love-struck look on her face; he looked confident and satisfied. But the strangest thing about the man was that he looked strikingly like Bob Marley, the legendary reggae singer from Jamaica. I felt a sense of paranoia wash over me and I wondered to myself that maybe I was too high or too drunk. I rubbed my eyes and looked again and this man, Robert, still looked like a young version of Bob Marley but without the long dreadlocks, a bushy afro in their place. I nudged Alfonso so he could see for himself but he was too busy eating pie so I grabbed my paranoia by the reins and reeled it in. Sometimes, you just have to do that when you're high. I took a deep breath and exhaled slowly.

"Is this who I think it is?" I said, pointing at the man she called Robert.

"Who do you think it is?" she said, curious.

This exchange snapped Alfonso out of the hypnotic state the pie put him in. He looked at the photo too and I think he saw what I saw, that distinctive face of the musical legend peering back at the two of us. It was weird.

"He sure looks a lot like Bob Marley," I said. Sarah smiled. "You're telling me you knew Bob Friggin' Marley?" She continued to smile.

"Whoa!" Alfonso said, taking the photo from my hands and examining it closely.

"Yes, I knew him for a short time while I was in Jamaica. He was very sweet on me until I found out he was married."

Alfonso and I got a kick out of that but then the doorbell rang--to the tune of One Love it seemed--and Sarah quickly got up to answer it. Me and my friend sat in a state of astonishment. It seemed to me that this elderly woman was way cooler than we were at that moment, WAY cooler. How could that be?

A few moments later she came back in the kitchen, her demeanor changed.

"Sorry, my friends, but something important has come up with one of my neighbors. I'm afraid I have to go help him." Alfonso and I looked at each other and disappointment sank in. Her story was just getting too good for her to stop at that point but we knew we really weren't there for a social call. We were just delivery boys. "But I'm very glad to have met you both. You are welcome back any time."

I stood up, wiping the crumbs from my lap, and extended my hand to her for a shake. She grabbed my hand then pulled me in for a hug, a tight hug like my mom used to give me when I was a boy. She hugged Alfonso too and led us to the door. After one more goodbye, we walked out the door, across the front yard to my Civic. I looked back to wave at her. She waved back then closed her door.

7. Party at the Slave Quarters with a Certain Other Employee

Alfonso's 1983 Honda Accord sat stranded in the parking lot of my apartment complex, covered in bird shit and june bug carcasses and dried leaves and cedar pollen, its tires partially deflated from sitting in one place for too long, its windows covered with palm prints from thieves looking inside then discovering just how worthless the car really was. Three of its hub caps were missing from too many tight turns on the way to work, and its license plate was bent at the bottom from scraping against one too many parking curbs. It was a real goddamn mess. Few other residents dared to park near it in fear that their cars would catch its disease, the pathetic-abandoned-poor-bastard syndrome. Alfonso had given up on starting it after trying unsuccessfully for an hour a few weeks before, punching its steering wheel and stomping its acceleration pedal repeatedly while violently cranking the key in the ignition over and over. The car just refused to start for personal reasons unknown to us. Rather than discuss it with Alfonso like a decent automobile--that would be a sight--it again decided on its own to die with a little bit of dignity, hunched over in its parking space, looking like a harpooned whale peacefully waiting to meet its watery maker. In spite of its desire for dignity, Alfonso was not pleased with his car.

"Piece of shit," he said. I snickered a bit as we walked by it. After looking the car up and down, he turned his head away. "I refuse to look at her anymore. She's a goddamn WHORE!"

"Maybe we can try to start her again on Monday. I think we're both off work," I said, trying hard to sound consoling.

"Maybe but I doubt she'll start. I probably just need to have her towed to a shop. I better start saving my money."

"Oh shit! That would cost a *lot* of money."

"Yeah, no shit, a lot of money I don't have."

"Ah, forget about it. Let's go to the party and have some fun tonight. All right?"

"All right."

My car was a row over. It was a little less shitty of a ride than Alfonso's car--mainly because it would start when I needed it to, it was a few years newer, and it had a few less dents. Still, it was no prize. It was just transportation, really. I unlocked the doors and we both hopped in. I lovingly caressed my car's steering wheel.

"I bet she'll start right up." I put the key in the ignition then winked at Alfonso.

"Fuck off," Alfonso said, folding his arms across his chest, his mouth twisting into an unhappy squiggle.

"And..." I turned the key and the car started immediately, sort of purring as it idled. "BAM!"

We put our seat belts on and were off, my Civic coasting down the hill toward the parking lot exit, turning north on South First Street, then east on Barton Springs Road to Riverside Drive. The party was at a P.W. employee's place, maybe the mooch Warren's place, maybe at the grumpy Levonne's duplex, somewhere on the East Side, who's house it was didn't really matter. All that mattered--to me anyway--was that a certain other employee would be there. They had an address scrawled on a piece of paper and the handwriting looked very similar to Levonne's crappy handwriting. Alfonso studied its juvenile scrawl, its shaky lines, its shriveled vowels, its wrinkly consonants.

"Is this party at Levonne's place or did he just write down the address for you?" Alfonso said.

"Levonne wrote it down for me."

"Is it his place then?"

"I don't have a clue."

"It would be weird if it was his place."

"Yeah, a little weird but who cares. It's a party."

"True. True. He is a little on the grumpy side to be the host of a party, though. You gotta admit, he's pretty sour."

"Like Lemonheads sour or like WarHeads sour?" I said. Alfonso placed his hand to his chin to think about this question, scratching his chin with his index finger. He took the question seriously, I could tell.

"*WarHeads* sour."

"That's pretty fucking sour!"

We yucked it up, Nitzer Ebb's *Hearts & Minds* slinky beat crackling from the blown-out speakers in the door panels, the reflections of fast food neon signs smearing across the windows then disappearing into the car frame. Alfonso attempted to light a cigarette with his Zippo but the night breeze slithering through the windows kept the flame from igniting off the flint. He put the Zippo in his pocket and pushed the car lighter button, the cigarette dangling from his bottom lip while it waited to be burned into a fiery, carcinogenic, nicotine delivery system.

"You think she'll be there?" Alfonso said, the cigarette, stuck to his lower lip, flopping up and down.

"Laura Ann?"

"Yeah."

"I hope so."

"I hope some other good looking chicks are there too." The car lighter button popped up and he lit his smoke. "I need to get laid." He pushed the cigarette lighter back in its place and took a long, deep drag off his cig, exhaling a plume of smoke to the ceiling through an exasperated sigh, his eyes fixed on the bright, pale yellow moon. "Man, I sure could use some trim. It's been a long, *long* time."

A turn here and there off Riverside Drive changed the landscape from fast food urban corporate sprawl to gentrified yuppie high-rise condos to down and out hoods to plain old-fashioned shit holes. I rolled down the windows all the way and the cool night breeze poured into the car, flushing the cigarette smoke out. The neighborhood street was lined on both sides with parked late model American cars, Lincolns, Caddies, Buicks, some with magnificent, sparkly, alloy rims, some perched on top of dusty cinder blocks with the dented hoods erected. As we slowly passed each home looking for the party house, we could hear various kinds of music that revealed the diversity of this particular hood--one house emitting the oompa oompa oompas of traditional Tejano music, another thumping the low-end stylings of the Funkadelic-inspired Dr. Dre, another with the beautiful squeal of Stevie Ray Vaughn finger-fucking his guitar. As we came to an intersection, I turned to Alfonso for direction but, knowing my friend knew as much about getting around town as I knew about astrophysics, I took the piece of paper from his hand and reread the address. A copilot from Rosenberg, Texas was worthless in Austin, Texas.

"Oh, almost there. It's up here," I said, tossing the piece of paper aside. I took a right and parallel parked my car in one fluid motion, squeezing my Civic between a maroon 76 Coup DeVille with a white vinyl top and a brown 74 Plymouth Duster with a flat tire and a smashed windshield. "Should be around here somewhere."

"Better lock your ride," Alfonso said. "This hood is sketchy." We got out of my Civic, dusting our clothes off, fixing our hair.

I nodded at Alf, locked my car, and we followed the sidewalk, our hands dragging along a chain-link fence with signs posted every three feet that said, 'Beware of Dog!'

"I don't see any dog," Alfonso said, peering through the fence, looking for a vicious dog worth posting a sign about.

"Yeah, me neither. This is 301. Two more."

The next house was also surrounded by a fence but it was the wrought iron kind, some parts of it painted black, some parts rusted, protecting a house that could barely stand up, looking like a drunk propped up on a bar with one wobbly elbow after being pummeled in a bare-fisted brawl in an alley. A large hole in the roof--remnants of a house fire long ago--was surrounded by poofy pigeons perched for their evening nap.

"Is this one even worth fencing in?" Alfonso said. "Look at it!"

"Really, it's a dump," I said, looking for the house number. I saw the number next to the front door except the zero was missing, adding a sad punctuation mark to the depressed exterior of the neglected house. "I think this is 303. The next one should be 305."

Once the wrought iron fence ended, the side walk revealed a large front yard at the next lot, a tall pecan tree with a thin canopy at the left of it and a massive oak tree with a bushy top to the right of the yard, both trees kept watch over a lush lawn of a mixed variety, St. Augustine and Bermuda grasses intermingling in a cross-hatch of wide and thin blades, some lawn chairs spread out in a haphazard fashion, and a keg of beer in a grey, plastic trash bin sat in the middle of a walk-way that connected the small, white, thoroughly kempt house to the sidewalk. A dozen or so people stood in the lawn in various small, social configurations, some of them we recognized from the P.W., some of them we didn't know at all but looked worth knowing. The party had started without us.

We approached the first group of folks that included that mooch Warren as well as the other mooch Paul and that bastard Fred. Just like any other place, cliques formed at the P.W. whether the employees wanted them to or not; that's the natural way. Warren, Paul, and Fred gravitated toward each other because they were kindred spirits, ones who were enamored with doing as little work as possible while taking as much from others as possible. Warren loved to mooch cigarettes while Paul was a master at mooching spare change and Fred was... well, Fred was just a contemptible bastard, the sort of coworker who seemed to get out of any side work, was always late for his shifts, never had his own pens or pads of paper, and who passed gas whenever possible in the close proximity of anyone he felt the need to fart on. These three were made for each other.

"Hey fellas!" said that mooch Warren. "It wouldn't be a party without you."

"Wazzup?" I said.

"'Zup," Alfonso said, his greeting more an acknowledgment than a kind regard.

We eyeballed the beers that the three bastards were holding, craning our necks to make sure the keg was still flowing. Warren extended his arm to keep us from leaving. I could tell he wanted something, that bastard.

"Can I bum a smoke?" he said.

"Surprise, surprise," Alfonso said, sliding his hand in his pants pocket as if to shield his pack of smokes from the despicable moochers. Warren looked hurt by Alfonso's gesture to protect his smokes.

"Come on, man. This is the last time I'll ask. Promise!"

"That is literally the thousandth time you've said it will be the last time that you ask to bum something," I said.

Warren eyeballed me, surprised that I seemed to notice, and then conceded a smirk.

"All right, then. This is REALLY the last time I'll ask," he said, slowly raising his palms to Alfonso, like a starved street urchin whose stomach pangs were too much to bear to suffer from the humiliation of begging.

"Fine, goddamn it!" Alfonso said, pulling the pack from his pocket and roughly pinching an unsuspecting cigarette, tossing it in Warren's grubby hands.

"Is this Levonne's house?" I said, looking around for more faces I recognized.

"Nah, this house here is Levonne's grandmother's. He lives in the slave quarters in the back," said the other mooch Paul, his palms slowly raising toward Alfonso, who grudgingly tossed a slightly bent smoke into his hand as well. Alfonso's face was flushed and steamy. That bastard Fred's hands began to raise when Alfonso snapped.

"I only have a few left!" he said. "I have to ration the rest."

Fred slid his hands in his back pockets, tilting his head back as if to say, 'That's fine.'

"Is his grandmother home?" I said.

"Nah. Bahamas," Paul said. "Levonne's around back. Some others from P.W. too, the dishwasher, some of the girls, even Paula."

"Paula's back there?" Alfonso said, surprised.

"Yep."

Alfonso nudged me and we bee-lined for the keg, leaving the dirty three behind who were two cigarettes richer than they were before. The keg was unoccupied, a sleeve of plastic cups duct-taped to the side of the trash can, a metal lockbox attached at the rim of the can with a colorful, hand-drawn paper sign that read: DONATIONS! A fat red arrow with an electric yellow outline pointed to the slot in the middle of the lid to the lockbox. Me and Alfonso rummaged through our pockets, slipping spare quarters and a few, wrinkled dollar bills into the slot. Alfonso unsheathed two cups and held them in front of the keg tap. He tilted his head toward the keg.

"You pump," he said. I obliged, pumping the beer tap, a glistening stream of golden liquid pouring out. I couldn't help but think that it looked like the keg was urinating in our cups, which wasn't too far from the truth considering how cheap the beer probably was. Soon, we each had two frosty brewskies and marveled that even cheap beer tasted mighty fine when it was very cold.

SALUD!

We surveyed the rest of the party-goers and concluded, with a disinterested sigh, that the backyard must be a more interesting place, particularly if Paula the Assistant Manager, who was also very, very pregnant, was back there as well. Surely, a pregnant woman at a late-night party was up to no good. Alfonso led the way with me close behind, around the front, careening around a small group of strangers to the left side of the house, through a metal gate to the crowded backyard. A massive oak tree jutted up from the center of the yard, maybe 20 feet from the back of the house, whose trunk must have been another 20 feet in circumference. 18-inch pieces of two by four were nailed to its side in a ladder-like configuration up to the crotch and we could see legs dangling from up there but we couldn't see who it was. The backyard was filled with an array of metal behemoths, an assortment of dead cars sleeping in the tall grass that would give Alfonso's piece of shit a run for its money--a 21-foot sail boat on a rusty trailer that had seen better days, a small, cinder block house that must have been Levonne's slave quarters, another keg in a plastic trash can with a similar cup sleeve / metal lockbox configuration, and a happy group of people drinking, talking, laughing, all generally having a good time. And even though we had never been there before, there was a feeling of contentment in the air that was palatable. I studied the dangling legs from the crotch of the tree some more.

"I wonder who that is up there," I said, tilting my head as if manually focusing my eyes.

Alfonso looked up there too, quickly studying the brand-new pair of Nike Air Jordans on the feet, the starched pair of khaki Dickies, the bright white tube socks with a red and green stripe. The leg dangled limply.

"Oh, that's just Reynard. I can tell by the shoes," he said. His observant tone surprised me a bit.

"Reynard the busser?" I said.

"Yeah."

"Hmmm. I hope he doesn't fall down."

"Whatever."

Behind the oak tree sat a cluster of lawn chairs, some occupied, a couple empty. Me and Alfonso made ourselves at home. We studied the crowd some more, noticing some familiar faces from the P.W., others complete strangers. Alfonso nudged me with his elbow, tilting his head in the other direction, emitting a sound from his mouth that could easily be translated as, 'Oh shit!' Sitting on the hood of one of the automobile carcasses was Paula the A.M., still as pregnant as can be, her stomach protruding in front of her and draped by an over-sized shirt, her arms wrapped around a young man who wasn't impeded by her incubating bun. The young man swooped down on Paula, attaching his lips to her neck. She squealed with delight, fumbling on the hood, almost losing her balance, breaking her fall by wrapping her legs around the young man's twigs for legs. Alfonso chuckled.

"That is NOT her husband," he said. I raised my eyebrows sharply with mock surprise. We leaned back in our chairs, wedging ourselves comfortably, and raised our plastic cups to each other. "A toast: To the night off."

We clinked our cups together.

"Cheers," I said.

"Have you seen Laura Ann?" Alfonso said.

"No, not yet. Have you?"

"Yep. Over there."

"Where?" I said, craning my neck, looking around.

"There, by the fence."

I turned to look, scanning along the fence at the side of the property.

"She's talking to that dude over there," Alfonso continued. "She looks happy. She looks good too. Damn, she's hot!"

I found her standing next to a good-looking dude, a guy who looked familiar but who didn't work at the P.W., maybe from a neighboring business or from the university. She talked casually with the guy, one of her hands on her hip, the other holding a cup of beer in front of her. She sipped her beer as she listened to the guy go on and on about something, laughing occasionally at something else, her head flinging back, a casual laugh flung into the air, then a another sip of her beer. They carried on together for a few extended minutes, talking and laughing back and forth as friends do, until the guy seemed to suggest that they explore other parts of the property, and the two walked off together. I watched them as they disappeared around the house, probably going to the front yard, maybe going to the backseat of his car. I sulked a bit. Alfonso noticed and sighed.

"You gonna go talk to her?" he said. I didn't respond. Alfonso started to console me when two giant hands crashed on our shoulders, like two giant boulders smashing boldly onto the floor of an unsuspecting ravine, thudding loudly. We looked up, surprised, a little of our beers splashing on our laps. It was Levonne, the grouchy cook, our grumpy host for the night. A smile stretched across his face that would make the Cheshire Cat jealous.

"Wazzup, motherfuckers!" he said, pushing down on our shoulders, giving them a little shake, a little more beer splashing on our crotches. Alfonso quickly wiped the crotch of his pants but it was too late. It looked like we peed our pants. Alfonso sighed, defeated. Levonne bellowed a deep, belly laugh. He was pleased with his handy work. "Don't let the ladies see you pissed yo self!" He pulled open a lawn chair behind us and sat down. "Glad you came to my motherfuckin' party, you motherfuckers."

"Thanks for having us," I said. "You have a nice setup."

"My grams lives in the big house, me and my fams lives in the small house over there. But they all gone right now. It's just me, alone."

"Where'd they go?" Alfonso said. He continued to wipe his pants even though it wasn't doing any good.

Levonne leaned back in his chair, a cup of beer in one hand, a huge sausage wrapped in a flour tortilla in the other hand. He alternated between the two, a sip here, a chew there. He was medicating his lonely soul.

"My grams is on a cruise, a Love Boat cruise. Going to the Bahamas. She went with an ol' folks group last week. She be back next week."

"Sounds nice," I said.

"Yeah, must be nice," Alfonso said.

Levonne raised his elbow to the arm of the chair, attempting to prop his chubby chin, but when he tried to rest his wide chin in his big hand, his elbow slipped, shuffling his body violently. Some beer spilled on his lap too and Alfonso couldn't help but laugh. We all looked like we peed our pants and Alfonso felt justified.

"Goddamn it!" Levonne said. "That's what I get, I guess. I can't do nuttin' right." He shoved the pool of beer off his lap. "Damn!"

"What do you mean?" I said, curious.

"My woman left me, took my kid too. They stayin' at her pop's house in Houston. She mad cause I be workin' all the time, stayin' at work late, workin' doubles and shit. But what does she want me to do? We got bills to pay, a baby to feed. Shit, a man's got to work, ya know?"

"True, true," Alfonso said. "But you have to make your woman happy, am I right?"

"I guess," Levonne said, a little deflated. "That's the Marvin Gaye answer, ain't it? I try to get all my shit done at work but it never ends. There's always more to do."

"When is your wife coming back?" I said.

"Shit, she ain't my wife. She just my baby mama," Levonne said, chomping at the sausage wrap in his hand, taking a swig of beer, and continued talking with his mouth full, spittle of food and beer spraying everywhere. "I proposed to the bitch but she say no, not until I treat her better."

"You could start by not calling her a *bitch*, I guess," Alfonso said, sipping his beer, his eyebrows slowly raising over wide eyes. Levonne gave him a stare that burned through his face and, for a quick moment, he regretted opening his mouth and saying anything, especially to the super, depressed host with boulders for hands. But soon, Levonne wheezed and laughed then slugged Alfonso on the back.

"Shit, you droppin' knowledge and shit. I need to sho' some respect, right? Even if she just my baby mama. I do love the b--" Levonne paused, collecting himself, taking a deep breath. "I mean, I have sincere feelings for the mother of my child." He sat up straight in his seat, putting on a dignified air about him, propping up his chin, before collapsing into a fit of giggles and wheezing and knee-slapping.

He whacked Alfonso on the back again, the sausage wrap leaving a grease mark, beer spilling from his other hand on my back. "You're a funny motherfucker, my man!" He stood up, spilling even more beer around, like a demented water sprinkler, splashing everywhere. "I gots to piss. I'll be back, motherfuckers!" He sauntered off, dropping the cup of beer on the ground then holding his crotch.

"Geez, he's wasted," Alfonso said.

"Yeah," I said.

"Say, you gonna talk to Laura Ann?"

"Nah."

"Why not?"

"Cause it looks like I pissed myself."

"You do!" Alfonso said, releasing a loud laugh, his head flinging back, then slumping in his chair. "Want to smoke a doobie instead?"

"I thought you'd never ask."

8. Life Can Be Gross

For my side work, I wiped bar glasses until they sparkled. Alfonso buffed silverware until it shined. We stood in the kitchen of the P.W., off to the side along an ancient brick wall originally built in the 1920s, dutifully ripping through our side work, assigned to us in a huff by Paula the Assistant Manager after she overheard us snickering about her adulterous behavior the night before at the party. She wasn't very pleased with herself for the way she acted but she was more upset that others noticed. Me and Alfonso were being punished for her lack of morals. The irony was not lost on us. Making the silver and glassware sparkle and shine was made all the more difficult by their cheap composition. 'You can make a turd sparkle if you can buff the shit out of it,' a brilliant man once said.

"Goddamn whore," I said, mumbling.

"Fucking bitch," Alfonso said, also mumbling.

"It's all our fault, though. We should have kept our fucking mouths shut."

"I guess."

Paula the A.M. overheard us as she made her way into the kitchen to announce that Dan the G.M. would be giving a little pep talk before the dinner shift. It wasn't like us to gossip or chatter or carry on about the other employees at the P.W. but sometimes these things had a way of getting ahold of people's common sense. Paula didn't care, though. She sent us a stare that would burn a hole through a steel-reinforced wall and we knew not to look directly at her searing eyes. She clapped briskly, the sound of her dry palms hitting together echoing throughout the enormous kitchen, ricocheting around and startling the other employees.

"Attention staff! Dan wants to speak to all of you in ten minutes. I want you all to gather around as soon as possible. Please grab anyone you know that is out on a smoke break or in the crapper or wherever. Got it? In 10!" she said, clapping some more, then stomping out of the kitchen, her thin legs gesticulating wildly under her immobile, bulbous torso, giving her the look of a spider scurrying away from a dropping human foot.

Laura Ann came into the kitchen after Paula escaped and noticed us against the wall--like kindergarteners being punished for disrupting the class--and knew something must have really upset Paula because of what we were doing for side work. It really was shit work, buffing and wiping those things, almost impossible to accomplish. She quickly found a package of table napkins--wrapped in brown paper and stamped with a logo of a panda bear wearing a chef's hat with a big shit-eating grin on its face--and quietly sauntered up behind me and Alfonso. She peeked over my shoulder, whistling a soft tune that sounded similar to the death march played when Darth Vader entered a scene in the *Star Wars* movies. I was surprised to see her behind us.

"Very funny," I said, huffing.

"What did you do?" she said, placing the brown paper package of napkins on the metal table, then tracing a figure eight on the table top, pretending to not know what happened but knowing full-well what happened. She was good at that.

"We said something we shouldn't have, about Paula," Alfonso said.

"Oh yeah?" she said, sarcastically.

"Yeah, we saw her at Levonne's party--"

"*You* were at Levonne's party last night? I didn't see you there."

"I saw *you* there," I said, looking up at her. She returned a quizzical look.

"Oh yeah?"

"But you left with some dude before I could say hello."

"I see," she said, continuing the figure eight on the metal table. "So what did you say about Paula that got you doing shit side work?"

"We saw her pawing on some guy last night, some guy that's not her husband. We were joking about it when she came into the kitchen earlier. We didn't know she was coming in."

"You mean, Jacques?" she said, drawing a smiley face on the table top, the warm impression from her finger remaining on the metal surface for a brief moment, the smiley face's toothy grin wide and maniacal, then vanishing. I perked up quickly and turned to Laura Ann who continued to look at the table top.

"Is that the guy's name?"

"He works at the salon next door," she said.

"I knew it! I knew he looked familiar!"

Laura Ann turned to me, squinting her eyes and wrinkling her nose as if to whisper, 'Dude, shut the fuck up.' I shut the fuck up.

"She's gonna give us shitty shifts, I just know it," Alfonso said. "Man, I have to make some money, my car won't start, we barely have any food in the fridge. This will be another turd dropped in our litter box called life. It's starting to pile up."

"That's gross," Laura Ann said.

"Life can be gross."

"I wonder what Dan is going to talk about," I said, placing the last bar glass into the plastic drying rack. I began to slide the rack over but Laura Ann stood in the way. I looked her up and down until she stepped back, giving me just barely enough room to slide by. I pushed the rack to the end of the table and placed it on a stack of other racks waiting to be pushed out to the bar, then to be hung up or put away by whoever was being punished over there. Alfonso's pile of silverware hadn't diminished at all so me and Laura Ann helped. I wiped some clean while Laura Ann rolled the clean ones in their napkins.

"Maybe somebody died," Alfonso said.

"Nobody *died*," I said, scoffing at the idea that one of our coworkers would be free from the hell hole that was the P.W.

"I heard there are going to be some changes made that will affect all of us," she said, looking at her handy work. "Some of our perks will prolly go away."

"Perks? Ha!" Alfonso said, slamming his palm on the table, rattling the silverware pile. "The only perk we've gotten lately is meeting a nice old lady who claims she knew Bob Marley."

"What?!" she said, her eyes opening wide, her mouth dropping. Then Dan came into the kitchen.

"EVERYONE! I need your attention," Dan the G.M. said, clapping his hands, then adjusting his grease-stained, paisley tie while also attempting to tuck his shirt into the back of his drooping, khaki pants. His fat gut protested his every move. "I have some important things to discuss with you."

Laura Ann squeezed Alfonso's shoulder as she leaned in front of him, squinting her eyes at his, trying to pull more information out of him about the Bob Marley comment with the tight gravitational pull of her stare. He smiled a big ass grin at her.

"I'll tell you later," he said quietly, then raised his finger to his lips and shushed her. Laura Ann huffed, crossed her arms, disappointed.

The staff huddled around Dan, 25 to 30 of them, from servers to cooks to bussers to dish washers to hostesses, even Paula rubbing her big belly like a fortune teller swirling her hands around a crystal ball, all of them heaped into a lazy formation, loose and tired. They didn't seem to want to get too close to Dan, as if he possessed the type of body odor that would permeate your own clothes and haunt your nose. Dan sighed.

"Come on, people. Get closer," he said, his head drooping forward while he raised his arms, waving for them to come closer.

Nobody moved.

"OK. I have some good news and I have some bad news. The good news is that you all still have jobs. That's good, right?!" he said, forcing a fake cheeriness through his teeth like an inexperienced comedian sensing his act was a complete bomb. "OK. OK. That wasn't so funny, I get that. Sheesh."

He motioned for them to come closer still and a couple of workers made a step or two but most stood where they were.

"All right, all right. So, here's the deal from corporate. As you know, all of you are entitled to meals at a discounted rate of 50 percent and that isn't going to change. But corporate feels that too much food is going out the door at 50 percent off so they are now limiting the number of meals per week that you can order food at 50 percent off."

"How many meals is that going to be?" someone said.

"Well, here's the catch. I know a lot of you people count on these meals and I hate to be the bearer of bad news--"

"How many?!" Alfonso said, his deep voice startling the others.

"Three per week." Heavy groans permeated the kitchen. Dan the G.M. placed his hands on his hips like a mother trying to cheer up her child after learning that the pet dog just got run over a few minutes before. "Come on, people. You still get *three* meals at 50 percent off. That's stupendous!"

"This sucks!" someone said, pissed off. Some tried to wander off to sulk.

"All right, all right. No one go anywhere yet. I'm not finished."

"You mean, there's more?" Laura Ann said.

"Yeah, one more thing. Corporate wants us all to mind wastefulness. Be good stewards of the inventory on-hand. Watch your portions when making salads. Watch your quantities when serving bread. Don't refill customers drinking glasses unless they explicitly ask for a refill. Mind wastefulness!"

"Is that all?" someone said.

"That is all," Dan said, shoving his hands in his pockets, rocking back and forth from heel to toe, grinning from ear to ear like he won a prize he knew he didn't deserve. "Wait! Before everyone man's their stations, how about we sing the Pasta Warehouse Birthday Song? Huh?!"

The heavy groans returned, some turned and walked away.

"Oh, come on. I'll lead! *From the pasta we make, to the bread we bake...*"

None of the employees joined in except for Paula. She clapped along as Dan sang loudly, holding his pant waist with one hand, twirling his other hand in the air like a crazed Italian pizza cook. Completely ridiculous. After another bar or two of the song was sung, a few employees joined in but it was the saddest birthday song ever sung by human beings.

SALUD!

***

After the dinner rush and the disappointing collection of meager gratuities, I walked out to the alleyway behind the P.W., alone, and sat on the edge of the walkway of the loading area. I looked up and watched the thin, wispy night clouds slither slowly across the white freckles of the night sky. A cool breeze poured in the alley from Town Lake a mile or so away, stirring up the dingy stench of the dumpsters, mixing in with the yummy exhaust of deep-fried foods from the neighboring restaurants. I thought quite a bit about my journey so far in my life that led me to the P.W. and wondered how it all came about. Did my choice of studying literature at the university lead me down a path of poor career choices to choose from after graduating from school or did I make concrete decisions that led me to work long hours for very little money at a restaurant with half-decent meals? I wasn't sure. I wasn't sure of anything, actually. I would ponder these things occasionally but with so little life experience, the pondering just led to confusion. I usually tempered the confusion with nicotine and alcohol and marijuana and ecstasy. At that moment, it was nicotine.

I lit a cigarette that I bummed from Alfonso a few minutes earlier with the brass Zippo I also bummed from my homie. As I inhaled the hot smoke, I felt a bit of gratitude inside for having met such a good person in Alfonso, a friend that felt more like a brother to me, a brother I never had. I enjoyed having him as a roommate, something else I hadn't planned for after graduating from school, another turn of events that I didn't see coming. Is that how life was going to be from now on after leaving the structure of college life, where things are fit into daily schedules and weekly events and blocks of semesters, one after the other with holidays and breaks sprinkled in between? I didn't know.

My thoughts pushed my brain into a vortex of internal monologues and event rehashing, churning through these questions and mental replays of good times at college parties, until the sound of glass clinking on asphalt echoed through the alley, disturbing my malaise. I looked where the sound originated from and saw a shadowy figure sitting hunched over on the ground at the end of the alley, picking up a glass bottle that tipped over, lifting the bottle above its head, mouth opened wide to accept any drops that may drip out of it. It must have been empty because the figure tossed the bottle. It crashed on the hard ground. I looked closer and recognized the figure. It was the same bum I'd seen before in the alley, the one who seemed to always appear when I was taking a smoke break with my coworkers. The bum tilted his head back, resting it on the building wall, and emitted a sigh as heavy as his heart. I felt ridiculous thinking about how shitty my life was when obviously, it could be much, much worse, like hobo-level-in-America worse or begger-level-in-a-third-world-country worse. I felt the internal machinations of self-pity swirl down like toilet water flushing away a bad meal when the back door to the P.W. swung open, crashing against the brick wall.

Levonne emerged from the P.W., pushing his rickety plastic cart out onto the walkway of the loading dock, the cart stacked high with aluminum trays. He pushed it toward me then stopped, placing his fists on his hips like a pirate in an old movie surveying something he was about to conquer. A scowl appeared on his sour puss. I felt my appendages whither as I was being scowled upon.

"How come e'ery time I come out here, you fools are sittin' around smokin', doing nuthin?" Levonne said. "It's goddamn ridiculous, if ya ask me!"

"I was just taking a quick smoke break."

"I can see that, fool," Levonne said, leaning over to handle the cart, pushing it again, its wheels rattling on the cement landing.

I felt like a piece of shit. I stood up quickly, tossing my cigarette on the ground, and said, "I can help you." Levonne kept pushing the cart. "I can help you get done quicker so you can get home early."

Levonne stopped in his tracks, looked back at me.

"You'd help me?" he said, his scowl turning into limp relief.

"Yeah, as long as you quit staring at me like you're going to murder me."

Levonne's head flew back and a deep, guttural laugh bellowed out, his hand clinging to his gut, keeping his shirt from popping out from his too-tight pair of Dickies work pants. After he laughed a bit, he sighed loudly, his hand wiping his brow. "Man, if wanted to murder you, you'd already be smoked. You're crazy."

"Maybe," I said, chuckling uncomfortably.

"But if you want to help me, I won't stop you."

"OK."

I jumped up onto the landing and accompanied Levonne toward the dumpster. When we reached the end of the landing, I turned to Levonne, placed my hand on his shoulder.

"I got it, man. Why don't you go home?"

"What?"

"I'll do this. Go home. Maybe your family will be there."

"Are you sure?" Levonne said, one corner of his mouth perking upward.

"Yeah, I got it."

"Thanks, my man," Levonne said, wiping his hands on his apron. "And if you could, write down on the clipboard how many--"

"Just go. I got it."

Levonne smiled and placed his hand on my shoulder. I could see that Levonne's yellow eyes had lightened a bit, a little sparkle appearing at the pinkish corners. Then he shuffled back to the door and disappeared inside the building.

I stood there peering at the cart, a clipboard dangling on its side, a ball point pen shoved into the clip. I grabbed the clipboard and examined the grid of lines and labels on the spreadsheet, names of dishes I was familiar with across the top and labels of quantities and sizes along the X's and Y's of the grid lines. I peeked under the aluminum foil of the top tray to see what was inside but all I saw was a swirl of tomato sauce and an occasional noodle protruding out. Without digging into it, I wouldn't know if it was lasagna or tortellini or ravioli. And there were a dozen pans, at least, to dig through. I decided to just fill in the spreadsheet as I saw fit, marking under each header randomly: two lasagna, one ravioli, two tortellini, etc. I was pleased with this decision. I grabbed the top tray with two hands and stepped over to the edge of the landing, hoisting it behind me, steadying myself to toss the tray into the dumpster, when curiosity struck me. 'What was actually in the covered tray?' I thought. I sat the tray back on the cart and pulled the aluminum cover back. I buried my forefinger in the saucy mound, lifting slightly to examine its ingredients, then placed my finger in my mouth. 'Lasagna,' I thought, 'and a practically full tray of it.' I stood there for a moment, my forefinger in my mouth, my eyes on the dumpster, an image of my empty fridge in my mind, and I debated if the trays of food would actually fit into my smallish apartment refrigerator. I decided that it would be worth finding out so rather than toss the trays into the dumpster, I sat them one by one on the edge of the landing, completely emptying the cart. I placed the filled-out clipboard on the cart and pushed it back inside the restaurant kitchen. A few other coworkers were still doing their side work, rolling silver, marrying ketchup bottles, and whatnot, but Levonne was gone. And I too was gone, out the kitchen, through the dining room, passed the host stand, and out the front door.

I ran as fast as I could, my apron swinging back and forth with loose change in it, as I looked for my parked car. Finding it a block away, I unlocked it and jumped inside, squealing out of my spot down the street toward the alleyway behind the restaurant. I parked behind the dumpster and popped my trunk. I loaded the trunk with the aluminum trays of food, stacking one after the other. With the last tray in my hand, I looked around to see if anyone was watching me. I saw the bum from earlier watching me from across the alley, his hands in his pockets, his head hung low. I raised the tray of food, as if to say 'this is for you,' and the bum quickly walked over. He grabbed the tray, looked at me briefly, then quickly ran off, holding the tray under his arm like an oblong football. I watched him round the building and vanish.

I closed the trunk of my car, hopped in, and drove home.

9. The Discarded Feast

When Alfonso was a little boy, he told me he refused to take a dump anywhere but at his home. He caused his mother an inordinate amount of grief because of this little problema. They could be *way* across town at a shopping mall with a perfectly good though mildly stinky bathroom for him to use when his adolescent sphincter would send him a warning and he would tug at his mother's pant legs incessantly. 'Mama, mama, we gotta go hooooome!' he would plead, clinching his butt cheeks together, his legs in a twisty shape. And because of her empathetic heart, she would drive him *all the way* back across town, cursing the whole way, so he could use the bathroom in the privacy of his family's home. What a little, pain in the ass! By the time Alfonso reached manhood, his little problema was ancient history but the memory of it tickled him whenever he took a dump in the dingy employee restroom at the P.W. He felt an ironic twinge tug at his insides and it wasn't lost on him that deep-down he still felt like the little boy he used to be in many ways, although he didn't have to go home anymore to take a dump. In fact, he quite enjoyed shitting at work. It was a great way for him to express his feelings about working at the P.W. in a very constructive way.

When he finished his business in the bathroom, he looked around the kitchen for me but couldn't find me anywhere. He asked the few employees still around after the dinner shift if they had seen me and nobody had seen me. Alfonso was stumped and a little concerned. He racked his brain wondering if I told him to get a ride with someone else but he couldn't think of it. He also worried if maybe he was drinking too much alcohol and smoking too much weed lately, bringing on early dementia or Alzheimer's or some other mind-deteriorating disease but then he knew he was just being paranoid. He was WAY too young for dementia, hopefully, he thought, but not too young to be paranoid. He looked for me a little more but when he came up short, he decided to try to bum a ride from someone. My apartment wasn't too far away.

He found that mooch Warren pretending to sweep the floor, raking over the same pile of crumbs and dust bunnies, near the walk-in cooler, hanging around on the clock to pad his paycheck. He decided to try to cash-in a favor he was owed by that moocher.

Alfonso placed his hands on his hips, looked down at the lousy sweeping job his coworker was pretending to accomplish, and said, "Hey man, can I bum a ride home?"

"I gotta finish my side work," Warren said. "You know, *sweeping*." He continued to barely sweep.

"It doesn't look like you're doing anything. Come on, I'm not going far and you owe me."

"What do I owe you for?"

"About 12,000 cigarettes, at least, not counting the spare change and pens I've given you."

"Oh yeah..." Warren said, a sly smirk appearing on his smug face. "I guess I do owe ya. You got a smoke for me?"

"If you give me a ride."

"Deal!"

"Come on, then, numb nuts."

Alfonso walked slyly out of the kitchen, hugging the perimeter so not to be seen by management, like an alley cat tip-toeing behind dumpsters and under fire escapes, trying to avoid predators or strangers. Warren slinked close behind, a goofy smirk on his face, a stiff gait in his step. They snuck out of the P.W. unnoticed, flinging the front door open, Alfonso's arms spread wide as if he had just crossed the finish line to a grueling marathon race--triumphant, defiant, satisfied. Warren, the opposite, shuffled into the street, his hands in his pockets, his body slumped over. Alfonso followed him to his car which, to his surprise, was a shiny, late model Mercedes-Benz. He looked on in disbelief as Warren fumbled in his pockets then his apron for his keys.

"Ah, hell no! This is NOT your car," Alfonso said, shaking his head.

"Yes, it is."

"How is *this* your car?"

"I bought it."

Warren unlocked the doors and the two sat inside. Alfonso marveled at the interior of the luxurious car, wedging his ass deep into the soft leather seat, rubbing his hands on the shiny leather dash. He was impressed, no doubt, and a little jealous.

"How could you buy this car on what we make?"

"Why do you think I bought it with what we make?"

"I don't know. Just an assumption, I guess."

"Where to?" Warren started the car, pulled out of the parking space, and sped away from the P.W.

"There's a convenience store on South First near Barton Springs. You can drop me off there," Alfonso said.

"OK. You got a smoke for me?" Alfonso gave him a smoke and quickly lit it for him. Smoke filled the expensive car's cabin. "Thanks, my man."

After that, the rest of the ride was silent, Warren sucking on his bummed cigarette, Alfonso feeling a bit out of place in the fancy car. 'How could that mooch Warren afford this car?' Alfonso kept thinking to himself. It just didn't make any sense at all. 'And if for some reason, he had a lot of money, then why would he be working at the P.W. and mooching shit from everyone?'

Before long, Warren pulled into the parking lot of The GODDAMN. He parked in a handicap space then unlocked the power locks.

"Is this the right place?" he said.

"Yeah, this is it. Thanks for the ride."

"I owed you one. I really did."

"Yeah." Alfonso got out of the car, slammed the door shut, and Warren screeched out of the parking lot, a cloud of dust and exhaust enveloping my tall friend. In a matter of seconds, his fancy-pants car was gone. Alfonso, dazed and dejected, went inside The GODDAMN.

The now familiar stench of bleach mixed with the aroma of hot dogs and coffee met him inside. The GODDAMN was never quite cool enough, a balmy humidity hung in the air as a deterrent for any customers who wanted to linger too long. Alfonso was pleased to see the tall boys were still on sale for 99 cents so he quickly scooped four beer cans out of the ice trough and thought about getting some packages of ramen for dinner and a can of food for Mr. Whiskers as his way of contributing to the household. He wanted to contribute, he had told me. He also wanted some cigarettes. Gerald the store owner sat behind his fortress of penis enlargement pills and energy drinks and condoms and candy, calling out to Alfonso, as if reading his mind, "Hal-oh! I got Marlboro still on special. Buy two, get two free. Want some?" he said.

"Yeah!" Alfonso said, barking from the other side of the store. He found a can of cat food and two packages of ramen and met Gerald at the front of the store.

"You, my friend, don't look so good." He sorted through Alfonso's things, zapping their bar codes with a laser scanner, dropping them into a brown paper sack with a caricature of his smug mug on the side. There was a cartoon voice balloon exploding near his cartoon face that read: 'Everything on special!' That always seemed true. "You want the Marlboros?"

"Yeah, I want 'em. Just having a bad day, I guess."

"We all have bad days, buddy." He dropped the four packs of cigarettes into the bag along with the other stuff, their meal for the night. He took a $20 bill from Alfonso's hand, his earnings for the night, and returned a few dollars and change. "The key to remember: it's just another day."

"True. True."

"You come back tomorrow. Last day of beer special! Bring your friend too."

"OK." Alfonso rolled the top of the brown paper bag down and placed it under his arm. "See you around, Gerald."

"See you, Chief."

Alfonso walked out of the store and across the street to my apartment complex. A car raced by after him heading toward downtown, the horn blaring away after it. Alfonso kept on toward the complex, his right arm extended to the sky, his middle finger defiantly at attention.

***

Mr. Whiskers licked his front left paw, sitting on the bar around the kitchen, as I stacked aluminum trays of food from the P.W. into my refrigerator. Every once and a while, the cat would look curiously at me, as if to ask, 'What has fortune brought our way?' Then he went back to licking his paw. I stacked as many trays of food as I could in the smallish refrigerator, taking up most of the inside of the practically empty fridge with the exception of a few cans of beer and a leftover Whataburger meal still in its original, greasy paper bag. I then worked on the freezer, which was also practically empty except for a plastic bucket of ice. I placed three trays of food in there then it was full too. My refrigerator and freezer had never been so full, ever.

Leaving two trays on the counter, I turned the oven on, set it to 350 degrees, then scratched my cat's head.

"We're eating good tonight, little buddy." Mr. Whiskers purred loudly, tilting his head to get more scratching coverage from me. "That is, if you like Italian food. I'm sure you'll at least try it. Huh, boy?" Mr. Whiskers replied with a loud, rumbling purr.

I placed the two trays of food in the oven, not even knowing what each contained. It didn't matter to me, though. They most likely contained something I thought at least to be reasonably delicious. I had tried practically everything at the P.W. and there wasn't one dish that I found to be uneatable or disgusting or not worth taking away from its demise in the dumpster. In fact, most of the dishes had been taste-tested so many times over the years by the P.W. corporate office that they all were winners. Mostly, I was just really hungry and was ready to chow down on something other than ramen noodles or mac and cheese made with powdered cheese packets and water. I didn't feel a twinge of guilt for taking the trays either. In my mind, they were on the way to the landfill anyway, a discarded feast, practically trash, not the P.W.'s property anymore.

I eagerly waited for my roommate's return and decided to take a quick shower before Alfonso got back from work. I wasn't sure how he'd get home since I left so fast without telling him but I knew Alfonso to be a resourceful friend and didn't doubt that he'd bum a ride from a coworker. I ran to my bedroom and jumped in the shower.

Mr. Whiskers continued to clean himself until he heard some familiar footsteps in the hallway outside the apartment. He hopped down from the bar and rubbed his ribs and hip on the wall near the front door, purring then turning the other way, rubbing the opposite side of his body in the same manner. Alfonso burst into the apartment, slamming the door against the wall, frightening Mr. Whiskers, who bolted for the bedroom as if Sasquatch had burst into the apartment looking to devour a plump, fuzzy house cat for a snack. This amused Alfonso.

"Honey, I'm home!" he said, tossing the brown paper bag from The GODDAMN on the kitchen counter. The smell of Italian food filled the apartment. "Shit, smells like the P.W. up in here. I need a beer." He pulled a tall boy out of the bag, opened it, took a huge gulp, and unpacked the rest of his groceries, tossing the contents onto the kitchen counter. He opened the can of cat food, the sound of its lid snapping off excited Mr. Whiskers, who appeared on the bar as if out of thin air, purring loudly, looking attentively at Alfonso. This amused Alfonso some more. He loved Mr. Whiskers. He grabbed a bowl from the cabinet, dumped the stinky, wet cat food in the bowl, and placed it on the bar. Mr. Whiskers devoured it.

"Shit, boy. You must have been hungry. I'm hungry too." He knelt in front of the oven and opened the drawer at the bottom. Inside, an assortment of beat-up pots and pans lay inside. He picked a small pot and set it on the stove top but curiosity captured him. He opened the oven and peeked inside, the delicious smelling hot air filling his nose. Seeing the familiar looking aluminum tray caught him off guard a bit.

"That's weird," he said, closing the oven door. He heard me rummaging around in the bathroom. "What's in the oven?" he said, calling out loudly.

"You'll see," I said, my voice muffled from inside the bathroom.

Alfonso sat on the couch, still hungry, nursing his beer. He watched Mr. Whiskers wipe his face with his right paw, then licked it, then repeated the motion over and over like a feline window wiper. I emerged from the bathroom wearing a grey t-shirt and black shorts, a big shit-eating grin on my face, rubbing my hands together like the villains in oldie movies used to do when hatching their evil plan.

Confused, Alfonso squinted his eyes, peered at me, and said, "What's going on?"

"We're feasting tonight!"

"Feast? I barely had enough money for beer and ramen at The GODDAMN."

"We're not eating ramen tonight but beer will do." I went into the kitchen then rummaged through the drawers. "Have you seen the oven mits?"

"Oven mits? We don't have oven mits. I use a towel."

"Yeah, I have oven mits," I said. "Somewhere in here--HERE THEY ARE!" I pulled out the two trays from the oven and set them on the stove top. "Come check it."

A deep sigh emitted from Alfonso's slit of a mouth and he reluctantly got up from his comfy spot on the couch. In the kitchen, he looked over my shoulder as I peeled back the top of one of the aluminum trays. Inside, steaming hot lasagna. Then I peeled back the top from the other: chicken parmesan. In both trays was enough food for 24 people, at least. Alfonso was beside himself.

"Ummm," he said, his hands on his hips.

"What?"

"How did you get this?"

"It was going in the trash."

"You got this from the trash?!" Alfonso smacked his forehead, his head tilting back, his tongue flapping out the side of his mouth. "What the fuck?!"

"No! It was about to be tossed out but I didn't toss it out. I brought it home instead."

"I don't understand."

So I caught him up, how I offered to help Levonne, the cart full of trays, the hungry bum, the cavernous dumpster, my rumbling stomach, their empty fridge. After all that, Alfonso seemed pleased.

"Right on, my brother!"

"So, you're cool with it?"

"Cool with it? I fucking love you. Let's eat."

And we ate like kings.

SALUD!

***

We sat on the small deck that jutted out from behind my apartment, a poor excuse for a patio but a leisurely place nonetheless, sitting in canvas chairs, smoking cigarettes and drinking cheap beer. Mr. Whiskers watched us from behind the glass sliding door, the stars watched us from above. Our stomachs were full but my mind wandered.

"Do you think anyone will notice that I didn't throw the food away?"

"Nah," said Alfonso, a poofy plume of smoke billowing from his mouth.

"Are you sure?"

"Nope, I'm not sure."

"I don't know why all of a sudden I feel all worked up about it. Levonne is so serious about tossing the food in the dumpster with his clipboard and all."

"Yeah. True."

"But he also seemed glad to let me take care of it."

"Why are you getting bent out of shape? It was gonna be trash. What's the difference if it rots in the dumpster or we make it into turds?"

"No difference, I guess."

"That's right. So don't worry about it."

"OK."

A moment went by, filled with more exhaled smoke and sips of beer. The song of a few cicadas could be heard coming from the trees around the apartment complex.

"So..." I said, rubbing my stubbly chin. "If the opportunity comes up again, then I should take it?"

"Most definitely," Alfonso said. "I'm going to get another beer. Do you want one?" He stood up and waited for my reply.

"Duh."

He slid the door open--Mr. Whiskers bolting out of his way--and went inside, leaving me alone with my thoughts. I kept thinking to myself that we really weren't getting much out of the P.W. besides measly gratuities and even measlier paychecks. Whatever perks we had before this night were slowly drying up in the form of corporate belt-tightening. But most of all, we were just hungry. The morality play that my heart and my mind were table-reading kept coming back to Alfonso's line: 'What's the difference if it rots in the dumpster or we make it into turds?' What was the difference? The difference was our survival and that was it for me. We were just surviving.

10. Birthdays at Restaurants and Other Diversions

When I was a little boy, I loved celebrating birthdays at restaurants. It didn't matter if it was a fancy restaurant or a fast-food restaurant, anywhere but home was infinitely more fun. And it didn't matter if it was my birthday or someone else's birthday. My love affair with restaurant birthdays started before I was in elementary school. I was in line at a McDonald's with my mother when I first saw a sign with a cartoon of Ronald McDonald wearing a birthday hat--his arms around a bunch of children, his big, goofy smile plastered on his face stretched from little white ear to the other little white ear, birthday balloons in the background, a pile of presents next to a pile of Happy Meal containers. I couldn't read at that age but I deduced quickly what the sign was implying.

"Mommy?" I said, tugging at my mother's arm. "Can I have my birthday party here? At McDonald's?!"

"Yes, it looks like they host them here."

'My favorite holiday at my favorite restaurant?' I thought. My little brain exploded.

BOOM!

Even after that fateful day, every birthday FOR EVERYBODY planned at a restaurant was an event worth waiting for. My sister's birthday at Pizza Hut?

BINGO!

My best friend's birthday at Chuck E. Cheese?

SHAZAM!

My mother's birthday at Naples Italian Restaurant?

BUON COMPLEANNO!

My father planned a birthday dinner for my mother at their favorite Italian restaurant and while me, my sister, and my mother anxiously waited for the delicious birthday meal, I spotted my father whispering in a waitress' ear, his hand draped over her shoulder, a wily smirk on his face. The waitress didn't pull away. I could hear her giggle as my father shoved a twenty dollar bill in her apron. My mother was oblivious as she flipped through the menu, her eyes wide with excitement. I was certainly my mother's son; I could barely contain my excitement as well. When the flirty waitress returned after the meal with a birthday cake and a band of singing servers, they sang my mother a boisterous birthday song. While they sang, I saw my father pinch the waitress' ass--my mother gazing upon the glowing candles in a trance--while my little sister tossed her silverware on the floor.

When I sang the birthday song at the P.W., I always thought of my father pinching that waitress' ass. I didn't know why I thought of that. I wasn't particularly upset about it but it seemed to be burned in my memory like the exploded remains of fireworks on the asphalt of the neighborhood streets the next morning after the Fourth of July. I couldn't help it.

Alfonso noticed a dire look on my face during a P.W. Birthday Song warm-up session in the kitchen before the lunch shift and nudged me with his elbow. Alfonso gave me a look of concern. I feigned a look of indifference that didn't convince him of anything. When the song concluded with limp clapping and forced hoorays, Alfonso put his arm around me and led me to the drink refilling station at the side of the kitchen.

"You all right, buddy?" he said.

"Yeah," I said.

"You sure?"

"Yeah."

"You don't look so good."

"I don't feel so good."

"Yeah? You feel sick?"

"No, just down, I guess. This shit is getting old, you know? The thrill is gone. Even singing this birthday song is weighing on me."

"I know."

Our coworkers slowly dispersed to their stations throughout the dining area as Paula the A.M. rushed into the kitchen, looking frantic and flustered and hot, all rolled into one and squeezed into a freshly pressed, pant suit. Her pregnant belly was larger than ever, pushing the limit of the seams of her outfit. She seemed relieved to find us.

"Oh good, the G.M. needs to see you two," she said, snapping her fingers. We pointed at ourselves, mock confusion all over our faces. "Yes, you. Get going!"

We weaved our way through the dining room, fielding odd looks from the other servers and bussers, walking in a way that emoted heavy guilt, as if to express that we knew we were busted, even though we had no idea what Dan the G.M. wanted. It was just more fun that way.

Inside Dan's office, it was sadder than ever. The stacks of papers and three-ring binders surrounding the office were higher than our last visit and we could feel his desperation, heavy in the air like a dense fog crawling over Town Lake on a humid, May morning. His arms propped up on the desk, he held his head in his hands, his face buried deeply into his palms. It was a sad sight, a grown man decaying in front of our eyes, his manhood wilting feverishly. Our footsteps activated the loose boards in the floor, the sound startling Dan to attention. He motioned for us to sit and we did. The view of the dumpster in the back alley on one of the security monitors mesmerized me; I was entranced and feared that I may have been seen out there, doing *the deed*.

"Good morning, boys. I'm assigning you to delivery duty again. You two all right with that?" Me and Alfonso perked up and sat up in our seats a bit. "I'll take that as a yes. Levonne will have your delivery ready for you in ten minutes along with the directions but I'm sure you'll find it again. It's the same address as last time." Alfonso laid his hand in front of me and gave me some skin, me then turning my palm upright so Alfonso could slide me some skin too. "Will you two get going, please?!"

"Yes, sir," we said simultaneously, leaving the sad office.

Weaving back through the dining room, we passed that mooch Warren as well as the other mooch Paul and that bastard Fred, toward the kitchen and our escape. I caught the eye of Laura Ann who was wiping down her tables and placing rolls of silverware on the clean table tops. She mouthed the sentence, "Where are you going?" I winked at her then disappeared into the kitchen with Alfonso.

***

The cabin of my beat-up Civic was filled with cigarette smoke as the grimy beat of Masta Ace's *Born to Roll* rattled the small speakers of the stock stereo system. We loved to blast our favorite tunes while driving around in my hoopty-mobile, the loud music camouflaging the sad sound of the engine wheezing and misfiring, its imminent demise just months away. Any signs of sadness or uneasiness on my part were gone, out the window along with the yellowish gray cigarette smoke, and replaced by gangsta, macking, karaoke rapping. We both knew all of the lyrics to this particular bad ass, hip hop classic. During the refrain, I said loudly, "It's the same house, right?"

Alfonso gave me a thumbs-up. Soon, my dusty Civic crossed over the South First Street bridge, over Town lake, passed the joggers, and past our apartment complex. Alfonso pointed at the complex and said, "What do you think Mr. Whiskers is doing?"

"Who knows. Licking his butt, probably."

"That doesn't sound good at all."

"It doesn't, does it?"

It was a hot day and the hot air rolled into the car windows with the heft of ocean waves, humid and dense, pushing things around on the seats and on the floor. Not far down the road, I turned right into Sarah's hood, slowed down to a crawl, turned the rap music off, rolled down my window all the way, and watched for kids or pets in the street. I rubbed my eyes and looked around and couldn't help but feel I had experienced this exact routine before, which of course I did, but marveled at my déjà vu nonetheless. Alfonso tossed his used up cigarette out the window and sat up.

"What do you think you'll be doing in ten years?" he said, running his fingers through his hair, trying to give it some shape, something other than a windblown mess.

"Shit, I don't know. I don't know what I'll be doing tomorrow."

"True. True. But do you ever think about what you'll be doing after our illustrious careers as servers are over?"

"Sometimes, I think what it would be like to make a living as a writer?"

"A writer?!" Alfonso slapped his knee and his head flew back into the headrest, a thunderous guffaw then belly laughter erupted from deep inside him. He could barely contain himself. "Why, I've never seen you write anything but someone's order on a notepad and even with that, you have shitty handwriting. Almost as shitty as Levonne's handwriting, I would say."

I found a place to park and pulled my hoopty over, parallel parked liked champ, turned the engine off, and turned to my friend. I was pretty annoyed.

"I studied literature *in college*."

"So? I studied political science *in college* but I'm not going to be President."

"Why not?"

"Cause that's a pipe dream for a Mexican, that's why."

"Well, I do think of a career as a writer. I hope to do that someday," I said. I leaned over and pulled a handle on the floor under my seat, releasing the trunk lid.

"I have some advice for you then?"

"What's that?"

"You have to actually *write something* to be a writer."

"Fuck off! I'll get around to it."

We opened our doors and got out. Sarah's house was just a few doors down and the neighborhood street was filled with playing children and barking dogs and bouncing balls. We gathered our delivery from the trunk--several bags of food cinched at the top, quite a bit more food than our previous delivery--and walked towards Sarah's house. There was a joyous bounce to our walk, almost like a skip, and we knew it. Without realizing it until we looked at each other, we were looking forward to seeing Sarah again and hopefully spending a little time in her company, even if it meant just sharing a smoke, or two, with more rum, hopefully. Reaching her house, we crossed the immaculate lawn, pushing and shoving each other with our elbows for the lead, and leapt for the front door. I pushed the "One Love" doorbell first then smirked at Alfonso.

"I won, bitch," I said.

"You're the bitch," he said, bitterly.

"Whatever."

"You didn't ask me what I would be doing in ten years?"

I turned to my friend and said, "I know what you'll be doing in ten years: P.W. assistant manager."

"Fuck you, bitch!"

The door opened, Sarah standing there with her pearly white smile and wearing a brightly colored dress. We weren't expecting that so quickly. We attempted to gather ourselves in a more professional fashion.

"Who are you calling a *bitch*? I hope not me," she said, giggling at the notion of us calling her that.

"Oh, so, so sorry, ma'am," Alfonso said, embarrassed. "We were--"

"And don't call me ma'am. My name is Sarah and I'd prefer to be called that, especially by you two boys. I thought we were friends?"

"Yes, Sarah, we are. We have your delivery for you. Can we come in?" I said.

"Of course, come in," she said, opening the door wider, motioning for us to come in the house. "You know I requested you for the delivery, don't you?"

Me and Alfonso stepped in the cool house, carefully maneuvering around Sarah so she could close the door. She greeted us with a warm, gentle hug. We blushed, a bit.

"Our G.M. didn't tell us that. He just sent us on the delivery," I said.

"Yeah, he never tells us anything important," Alfonso said.

"Well, quit standing around. I have someone I want you two to meet. Come in the kitchen." Sarah pushed the two of us toward the kitchen then she led the way. We followed her, stepping in tune to a reggae song playing softly from some small speakers on a window sill. "Are you boys hungry?"

***

Me and Alfonso entered the breakfast area off the kitchen and saw a man we had never seen before sitting at the table. A bottle of rum sat in the middle of the table, surrounded by small glasses. The man's glass was full of rum. Sarah patted us on our backs and motioned for us to sit down.

"Boys, this is Arthur Singleton, one of my neighbors, a kind man with a generous heart and a pleasant smile."

Arthur extended his hand to us and we took turns shaking it. Even though Arthur was older than us, he still had a grip to his handshake that was as firm as a vice on a steel rod.

"Nice to make your acquaintance," Arthur said.

We nodded then rubbed our crushed hands. Arthur chuckled a bit before taking a swig from his glass. He was stout like a bull dog, his wrinkled, thick neck protruding out of the tight neck hole of his Hawaiian shirt like an oak tree stump. He was in great shape for his age, being that he looked considerably older than Sarah by at least ten to fifteen years. Despite his age, he still had a thick head of hair, white as snow on a mountain top and cut into an angular peak at the front and a flat plateau at the crown of his head.

"Arthur lives in the house right next door. Our yards practically hold hands."

"That's the truth," he said, smiling. "I used to cut Sarah's lawn before my sciatica decided it was time for me to stop."

"Now we use a lawn service."

"Those Beaners sure know how to make our yards look like a golf course." This comment caught Alfonso off guard and Arthur noticed, assuming the color of his skin was similar to the Mexican fellows who cut his yard. "No offense, son."

"None taken," Alfonso said. "Those Beaners sure can be lazy, too, when they want to be. They're probably cousins of *mine*. Lazy bastards. I'll take some rum, too." He raised his glass and Sarah filled it as well as my glass and her own. Arthur was still nursing his rum.

"Sarah," Arthur said, quietly. "Do you mind telling these boys about my condition?"

"Oh... certainly. Arthur suffers from a curious cognitive condition--a by-product of his time in the military--that keeps him from filtering his thoughts sometimes before he speaks. He's not a racist or anything. He hopes you understand."

Arthur nodded his head approvingly to Sarah.

"What war were you in?" I asked, sipping my rum. The burn of the alcohol in my throat pleased me very much.

"I served during World War II. I was in the Army."

"Yes, and as a token of my appreciation, I have Arthur over for lunch as a way of saying thank you for serving our country."

"Now, Sarah, you know that's not true," Arthur said, then lowering his voice and shifting in his seat uncomfortably. "Everybody knows that I lost my entire fortune and that's why you have me over for lunch."

"Well, Arthur, my way of explaining our lunches sure sounds nicer. You know? Not so bleak and all," Sarah said. Arthur smiled then took a sip of his rum. Sarah turned to us and said, "Arthur is quite the story teller. He loves to tell his stories. They are truly amazing, actually. He's lived a very colorful life. Do you mind telling them a story, Arthur?"

"No, not at all. I do have quite an interesting story to tell. Are you boys interested?"

We looked at each other then looked at Arthur. We nodded in approval.

"How about I start serving some food while you tell it?" Sarah said, getting up from the table and walking toward the oven. "You boys are staying for lunch, right?"

"Yes," Alfonso said.
"Yes, we are," I said.

11. He Sounds Like a Super Hero

"In 1942, I was 17 years old when I was drafted by the Army. I was pretty big for my age so when I showed up at the recruiting office, they had big smiles on their faces. Up until that point, I had done nothing but play sports, football, baseball, wrestling, and shoveled food into my face. I was a big boy, not big like tall, but big like muscular. I was a strapping young lad as they used to say. Those Army bastards knew exactly what I was when I walked through their door. I was going to be a fighting machine: their fighting machine.

"They weighed me and measured me and while they were doing that, they kept asking me, 'How many Nazis are you gonna kill for Uncle Sam?' And I kept telling them, 'I'll kill 'em all.' They got a real kick out of that. They were some real knucklehead bastards," Arthur said.

He had a peculiar cadence to his voice when he told his story, like an actor from a 1940s movie, kind of fast and sharp and punctuated with outdated obscenities. We got a kick out of listening to him tell his story. We slowly ate our food as we listened, our eyes set straight on him, sipping rum between bites of lasagna and baked chicken parmesan. We were mesmerized. Sarah got a kick out of watching us watch Arthur. He hadn't had that much attention in years. None of his family came to visit him anymore; Sarah's family didn't visit her either.

"All I had on me was $3 that my dad gave me, a photo of my girlfriend Maggie, and a Bible my grandma gave me. That's it. They threw me on a bus and the next thing I knew, I was on a plane to Fort Bragg to train to be a paratrooper, one of the type of soldiers that were thrown out of a big plane, ready to fight, guns a blazing from the sky. Most of the guys I was with were pretty gung ho about killing Germans. I was too, I guess. Mostly, I wanted to see the world, even if the world I was going to see was on fire. I hadn't seen much outside of Amarillo, Texas and the idea of going anywhere was exciting. I had mostly seen the world through movies on the big screen. I wanted to see the world with my own eyes.

"My short time at Fort Bragg was pretty fun to me because it was a lot like football practice, running laps and climbing on obstacles and tossing stuff around and swinging from bars and laying in the dirt. And eating the food there was a lot like the food from the high school cafeteria, all sorts of gloppy and runny and not so good at all. The only real difference from high school was that there weren't any pretty girls around, actually, there weren't any girls at all. Only men. And let me tell you, that's rough for a 17 year old strapping lad. In fact, I don't think I choked my chicken as much as I did at Fort Bragg for the rest of my life. Sorry Sarah."

Sarah smiled and nodded. "It's OK, Arthur," she said.

Arthur looked at our two friends, pointed to his head, pressing his index finger to the temple of his skull, and said, "No filter."

"No problem," Alfonso said, eating his food, sipping his rum.

"Yeah, keep going," I said.

"OK. I'll keep going. Gimme some more rum," he said, raising his glass. Sarah poured him some more. "No girls, all men, all work all the time, they got us pretty wound up. After six weeks, all us basic training knuckleheads were packed on a plane and flown to Europe to fight the big fight. They probably told us where we were going but I don't remember. All I remember was the boredom and the smell, the smell of those stinky bastards on the plane. They fed us peanut butter sandwiches, apples, and water, bottom of the barrel stuff. We couldn't see out of any windows either; all we got to look at was each other. And, boy, let me tell you: looking at other soldiers is no fun!"

We laughed. Arthur laughed a deep laugh, an amiable guffaw that could have come from the baritone gut of Johnny Cash or some such old timey country singer. He had a sweet, wrinkled disposition yet slumped over in his chair in a painful arch of worn muscles and brittle bones. He seemed pleasantly exhausted.

"You all right, Arthur?" Sarah said.

"Yes, thanks for asking. Just a little tired."

"You can finish your story another time."

"No, I can go on. Just need to catch my breath."

"OK," Sarah said, smiling.

"Once we got to where we were supposed to be, I heard rumors we were near Stalingrad but I really didn't know. They didn't say much as we got ready to jump out of the plane. The commanding officers kept telling us we'd be killing Germans soon and, boy, did we want to kill us some Germans. It was a long way from home and we were tired and lonely and hungry. Killing Germans was going to make us feel better."

"I can't imagine wanting to kill someone," I said, shifting in my seat uncomfortably.

"But this wasn't just someone, anyone. They were Nazis, our enemy. We were going to be heroes and we were looking forward to it. Then--BAM! A loud noise came from the back of the plane. They were opening the back so we could jump out. And then, before I knew it--" Without warning, Arthur keeled over in a fit of coughing and hacking, wheezing and coughing. He looked up at us for a moment, a plea for help all over his red face, then he grabbed his throat, his tongue protruding from his mouth in a way that let us know he was not good at all. Sarah patted him on the back, at first softly then more abruptly, but he quickly crumpled to the floor, sending his chair flying. Sarah screamed.

"Boys, help him!"

Me and Alfonso quickly huddled around him but we didn't know what to do, not really. We looked at each other and quickly realized that if either of us was in a life-threatening situation and we hoped that the other would help out, then we were most definitely doomed. But there wasn't time to ponder why we had never paid attention in high school health class to CPR or Heimlich maneuver techniques. We just had to act and we did. Alfonso, being the bigger of the two of us, picked him up from underneath his arms while I maneuvered his legs. We got him back in his chair and--quite miraculously, actually--he seemed OK all by himself. His breathing was easier although his face was red as all hell, his eyes bulging and bloodshot. He seemed quite relieved. He patted us on our shoulders and smiled.

"Thank you," he said, then turned to Sarah. "Can everybody help me home?"

"Can you boys help him? I'm not strong enough."

We immediately helped him to his feet, although, it was a struggle. His bull dog frame was as heavy and dense as a boulder but we got him up, one of his arms around Alfonso's shoulders, the other arm around my shoulders. We guided him out of the breakfast area and through the living room--Three Little Birds by Bob Marley was playing, which I thought was weird--then through the front door. We crossed Sarah's front lawn to Arthur's, all the way him whispering to us, "Thank you. Thank you." When we got to his front door, he fumbled in his pocket for his keys.

"I think I can take it from here," he said, opening his door.

"Nah, we'll make sure you're OK," Alfonso said and we helped him to his bedroom where we made sure he sat upright on his bed. His house was a cluttered affair, a little dustier and messier than Sarah's house, with the smell of mold and mildew in the air but in a way a fine cheddar cheese emits its unusual odor, discreetly instead of pungently. I also detected a hint of eau de moth balls as well, a scent I was all too familiar with from my own grandparents' house. The bedroom was tightly packed with old furniture and cardboard boxes and piles of clothes, some neat and some haphazard, so when Sarah made her way in to the bedroom, there wasn't a lot of empty room to move around. She made it clear that she wanted to check on Arthur and when she moved by me, I clumsily stepped back and my foot smashed an unsuspecting shoe box that lay in front of a dresser. Once I stabilized myself and I looked down at the crushed Jarman shoe box, I realized $100 bills were protruding from under the lid and some of the bills were poking out of the new cracks I made in the seams of the box. It was an unexpected sight to see, for sure. No one seemed to notice but me. I quickly pushed the box with my foot around the side of the dresser.

"Arthur, you doing OK now?" Sarah said, pushing the short white hairs from his moist forehead to the side. He smiled and nodded. Sarah turned to us, smiled, and said we should go.

As she left the room with Alfonso not far behind her, I knelt down as if to tie my shoe, pinched one of the protruding $100 bills from the shoe box, shoved it inside my shoe, pulled the strings of my shoe as if securing it, stood up, and looked over at Arthur, who was laying down on his bed, his belly protruding upward, his breathing deep and easy. I thought of putting the $100 bill back in the box but I didn't for some reason. I just followed Alfonso and Sarah out of the house.

We crossed the lawns together back to Sarah's house. As we walked, Sarah put her arms around our waists, pulling us close to her with sincerity and gratitude.

"Boys, I'm glad you were here to help. I never would have been able to pick that man up by myself. I'm sure he weighs a ton!"

"You're welcome," Alfonso said.

"Glad to help," I said.

We followed her back into her house and returned to our places at her breakfast table. She poured us some rum and offered us some pie that she had in her fridge. Who were we to turn down pie and rum?

SALUD!

"Since Arthur didn't finish his story, I'll be glad to tell you the rest of his story if you're interested." We nodded as she placed slices of pie in front of us. "Very good. After Arthur jumped out of the plane, he and his troop landed at the outskirts of a massive battle, ground troops pummeling each other, his calling to kill Nazis in front of him. He killed dozens of them as he ran on foot straight into carnage, some he shot with his handgun, some he stabbed with his big knife, and as many soldiers around him both friend and foe fell to the ground, he witnessed a Nazi officer in the distance standing at the top of a hill. With Arthur's senses heightened with adrenaline and fear and uncertainty, his vision locked onto the officer with laser focus as the battle between foot soldiers raged around him. A path cleared in front of him toward the hill and he ran as fast as he could toward the Nazi officer, his eyes locked on him as he sliced and shot his way through the battle field."

"Whoa! He sounds like a super hero!" Alfonso said, his mouth full of pie, crumbs raining down on his shirt as he spoke.

"He had been trained to kill and deprived of any enjoyment for months. He was primed to kill and he wanted that officer. He told me he wasn't sure why it was so clear to him that he was to kill the officer but he acted on his instinct, running as fast as he could toward him. As he got closer, more and more soldiers attempted to impede his way but they weren't successful; he killed them all. He rounded the base of the hill, moving behind where the officer stood at its peak. He ran up the back of the hill with the dexterity of a monkey climbing a tree for a fruit, his traction firm, his stride long. When he reached the top, he grabbed the officer from behind, his arm around his neck, his knife in the other hand ready to slit his throat. The Nazi soldiers there to protect him were caught off-guard and didn't notice their commanding officer was captured until he screamed for help--in German, of course. When they turned around, they saw Arthur there with their commanding officer in his grasp and dozens of other American soldiers behind him, who had followed him up the hill when they noticed his attack. The Germans scattered in every direction and Arthur, unaffected by the screams of the Nazi officer, killed him on the spot by slitting his throat."

"Man! That's crazy!" I said. "That's like something straight out of a Rambo movie."

"When the officer fell to the ground, a sword he had in his belt fell to the wayside. Something red sparkled and glistened as it hit the ground. Arthur picked up the sword and quickly slid it in his pant leg, keeping it for later. The battle ended soon after. The Germans surrendered and either retreated or were captured and it would be a good twenty four hours before Arthur would get some rest and sleep back at the camp."

"That is one crazy story," Alfonso said.

"What did he do with the sword?" I said.

"Back at his camp and after a good night's sleep, Arthur remembered he had the sword and examined it. The sword had an intricately engraved handle and a very large, red jewel in the pommel at the base of the grip. It looked like something of great monetary value so he pried the jewel from its golden bezel and hid the jewel with the rest of his belongings. The sword was eventually confiscated and when asked about the empty pommel, he shrugged. But rather than be questioned more about it, he was commended for his brave and successful attack. More rum?" she said, raising the bottle to us.

"Yes, please," I said. She poured some more for the three of us.

"On the way back to the United States, Arthur befriended a fellow soldier and, upon learning that the soldier was Jewish, confided in him the secret he had been keeping. His new friend promised that his family could help auction the Nazi jewel and that Arthur would make more money than he could ever imagine, with a cut going to his new friend of course. When they returned to the United States, he followed his friend to New York, where he introduced Arthur to his family, all of which were in the jewelry business. They enthusiastically helped Arthur auction the jewel and in return, paid him tens of thousands of dollars for the Nazi ruby, and he came back to Texas and opened a car dealership selling Ford trucks and automobiles here in Austin soon after. He became very, very successful."

"That is one crazy story," Alfonso said. I agreed with him. It was a very crazy story and far more interesting than any story we had heard from any of the shitheads down at the P.W., whose stories mostly consisted of who got fucked up on what and where they got fucked up and how hung over they were while telling you how fucked up they were. Just stupid. But this--this story, Arthur's story, as well as Sarah's own story--was way more interesting than anything me or Alfonso had experienced around Austin. What Sarah and Arthur experienced in their lives was nothing short of epic. The only thing epic about me and Alfonso was how broke we were.

"Well, I guess it is kind of crazy," Sarah said. "But that's life. That was part of his life. It only seems crazy because you can't imagine it but it happened to him. So, rather than being crazy, it's actually just the truth."

"Does Arthur have any family?" I said, sipping my rum.

"He did have a wife but she passed away ten years ago. Cancer. And he had three kids but one died in a car wreck. The other two live on the west and east coast respectively. They do not come to visit him. He used to visit them quite often but he's traveled less as his health has deteriorated."

"I see. He must be lonely."

"Shoot, Arthur and I have a hoot with some of the other neighbors we have. We've formed our own little family, the old folks we are, abandoned by our children or families or whatever. We take care of each other."

"Sounds nice," I said, feeling a little envious, a little jealous. "It's nice having support and friendship."

"Yes, it is. Oh my!" she said, looking at a wall clock, realizing the amount of time that had flown by. "I don't want to keep you boys from work."

"You're not keeping us," Alfonso said. "We'd rather be here, actually."

"Well, if you boys don't mind giving me your phone number, I'll call you next time we have another get-together with Arthur and the neighbors. The other neighbors have wonderful stories, too, to tell. I'm certain you'd enjoy yourself."

"That would be great," Alfonso said.

"Yes, I'd like that too," I said. She slid a pad of paper and a pen across the table to me and I wrote down my phone number. I pushed the pad of paper back toward her, placed the pen on it. "I'd like that very much."

12. Goodbye, Puss Face

One of the frustrating things for me and Alfonso about working at the P.W. was that we were required to look and dress like a million bucks even though we didn't have a million bucks. In fact, we didn't even have a million cents to our name, for that matter. The management wanted us to wear pressed and starched shirts, nice silk ties, pressed slacks, nice dress shoes, and so on and so forth. They really impressed upon us that it was important to present ourselves in a very professional manner to our customers, which was fine and all, except that was very hard to do when you didn't have any fucking money! I mean--seriously. I basically had two dress shirts, two silk ties, two pairs of slacks, and one pair of shoes to cycle through for what usually amounted to working six days a week, sometimes all seven days. It doesn't take a genius to figure out the wear and tear those clothes took in a short amount of time. To top that off, imagine the amount of food and beverage and bodily fluid shrapnel the average food service worker needs to dodge to try to keep their uniform clean or at least reasonably free of marinara sauce spots or salad dressing splatters or hot oil stains or parmesan flecks. It was practically impossible to do--really.

But we tried our best to look clean and pressed and put-together in an elegant way on very little wages. We concocted a system where we would rotate our clothes with the ones we wore the day before by hanging the next shirts and pants in the bathroom and hope the steam from the hot showers would at least permeate our clothes in such a way to loosen the food particles and relax any wrinkles and combat the body odor and make for a smoother ironing job. We had a make-shift pressing station that consisted of an ironing board--one I bought from a nearby thrift shop--that stood in the corner of my bedroom and a $10 iron purchased at the grocery store that was coated with rust and mineral deposits from the hard water that flowed through its steam holes. It wasn't the best solution but it was all we had.

Almost every day before every shift, we went through the same dance routine of attempting to look like a million bucks with clothes that may or may not have been washed in a week or so, pushing our greasy hair into a style that looked somewhat elegant, and dealing with facial hair that may not be shaved for lack of a decent razor or a can of shave cream with actual shave cream in it. Sometimes, we had to share the small bathroom together, fighting for space in front of the mirror like two teenage sisters, elbowing each other while combing our hair or straightening our ties.

"Fuck off!" I said, my elbow to Alfonso's ribs in retaliation for his elbow in mine.

"Don't be a bitch!" he said.

"You're the bitch!"

"YOU'RE the bitch!"

Then a short truce.

"We should try to start your car," I said, combing my hair back in place.

"It won't start," he said, annoyed.

"We should at least *try*."

"Why? It won't start."

"How do you know?"

"I just *know!*"

"You're such an optimist," I said, sarcastically.

"Fuck off."

Mr. Whiskers enjoyed this type of interaction between me and Alfonso. He'd jump up on my bed and peer into the bathroom, his tail slithering back and forth like some vertically-inclined, insane snake, pacing back and forth at the end of the bed, meowing occasionally. When we were done primping, I scratched Mr. Whisker's head after getting out of the bathroom then gathered all the things I needed for work: my apron, a pen, a pad of paper, some coins, a pack of cigarettes, and a cheap plastic lighter.

"You ready?" I said. Alfonso was still in the bathroom, primping.

"Beauty is hard work," he said. We both laughed out loud.

"I think we should try to start your car really quick."

"Fine," he said. "But if it doesn't start then you owe me $50."

"$50?!" To me, $50 might as well have been $1,000. It was absurd.

"That's right. $50," he said, combing the last loose strands of hair in place on the top of his fat head.

"Jesus! You suck. Goodbye, Mr. Whiskers," I said, patting his back then leaving my bedroom.

"Goodbye, Puss Face," Alfonso said, patting my cat after coming out of the bathroom. He followed me out the door of my apartment.

***

We stood next to Alfonso's dead car and stared. It was covered in more bird shit and more June bug carcasses and more dried leaves and cedar pollen than before, its tires totally deflated, literally looking like a relic from another time, maybe 1983, maybe 1982 depending on when it was manufactured, covered in dust and shame. In all the years that Honda tested this model of car for safety and durability and comfort and stamina, I'm absolutely certain they never imagined the state it would be in now, some 10 years or so later, stranded in my apartment complex parking lot, looking like Godzilla just shit it out after devouring a pile of cars in an unsuspecting parking garage somewhere in Japan. I'm sure it was a nice car when it was brand new. I'm sure someone was proud to own it at some point in its young life. That certainly wasn't the case while we stared at it.

"Piece of shit," Alfonso said.

"Mmm hmm," I said.

"She's still a goddamn, dirty whore."

"Now, now, no need to talk that way. I'm sure she was your sweetheart back in the day."

"I guess."

"Maybe you'd be happier if she started."

"She won't start," he said, his head drooping.

"All you can do is try. She might surprise you!" I patted him on the shoulder. He looked down at me, a look on his face I could only describe as "certain defeat," and he nodded. He fumbled in his pockets for his keys, found them, unlocked the door, and opened it. Leaves and empty aluminum cans fell to the ground. He sat inside--his left foot pushing the trash on the floor board away from the gas and brake pedals onto the ground as well--and he put the key in the ignition. I'd not known Alfonso to pray but he closed his eyes and mumbled something under his breath that I can only imagine to be a prayer of some kind--maybe a Catholic one that was lodged in the outer places of his memory where the dreams and mental images of his childhood resided--as he gripped the steering wheel with his left hand and tightly pinched the key with his right. Then, unceremoniously, he turned the key in the ignition. His car made a noise that sounded like an old lady coughing up phlegm, and then it roughly started. A look appeared on his face that reminded me of those people you see in lottery commercials--the ones that supposedly won big with a scratcher or whatever--and he jumped out of his piece of shit car, his arms extended to the sky like he was the champion of the whole fucking world.

"It started!" he said, yelling toward the sky, his voice echoing through the trees around my apartment complex, and grackles escaping the noise. We gave each other high-fives. He turned to look at his ride, still surprised, *really* surprised. "Kinda rough but she's running."

"Yep." I was happy for him. It really was like he won the lottery or something.

"I can't believe it. This whole time..."

There are times when you are so far down in the dumps, so far down a pit of despair from bad luck and bad circumstance and bad choices that it just seems like you never, ever catch a break, and when it finally comes, even just a little break, it feels monumental. It feels like the best thing that has ever happened to you. It feels like winning the lottery, even if it's only your piece of shit car barely starting and running after sitting for what seemed like months. Alfonso's car starting felt like that--like he won something, like it was his time. It felt like we were heading in a new direction, like good things were about to happen. Do you know that feeling? I bet you do.

"Too bad the tires are flat as fuck," I said, laughing. "We need to figure out how to air them up."

"No doubt," Alfonso said, rubbing his hands together.

"And maybe invest in a few things to tune it up, spark plugs and filters and whatever."

"Yeah." He leaned into his car and cut the ignition. The car burped back to sleep. "I need to make a plan to fix it up."

"I'll help you, buddy." I patted him on the back and he closed the door to his car. We found my Civic, jumped in, and went to work.

***

There was a strange energy in the air at the P.W. when we walked inside. The wait staff huddled around the podium even though Paula the A.M. was not there. They all mumbled about her whereabouts but nothing concrete was said. I looked at Alfonso and he looked at me. We shrugged and hung in the background, finding a spot against the wall to lean on, hanging out. As I looked at the throng of impatient servers, I saw Laura Ann peering at us. I tilted my head up as if to say, 'Wazzup?' She tilted her head back at me as if to say, 'Huh?' She broke through the others and stood next to me. She nudged me with her elbow.

"No one knows what's going on," she said, whispering.

"I see," I said, mock whispering.

"It would be nice to know what are assignments are."

"Yeah."

"I could use the money."

"Me too."

"Do you ever consider what it would be like working somewhere else?" she said, extending her leg forward and drawing figure eights and stars with the toe of her shoe.

"At another restaurant?" I said, curious.

"Yeah."

"I think if I had to leave here that I wouldn't go to another restaurant. I'd probably look to find something new."

"Like car salesman?!" Alfonso said. I looked at him, giving him a burning stare. "You can make fat cash as a car salesman."

"I'm not a car salesman," I said. "That's not a part of my personality."

"I hear they are hiring at the lake for next season. I know this chick who worked at Señor Toad's. She told me she made a lot of money last summer working out there."

"Yeah? How many guys did she have to blow?" Alfonso said, sarcastically.

"She didn't have to blow anybody!" she said, punching him in the gut. That caught him off guard. Pretty funny, if you'd asked me. I couldn't stop giggling.

"Just asking. Shit," he said, rubbing his stomach. I looked at him and motioned with my eyes for him go away. He rolled his eyes, annoyed, and straightened his shirt. "I see I'm not wanted here." He walked away.

"Where's he going?" she said. "Did I hurt his feelings?"

"Nah. He'll live."

"OK." She drew something on the floor that I can only imagine was a flower.

"Can I ask you a question?" I was nervous. I slid my hands in my back pockets, holding myself upright, bracing for a possible negative reply.

"Oh, OK."

"That dude I saw you with at Levonne's party. Is that your boyfriend?"

"What? Ummm, Mick? Oh God, no! No, no, no, no."

"Really?"

"Mick is my roommate's boyfriend. We're just friends. He's nice. And he's nice to my roommate."

"Oh... good. I mean, that's good."

"We were probably just waiting around for her to go to the bathroom or something. She was at the party too and--"

"Would you like to hang out sometime? Like, maybe after work tonight?" I said. I felt like a real dufus, too, all of a sudden, for asking. I don't know why. I just did, OK?

"Ummm."

"If you're busy then I understand."

"No, sure. Let's see. I don't have any plans after work tonight. What do you want to do?"

"I don't know. I wasn't planning on asking you to hang out. I guess we could just hang at my place, talk, eat something."

"Well--"

"Alfonso will be around too. He lives with me, if that's OK. I mean, he's my roommate."

"I figured he was since you two always seem to be around each other."

"So, is that a yes?"

"Yes," she said, smiling at me, the toe drawing continuing again.

SALUD!

"Great!" I said, excited then tempering my excitement, not wanting to sound too bonkers about it. "So, what's going on here? Where's Paula?"

"I don't know. There's rumors that her and Dan are upset about something but I don't know what it is this time."

"I see. So, tonight then? Us, hang out?"

"Yes, tonight."

"Great! I'm going to check on Alfonso, make sure his feelings aren't hurt."

"OK."

I went to look for Alfonso.

13. Dinner, a Confession, and a Novel about Something

Mr. Whiskers displayed a level of whorishness on Laura Ann's leg that I had never seen before. The minute she stepped inside my apartment with us, he commenced to rubbing his head and neck on her leg in such a way that would make a hooker from Silicon Valley embarrassed. I mean, he just wouldn't stop. I didn't know what to say. Thankfully, Laura Ann thought it was cute (lucky for him). I was ready to toss his fuzzy ass out the window.

"Your cat is so affectionate," she said, kneeling down to pet him. She started at the back of his head and stroked him the full-length of his body. Wads of fur came off in her hand as she pet him, plumes of loose fur twirling in the air, his purring getting louder, his whorishness more aggressive. "Sooo cute!"

"Ummm, thanks," I said, closing the door behind us. Alfonso got a kick out of Mr. Whiskers unsavory behavior, chuckling at the brash display of favoritism toward our new guest.

"Hooker," he said, setting his things on the side table next to the couch, his makeshift bed in the living room which was really his makeshift bedroom. "That cat is straight-up, a hooker."

"Awww, you guys are so mean," she said, continuing to pet him. I stared at her for a moment, shocked at the idea that the beauty I had crushed on for the past few weeks was actually in my apartment, kneeling down and petting my cat. There was something inherently good about her--without a doubt I could tell--that emitted from her like warm rays from the sun, like the sound of ocean waves crashing on a remote beach, like the sound of the rain tapping on a roof. It was an undeniable truth, something good. I could see it in the way she carried herself, in the way she presented herself to the world, in the way she pet my cat and said yes to coming to hang out with me. She had a way about her that said, 'I'm a good person' and I believed that to be true. I liked that about her and Mr. Whiskers did too, obviously. "I miss having a cat."

"You can have mine," I said. She thought that was pretty funny. "There are hundreds of cats down at the shelter too. You could go adopt one."

"That's a great idea. I may just have to do that except... I'm never, ever home. I work too much. Maybe it's not a good idea after all," she said, giving Mr. Whiskers one last scratch then standing up. She looked around, investigated, wiping her hands together, releasing the loose fur into the air. "So, this is where you guys live, huh?"

"Yup," I said. "The Palace on South First Street!"

"The Chateaux of Shit!" Alfonso said.

"It's not sooo bad," she said, maneuvering around my small apartment, trying her best not to knock anything over. "It's just a little cramped but nice."

"Alfonso sleeps out here," I said, then pointing to the bedroom. "That's my room back there."

"Can I see?" she said.

"Sure." I watched her walk into my room and I looked at Alfonso. He shrugged. I followed her in.

My bedroom was sparsely furnished. I had a pretty nice double bed although I rarely made it. I had an antique nightstand my father gave me with a digital alarm clock on it, an ashtray, some coins, a lighter, and a framed photo of Mr. Whiskers when he was a kitten. Laura Ann thought that was cute. The only other piece of furniture I had was a massive drafting table that I used for a desk, its tilt-able top set at a perpendicular angle to its base, with a beat-up Toshiba portable computer on it. There were some papers scattered on it too, some pencils, and some empty cigarette boxes. It was a pathetic excuse for a desk, really.

"What do you do with that?" she said, pointing at the computer.

"I write on it, sometimes."

"Write? Like what?"

"He keeps telling me he wants to be a writer but I've never seen him write anything," Alfonso said, looking into my room through the door.

"I've been too distracted lately," I said.

"What are you writing?" she said, standing closer to me.

"I've been working on a novel... kinda."

"Can I see?"

"Sure." I turned around and opened my closet door, revealing a small walk-in closet, big enough for one small person to step into, which I did. I reached for a cardboard box up on a shelf above my hanging clothes and pulled it down. Stepping back out of the closet, I set the box on the desk and opened it. Inside, a stack of white papers with a title page on top looked back at us. The title page said, "Untitled" with my name below that. "See," I said.

They both looked at the box with part amazement and part befuddlement. There obviously was a stack of a few hundred sheets of paper that was a couple of inches thick in the box, some typed text on every page, which meant a lot of time and effort must have gone into creating them. But what did it mean? What was it really? A novel? A book of stories? I wasn't even sure myself.

"Holy shit," Alfonso said. "You *are* writing something. I'm sorry, homie. I didn't mean to give you a hard time."

"What kind of novel is it?" she said. "You know, is it a mystery? Science fiction? What do you call that?"

"You mean, what genre?" I said.

"Yeah! What genre is it?"

"I have no idea. I don't even know what I'm doing, really. I just feel that since I studied literature in college then I should write and try to be a writer. I'm trying anyway."

"You can do it!" Alfonso said, slugging me on the back then he left my room for the living room.

"Thanks."

"Well, I'm impressed, Seff. I had no idea that you were following your dream, wanting something more than working at the P.W. I admire that. Me and my roommate, all we do is work. Most of the people I know, that's all they do, just work. You're the only person I know following a dream, doing more than just work."

"Do you want something to eat or drink?" I said. I was so embarrassed from the attention that she was giving me that I didn't know what else to say.

"Oh, OK," she said, caught off guard.

"We have lots of food and wine. Food or wine? Just wine?"

"Either or all of it is fine with me."

I motioned for her to lead the way out of my room then after she left, I quickly shoved the cardboard box with my writing project back up on the shelf in my closet.

In the kitchen, Laura Ann was petting Mr. Whiskers again while Alfonso listened to a message on the answering machine. I could make out a few words here and there in the message but I didn't know who it was. I was too busy looking for a cork screw for the bottle of wine to pay attention.

"Who called?" I said to Alfonso.

"I think it was Sarah. Weird."

"Really? That is weird."

"Who's Sarah?" Laura Ann said, curious.

"A very cool, old lady we met not long ago. Get this! Dan sent us to deliver food one day a while back and we met the coolest old lady with the coolest story."

"Really? I have never delivered food. How interesting."

"Yeah, then we went back again on another delivery and met a neighbor of hers who also had a very cool story. They both had WAY more interesting lives than us. I mean, infinitely more interesting. Plus, their families have kind of abandoned them so it was nice hanging around them, listening to their stories."

"Are you going back?" she said.

"Yeah, hopefully. What do you think, Alfonso?"

"We're going back."

"Yeah?" I said, pleased.

"Yeah, she invited us back over. That's what she said in the message."

I found my cork screw in the knife drawer, opened a bottle of cheap red wine, and poured a couple of glasses of wine. I didn't pour one for Alfonso because I hoped he'd get the hint and take a hike. He didn't get the hint. I slid one glass over to Laura Ann and the other was for me. When we clinked glasses, Alfonso looked over.

"Where's my glass?" he said. I tilted my head toward the door, slowly craning it as if to say, 'Your glass is somewhere else.' Then he got the hint. "Fine. Let me just change my clothes first before I go." He got up with an armful of clothes and went into the bathroom.

"He doesn't have to go anywhere," she said, embarrassed.

"Are you sure? It just seems--"

Calling from the bathroom, he yelled, "I suppose you're going to eat all of our discarded feast, too?" Laura Ann looked at me and I looked at her. I wasn't expecting my roomie to blurt that out but he did. He came out of my room, pulling his shirt over his head and into place on his barrel-shaped torso. His hair was a tangled mess. "Are you?"

"What's a discarded feast?" As she said that, I felt a rush of electricity through me, a confessional streak of lightning. I looked at her and looked at my roomie and all I could think was, 'Uh oh.' I turned around and opened the refrigerator and the freezer, revealing stacks and stacks of aluminum trays that were obviously from the P.W. When I turned back to look at Laura Ann, her mouth dropped open.

"Oh shit," she said.

"Oh shit is right!" Alfonso said.

SALUD!

***

Alfonso left to go run an "errand" and said he'd be back later, probably to go mope around The GODDAMN or something like that. While he was gone, I told Laura Ann the truth about the food and how it was just a few seconds away from turning into trash. She didn't seem surprised at all that we brought the food home. It was decent food and more than edible--better than trash really. More than anything, she was surprised that she didn't know of anyone else taking the food home too, like Levonne or any of the other mooching servers like Warren the mooch or the other mooch Paul. Info like that got around quickly at the P.W. and as far as she knew, no one else was doing it. She had, on occasion, hung out with several of the other servers and kitchen staff from the P.W. at their homes or apartments or condos or duplexes and not once did any of them mention the idea of taking home the leftovers after the P.W. closed. Not to say that no one noticed the sheer volume of food being wasted in the nightly dumpster toss. It was plain as day what Levonne was doing, pushing the cart over to the dumpster, and heaving the trays in there.

"But WHY did you do it?" she said, turning her chair to get a better look at me. We had moved to the patio for a smoke break shortly after finishing our meals. It was a nice night, especially since Alfonso was gone. "What made you bring all that food home?"

"I don't know," I said, lighting another cigarette. I felt like I was part of an informal inquisition. I started to sweat a little.

"You don't know? Really?" She reached for my pack of smokes on the small patio table and held them up as if to ask if she could have one. I nodded. She lit one and exhaled, a sexy plume of smoke erupting from her mouth.

"Really. I was ready to heave the trays into the dumpster and something told me to bring the trays home. Maybe it was because we're dirt poor. Maybe it was because, deep down, I felt like the P.W. was screwing us. Or maybe I just really felt that it was a waste of good food."

"I get that. I really do but... you could get in trouble."

"How could I get in trouble?" I said, sitting up, actually curious. I didn't think of myself as a thief for taking the garbage home but I guess, technically, I probably was, maybe more like Robin Hood. Maybe.

"Isn't it stolen property?"

"But isn't it just garbage the minute it leaves the building? I mean, that's where it was intended to go--in the garbage."

"Who knows what corporate would do."

"Are *you* worried about me?"

"No!" she said, immediately. Even though I was joking, deep down, I hoped she'd say yes. I was crushed a little bit. "No, no, I'm not worried. Just saying."

"Oh, OK."

We sat together for a few quiet minutes, finishing our smokes, enjoying the night sky. Mr. Whiskers batted at a bug on the other side of the sliding glass door, his paw tapping the glass. We looked at him and laughed. He was being really cute.

"So," she said, pausing while she crafted her thought. "Are you going to do it again?"

"Do what again?"

"Load up your refrigerator?"

"I don't know. Probably. Maybe. You got me all paranoid now."

"*Now* you're paranoid?" she said. We both laughed. It was pretty funny. Hearing her laugh was an aphrodisiac and I found myself daydreaming about kissing her, caressing her hair, touching her skin. A moment of silence set in as we extinguished our cigarettes. I crushed my smoke in a tin can next to my chair and she did the same. As she leaned over, making sure that her cigarette was out, I locked my eyes with hers and I looked deep into them to that place that everyone knows to look for a connection. I could see something there. She didn't look away. The corners of her mouth turned up slightly. Then she said, "I'm not going to kiss you, Seff."

"Right, of course not," I said, startled a bit. I sat up, embarrassed, straightening my shirt. "My bad. Sorry, so sorry. I wasn't trying to--"

"Well, I'm not going to kiss you tonight but that doesn't mean I won't kiss you another night."

"Really?"

"Really," she said. "If you play your cards right."

"Sorry if I spaced out there for a moment."

"Don't be sorry. Just not tonight, OK?"

"OK."

"So, what would you say if I helped you with the next discarded feast?"

"Huh?" That caught me more off-guard than the kiss rebuff. I sat up in my chair. "What do you mean?"

"You know? The next time you bring home the food the P.W. throws away?"

"Oh, I don't know. I don't know if I'm going to do it again. I really don't want to get in trouble or lose my job. I have bills to pay."

"Who doesn't?" she said, looking up at the clear sky, the stars sparkling.

"It is stolen property, right?"

"Who knows?"

"Right, who knows. Besides, there would be so much, I'd have to give a lot of it away. My fridge is still full. Maybe I'll give some to the old folks we met--Sarah and Arthur. You'd like them."

"My refrigerator isn't full. It's practically empty." She leaned back in her chair and extended her hand towards mine. I put her hand in my hand and held it gently. The touch of her skin against mine sent goose bumps up my back. "I wouldn't turn down free food."

Mr. Whiskers tapped at the sliding glass door some more and I thought he was trying to get our attention but he was swatting at a roach, hoping to maneuver it into his mouth. We watched him wrestle with the bug, attempting several times to have it for a snack.

Laura Ann pulled at my hand, getting my attention, then said, "Can I read what you've written so far?"

"You want to read my book?" I said.

"Yes."

"OK. If you really want to."

"I really want to."

"I'll let you take it as long as you bring it back when you're done. That's my only hard copy."

"I'll be careful with it. I promise."

Mr. Whiskers finally got the bug into his mouth and ate it.

14. Spanish for White Bread and Party for Mooches

Once the bread was 86'ed, the entire wait staff was toast. Alfonso and I wished for a good night of tips but it wasn't meant to be that night. You see, once the complimentary bread was gone, everything else went to shit. We didn't know why that was, although, we had plenty of theories. 1) Our customers loved the free bread more than the actual meals and even though they paid for the meals, they really just wanted to stuff their pie holes full of free bread. 2) The free bread curbed their hunger until they could stuff their faces with cheap pasta but without the bread, their hunger turned our already grouchy customers into even worse tippers. 3) I could go on forever with our stupid theories. Mostly, when Dan the G.M. or Paula the A.M. came into the kitchen and yelled '86 bread!' then we knew our shifts were done. We weren't going to make any money, no matter how hard we tried. It was over like Donkey Kong grabbing Pauline and climbing up the girders, leaving Mario to stare blankly at the emptied scaffolds, empty handed. We were powerless. Me and Alfonso stared at our empty sections knowing full-well that we were going to be hard pressed to pay rent.

"This shit sucks," Alfonso said.

"You're telling me," I said.

"Might as well enjoy the rest of our night. Smoke break?"

"Duh."

We abandoned our stations and careened around the perimeter of the dining room, passing the other staffers, some pretending to work or others just standing around. Warren the mooch asked to tag along (we didn't say he could, by the way) and followed us. Soon after, Laura Ann followed us too. We barreled through the kitchen, all in a line like segments of a crazed centipede, and out the back door to the alley before anyone could tell us to start side work or sweep the floors or wipe down menus or whatever busy work was waiting to be done. The night air was clean and crisp and it was very apparent that doing anything else besides standing around in the P.W. not making money was the right thing to do.

"Who has smokes?" Alfonso said. He looked at me then Warren then Laura Ann. We all shrugged. "You cheap motherfuckers! Why am I always the one handing out cigarettes?" He stomped his feet.

"Because you're the best!" Warren said, his hands in his pockets, rocking back and forth on his heels, his teeth yellow and slick through his Cheshire Cat smile.

"Fuck all of you, bastards," Alfonso said, pulling a crumpled pack from his pants pocket with a huff, opening the top, and revealing four not-so-perfect, white cigarette filters. "But you're in luck. Look at that! Four motherfucking cigarettes for four cheap bastards."

The three of us said 'Horray!' in sarcastic unison. All of us got a cigarette and Alfonso lit them all, displaying his ninja skills again, opening and lighting his brass Zippo with one hand. He really was a master at that--by the way--something that is harder to do than it looks. The four of us sucked our smokes to life, releasing nicotine smoke to the night sky. It was chillier than it was when we arrived for work earlier in the day. Laura Ann shivered a bit while she smoked her cigarette and I tempered my urge to put my arms around her and snuggle her.

"Thanks Alfonso," Warren said. "I know the perfect way to make it up to you."

"Oh yeah? Wha' cha got for me? You've bummed at least $100 worth of my tobacco."

"I'm having a party at my place later. Wanna come?"

Alfonso didn't skip a beat and said, "Shit, yeah I wanna come but I'm bringing my homies right here." He motioned to me and Laura Ann. "Cool with you? I'm not going to no party without my homies."

"Yeah, I have to give him a ride since his car won't start," I said.

"It starts, goddamn it!"

"Barely," I said, snickering.

"That's fine," Warren said. "You are all welcome to come. We'll have a keg and some booze and some weed, maybe some ecstasy but I'm not sure yet about that."

"That's all you had to say, bolillo. We'll be there. Want us to bring anything?"

"Nah, only if you want to." Warren said. Puzzled, he continued, "What's a bolillo?"

"It's Spanish for white bread."

We all laughed at Warren's expense. He laughed too, a little, slightly uncomfortable laugh. It was pretty funny, though.

"Well, I'm going to start my side work," Warren said. "I want to get out of here and go pick up the keg." He flicked his smoke down the alley, its cherry bursting into fiery dust on the ground, and went back in the P.W.

"What do you say, home slaps? Wanna go party at Warren's pad? He owes me--us! I mean, he's bummed so many smokes I can't even count."

"I'm in," I said, looking over at Laura Ann. "Want to go?"

"Sure, I don't have any plans tonight. I'll call my roommate and tell her not to expect me home til later. She waits up sometimes."

"Great! It's settled," Alfonso said, then taking a deep drag off his cigarette.

As he exhaled, the back door to the P.W. slammed open and in the doorway stood Levonne, his backside facing us, his leg propping the door open as he maneuvered the plastic cart through the doorway. It was stacked high with aluminum trays, more than usual, probably because it was an unexpectedly slow night. Once through the door and out a few feet, he stepped around to the back side of the cart and slowly pushed it onto the landing area, careful not to let the trays spill over the side of the cart. I looked at my two friends and they looked at me and we knew we were all thinking the same thing: it's time to fill our refrigerators. Alfonso nodded at me and Laura Ann winked. I knew exactly what to do.

"Hey Levonne!" I said, tossing my cigarette to the ground then jumping up on the landing area. "Need some help?"

"Nah, thanks my man. I go it." He continued to slowly push the cart toward the dumpster.

"Seriously. I finished all my side work," I said. I lied.

Levonne stopped and took a few labored breaths, wiping some olive oil-infused sweat from his brow onto his shirt sleeve.

"Are you sure, my man? There's a lot of shit here to deal with."

"I don't mind at all."

"Seriously?! Shit, negro. That's all you gots to say. It's all yours."

"Cool," I said, taking a hold of the cart. Levonne shuffled back into the building and I looked at my friends and they looked at me and it was time.

"What do we do?" Alfonso said, tossing his smoke to the ground and crushing it under his shoe.

"Here," I said, taking my car keys from my pocket and tossing them to him. "Go get my car and park it behind the dumpster." He ran off--at top speed--to go find my car.

"What do I do?" Laura Ann said, looking clueless and excited at the same time. She looked sexy too but that had nothing to do with what we were doing.

"I think you should keep a look-out at the door, maybe keep anyone from coming out here?"

"Seriously? What would I say?"

"I don't know. Make up a story."

"But you're the story teller."

"True, true. But you're WAY better looking than I am and WAY more convincing. They'll listen to you."

"Not Paula. She hates me," she said, putting her hands on her waist.

"Paula is too pregnant to come out here."

While we were arguing over details that didn't matter, Alfonso sped my car into the alley and passed us on his way to park behind the dumpster.

"Oh shit!" I said, frantically pushing the cart toward the dumpster. "Just keep a look-out. OK?"

She waited by the door, her foot propped at the bottom to keep it from opening. I made my way toward the dumpster. The cart was so overloaded with aluminum trays that the wheels went every which direction but straight, one spinning in circles, another angled left, another jammed with hair or something that looked like hair. It made for a difficult push to the dumpster. Alfonso parked my car behind the dumpster and got out, his head poking up from behind the metal trash container.

"What's taking so long?" he said, excited but trying to keep his voice down. He saw me struggling with the cart which must have been a sight. "Do you want me to help you?"

"No, I got it. Stay down there." I tried to keep my voice down too but it was hard with all the struggling. I eventually got next to the dumpster and Alfonso stood on the ground next to the landing. He had already popped the trunk open and my car waited there, patiently, like a hippo in a shallow pond waiting for kids to dump bags of peanuts in its mouth. I quickly passed a tray of food down to him. It was still quite hot, hotter than I expected. "Here--FUCK!" I sucked on my fingers quickly after giving it to him then got back to work.

"Oh man, it's hot!" he said.

"Yeah!"

"What are we going to do with all this food? I don't think it'll all fit in our fridge."

"We'll give some to Laura Ann," I said, handing him another, then another, as he placed them in the trunk. "She told me she'd take some. Her fridge is empty."

"I don't think she'll have room for the rest. We'll have a lot leftover. There's a shitload."

I handed him another, then another. He was right. There *was* a shitload, more than would fit in two crappy, apartment refrigerators. It seemed absolutely ridiculous to me that so much food was being wasted on a daily basis, just marked for tax purposes then tossed in the trash. What a waste.

"Maybe we can take some over to Sarah and Arthur. They're nice people and would appreciate it," I said.

"Sounds good."

I handed him the last one, 17 trays in all, and he closed the trunk, then swung my key ring around his index finger as if he was ready for a high-speed getaway from dozens of encroaching police cars.

"Now what?" he said.

I put one hand on my waist and scratched my head with the other, then said, "Go park around the corner. I'll take the cart back in, tell Laura Ann, then clock us both out. Give me your card."

He handed me his employee card, the one I would need to swipe on the computer and clock him out, then he hopped in my car and sped off. I turned around and pushed the cart back to the door. All of its wheels were cooperative, none stuck, all turning in the same, easy direction. Fucking cart.

Laura Ann was gone, disappeared. Maybe she saw someone and went in to distract them or maybe she had to go to the bathroom. I don't know. But as I started to push the cart into the door, there was good ol' Levonne, trying to come back outside. He was so big he clogged the doorway. I couldn't get passed him.

"Lemme check to see you did it right, home boy," he said, trying to grab the clipboard from the side of the cart. I swatted his hand away and put an arm around his massive frame.

"We're going to a party at Warren's place. You going?" I attempted to maneuver his body, to turn him around. He was a granite boulder to my skinny, twig-like arms.

"Don't know about no party," he said, still trying to get the clipboard.

"I did it right. Relaaaaaax," I said, soothing the man. He was pretty hot under the collar for some reason.

"I just needs to know," he said, looking me serious in the eyes, pulling me close by my shirt. "Did you do it right?" He looked like he could pulverize me with the flick of the wrist.

"Yes, of course." I lied but he relaxed, eased up. I could tell he was really worried about it. He was a good employee, really. He was proud of his work ethic (which was weird to me since it was just the P.W. of all places), something I didn't have.

"OK... Thanks, home skillet. Say, where's the party at?"

"At Warren's."

"Where's dat?"

"Shit, I don't know. Let's go find out."

We both walked back to the kitchen, my arm draped over his massive shoulders. The back door slammed shut behind us.

***

I drove north on Loop 360 in my Civic with Alfonso riding shotgun, looking for the entrance to the neighborhood where that mooch Warren lived, while Laura Ann and her roommate followed behind in her car. There weren't many lights on Loop 360 so I knew it was going to be difficult to see where the entrance was at night. During the day, Loop 360 took you through a scenic view of west Austin, complete with rolling hills covered with oak and cedar trees and upscale neighborhoods with McMansions speckled across the landscape like gaudy ornaments jutting from the branches of a Christmas tree. At night, the drive was a dark road stretching into the abyss. Alfonso did his best to lookout for the entrance, squinting his eyes at each passing sign or telephone pole or boulder, but he wasn't a very good navigator since his eyesight was so bad. It would have been just as good if he didn't try to navigate at all.

"I don't know why you never wear your glasses," I said, annoyed.

"They make me look funny," he said, still squinting. I thought of that old cartoon character Mr. Magoo and his stubbornness at admitting he couldn't see shit without his glasses. Alfonso was my Mexican version of Mr. Magoo.

"And you think the way you look right now without them isn't funny?"

"What do you mean?"

"Nothing." I looked in the rear view mirror to find the familiar shape and glow of the headlights of Laura Ann's car. She followed close enough that another car couldn't slide in between us but far enough that I couldn't make out her face through the windshield. I occasionally saw silhouettes of her and her roommate in the car. "What was her roommate's name again?"

"You got me. I already forgot."

"That won't bode well for you if you're going to mack on her."

"Man, I don't need to know a girl's name to mack on her," he said, pounding his chest with his fist. "I got game! I got ALL the game!"

"Mmm hmm. You can barely see past your nose."

"I'm not going to let you disparage me and my slight visual impairment," he said, sarcastically. "You, my friend, are jealous of my good looks."

"Ha! That sure is some shit you're talking about. Besides, her roommate has a boyfriend anyway. He's the dude Laura Ann was talking to at Levonne's party--There, there it is!"

Pointing with my left hand and steering with my right, I pulled my car into to the turn lane and Laura Ann followed behind. We turned left into the neighborhood and slowly made our way up into the hills, my Civic's engine rattling at the sudden steep incline. Unlike Loop 360, a street lamp appeared here and there, illuminating brick mail boxes sitting in front of vast yards with very large homes at the far edge of the lamp's glow. I couldn't tell if they were mansions but they were big houses, a lot bigger than I could ever imagine that mooch Warren being able to afford.

"Maybe I should put my glasses on," Alfonso said, reaching into his pants pocket then putting on his large, coke-bottle glasses. "Ah! Much better. What's the address?"

"He said it was on this road, that we wouldn't miss it, to just drive up the hill a ways and it's on the left."

"You gonna make the moves on Laura Ann tonight?" he said, pretending to cast a fishing line out into an imaginary pond of eligible ladies and then reeling it back in.

"Maybe."

"Your window of opportunity is closing."

"Why do you say that?" I said, annoyed.

"Women's windows are *always* closing. Don't you know anything?"

"Oh, shut the fuck up."

I could tell I was getting to the top of the hill because the road started to level out and my Civic stopped rattling so much then we found ourselves in front of a house with dozens of cars parked in the street as well as in the driveway and on the front lawn. The house was a sprawling, ranch-style, one-story place made of tan stone and tan siding and tan shutters galore. The roof had a low pitch and hung long from the sides of the house, like a sombrero that had been mushed down and rained on quite a bit. At one time, early in its history, I imagined this house to have been a pretty fancy place. It had remnants of its fanciness but was starting to look a little haggard, like a party-girl heiress who smoked and drank too much through her youth but was edging past 40 with wrinkles and skin spots and dark circles under her eyes. I rolled my window down and I could hear the faint thump of rap music and the buzz of people talking and laughing. There was definitely a party going on.

"This has to be it," I said, looking for a spot to park my car. There were cars everywhere. Down a little ways from the house, the property extended into the distance, cedar trees and cactuses and rocks fading to black from the edge of the street into the night, with a random car here and there parked haphazardly as if they'd fallen from the sky or been randomly shat out by a prehistoric monster who'd recently stomped through. I found a place between a cedar and a live oak and parked my car. As Alfonso and I got out, Laura Ann parked a few trees over, her front bumper scraping against a large rock jutting from the ground. When she turned off her engine, I could hear Tone Lōc's *Wild Thing*, faintly thumping in the distance.

"This should be interesting," Alfonso said, pushing his hair into some semblance of a style. "I'm going to ask Laura Ann's roommate what her name is."

"Good idea."

They appeared quickly, unexpectedly, like cats.

"What's a good idea?" Laura Ann said.

"Oh, he wants to know your roommate's name," I said, extending my elbow towards her. She interlocked her arm within mine and I escorted her towards the house, leaving Alfonso dumbfounded with her roommate, who looked about as excited as a kid with a bowl of pea soup in front of her. "What is her name again?" I said, whispering.

"Constance. It was her grandmother's name but I call her Con."

"I see. Is she cool?"

"Most definitely. But she has a boyfriend, remember?"

"I told him that already."

We walked along the street then through the front yard of what we believed was that mooch Warren's pad, empty beer cans and crushed cigarette packs strewn across the Bermuda grass, the smell of spilt beer and marijuana smoke in the air, the buzz of conversation. The front door was already partially open so we just walked inside.

The music was considerably louder but there weren't as many people as we expected in the living area, a massive, wide-open room with a sunken area in the middle, a humongous, brown sectional couch big enough to seat 20 people--at least--and a large screen TV surrounded by cabinets of Hi-Fi stereo equipment. One couple sat on the couch drinking beer. Another couple stood near the stereo. There wasn't a thing on the walls or any other furniture. It was a bachelor pad, for sure. Nintendo Zelda was on the TV but nobody was playing and the song *Wild Thing* morphed into *Bust a Move*.

"Sounds like more people are back there," Laura Ann said, shouting and pointing to where the kitchen seemed to be. "Let's go check it out."

I nodded and looked back to see if Alfonso and Con were behind us. They weren't. Maybe Alfonso's mack game *was* as strong as he claimed? We made our way to the kitchen where we found that mooch Warren as well as the other mooch Paul and that bastard Fred, playing a game of Quarters on the kitchen island. The Three Fucking Mooch-keteers. I had a feeling they all lived here in this monster house but I wasn't quite sure. I really didn't know them all that well. They were all wearing Levi's and Izod shirts and loafers like some kind of preppy gang. It was weird and kinda creepy. Warren saw us and smiled.

"Ah!" he said. "You made it. Come in. Want some beer? There are kegs on the patio." He tilted his head toward the back of the kitchen and out a large window above the sink, I could see dozens of heads bobbing outside. "Or I have some whiskey here. Wanna shot?"

"Sure," I said, looking at Laura Ann. She nodded. Warren opened a door under the island counter and pulled out a bottle of Jack Daniel's whiskey, then opened a drawer which contained loose bottle caps and wine corks and cigarette butts and cork screws and church keys and shot glasses. He fished around in the drawer and pulled out two shot glasses, a glass one that said on its side, 'I got shipwrecked in Port Aransas!' with a cartoon of a pirate who looked drunk and sunburned. The other shot glass was a little ceramic one in the shape of a woman's boob, flesh-toned with a large, pancake-shaped, bright pink nipple. It didn't say anything on the side; the nipple was statement enough. He filled them up and slid them to us--me getting shipwrecked and Laura Ann getting the ugly boob cup. "Drink up!"

I clinked glasses with Laura Ann and we drained the shots.

SALUD!

After exhaling some burning fumes and wiping my mouth, I said, "Who all lives here?"

"Just me," Warren said. "Well, I have some people staying here with me. These two dopes." He pointed at Paul and Fred. They smirked the way I imagined two goblins possessing some secret that would obliterate the universe would smirk, sinister and passive-aggressive at the same time. "But this is MY house. I don't have any roommates but I do let friends stay here, if they want. Want a hit from the freezer bong?"

"What's that?" I said, puzzled.

Warren looked at Paul and tilted his head toward the refrigerator. Paul walked over and opened the freezer top to reveal a series of hoses and chemistry lab tubes and glassware, not one single frozen dinner or tub of ice cream inside. On the outside of the refrigerator was a hose that was coiled up on a hook. Closing the door, he unraveled the hose and brought it to us. After he placed the hose in my hand, he walked back to the refrigerator and stood by the right side of it, the water chamber and weed bowl section of a bong protruding from the side. He stood there holding a Bic Lighter in his hand, ready to ignite it.

"I converted my freezer into a bong. When you're ready, he'll light the bowl and you suck on the hose." The look on Warren's face alone sent warning signals through every nerve in my body. Red alert was in full effect! I set the hose in Warren's hand. Disappointed, he said, "Are you sure?"

"Yeah, man. I'll stick to whiskey or beer for now."

"Ok, OK. But don't say I didn't offer. You?" he said, looking at Laura Ann. She politely shook her head. Smart girl. "Man, rejected twice in such a short time. Maybe later." He handed the hose back to Paul, who reluctantly coiled it back on the fridge.

"How can you afford this place working at the P.W.?" I said. "We don't make THIS much money."

"Ha! I couldn't afford this place on what we make at the P.W. Shit! I just work there to make friends. I actually don't even need to work."

"Why's that?" Laura Ann said, curious.

"Well, I don't want this getting around but... I inherited some money a few years ago. My parents died in a plane crash and I inherited their estate. I also got a settlement from a class-action lawsuit. I was rich overnight!"

"So, if you're rich, then why work at the P.W.?" I said, pushing my shot glass forward. He filled the two glasses up again.

"Like I said, man, to make friends. I got lonely. Just don't tell anyone else, OK?"

"Why not?"

"Because I don't want to be treated differently."

"But you just told us."

"That's because I'm high as a kite!" He cackled.

"If you're so rich, then why do you mooch off everyone?" Laura Ann said. I looked at her, proud of her moxy. It was a very important question, after all.

"The rich don't stay rich by spending their money when they can get things for free. Am I right?" he said.

"I wouldn't know. I'm not rich," she said.

"Cam down, calm down," he said, raising his hands as if to surrender. "I realized that I've asked a lot of people at the P.W. which is why I threw this party--to give back to everyone. So drink up. Hang out. Enjoy the view on the back patio. It really is spectacular, even at night."

"OK," she said.

"Thanks Warren," I said, lifting my chin as if to accept his surrender. "Let's go check it out." Laura Ann and me made our way out back.

Outside, that's where the party was really happening. The back patio was at least 50 feet wide and 25 feet deep with dozens of party-goers drinking beer, smoking cigarettes and joints, circling the kegs like frontiersman protecting their last rations, talking, dancing a bit. It was a miracle the wood deck could support so many folks. I could feel everything through the wood planks, every stomp and every shuffle of someone's feet. I pulled Laura Ann's hand and led her around the perimeter of the deck to the railing. Once there, a spectacular night view stretched all the way around us and we could see for miles and miles. Even at night, the view was something to behold, hill after rolling hill speckled with various colored lights from homes and businesses and schools and country clubs and whatever. Holding the rail with both hands, I leaned my head over to look down. The deck was jutting out from the top of the hill. There was a least a 50 foot drop before the hill slid into darkness beneath us. A cool breeze hit our faces as we looked down.

"That's an amazing view," I said.

"No shit," she said. "Must be nice to have a pile of money just drop in your lap."

"Well, his parents did die, you know?" I said, sarcastically.

"Everyone's parents will die. Might as well get some money out of it." I was caught off-guard by her comment, which she tossed out like a grenade but refused to take cover. I didn't expect such a bitter comment to come out of her mouth but there it was. She quickly realized the unattractiveness of saying such things out-loud and quickly recanted. "I'm sorry. That was an ugly thing to say."

"It's OK. No worries."

"My parents died too in a freak accident. A drunk driver plowed into them when they were driving home from a charity event. When the police came to our house, they first told the babysitter who then had the difficult job of telling me and my little brother. We were crushed."

"Oh no!" I said, feeling extremely guilty that my parents were still alive and only lived a couple of hours away, even though I hadn't seen them in quite a while. At least, if I wanted to, I could hop in the car and go visit them on a whim. Laura Ann didn't have that choice. "I'm so sorry. I didn't know that about you."

"It's OK, really. It was a long, long time ago. But I didn't get any money out of it. Warren can gloat all he wants but I'd rather just have my parents back than have a lot of money. It's kinda pathetic that he's bragging about it like that."

"Yeah."

"I mean, it's just so insensitive--Hey! There's Levonne." she said, craning her neck to see him. "He's coming over here and he looks pissed!"

I turned around to find Levonne, mad as hell with a look on his face like he was going to demolish me, as he grabbed me by my shirt and pulled me close to his face. The whites of his eyes weren't white at all but red and sinewy with lines crisscrossing on them like miniature highways to hell. And his breath--hot and dense and rank with anger--hit my face hard.

"Why you givin' food to bums, nigga?!" he said. Boy, was he pissed, really pissed. I could tell. I felt some droplets of urine hit my inner thigh. "You takin' shit that's not yours?"

"I don't know what you're talking about," I said. I lied. I knew exactly what he was talking about but I wasn't going to give up the ghost like that.

"Oh yeah?" He pulled me even closer, even tighter in his grip, his stinky breath enveloping my head like a toxic fog. "After you split, I went out back to check that ya did yo' job correct and some dirty bum came frontin', asking me for food and shit, saying you gave him food. And I was like, 'Oh yeah?! Who been givin' ya food?' And he said some scrawny white boy who I can only surmise was yo' ass!"

"I didn't--" I was having a hard time breathing, the way he was holding me to him. I gagged a little.

"Hey! Let him go, goddamn it!" Laura Ann said, yelling and trying to release his grip but he was too big and too strong. He didn't let go no matter how hard she tried to tap on him with her fists.

"Then, then, that dirty motha'fucker tells me you been stealing food, not tossin' the shit like ya suppose ta, like I told ya. He said he been watchin' yo ass in the alley. Is this true?!"

"Wha?!" He was pulling me so hard that I was about to confess, just about to let it slip and tell him the truth, tell him I did it all, that I gave the bum some food and that I took the rest cause I was poor and hungry and felt slighted by the P.W. and how it was just going to be garbage anyway and who gave a fuck about the discarded feast. Really? Who gave a fuck, anyway, dude?!

But, in the way that most melees mysteriously happen, a flurry of fists appeared before my eyes in a blurred whirlwind with grunts and spit and the sound of flesh absorbing punches and the next thing I knew, I hit the deck with my face and I heard Alfonso's voice, a deep, angry growl of a voice. I looked up to find my friend on top of Levonne, pummeling his face, hard and fast and relentless. Levonne somehow rolled out from underneath Alfonso and jumped to his feet, his fists at his waist, his hair a mess, his left eye swollen and puffy and wet. It happened so fast that the rest of the people didn't notice until it was over. The party-goers closed in as Alfonso and Levonne squared off, giving each other death stares, their chests heaving in and out. Levonne looked even more pissed than before but haggard, off balance. He wiped his mouth with his hand.

"You motha'fuckers are fucked! That's all I gots ta say." He turned around and walked back into the house.

Alfonso turned to me, placing both of his hands on my shoulders, looked me straight in the eye, then he said, "You all right, homie?"

"Yeah, I'm all right," I said, shaken up.

"Glad I was coming back here or you would'a been destroyed. He was pissed. What was his problem?"

The party-goers dissipated without the promise of a fight on the patio deck. Something warm and wet appeared on my upper lip.

"Your nose is bleeding," Laura Ann said, dabbing the blood with a napkin. I liked the attention she was giving me.

"He said that bum from the alley told him that I was giving him food and taking food home. He was mad cause I didn't follow his directions."

"Fuck Levonne! Who is going to believe his fat ass anyway? What's he going to do? Tell the G.M. that a dirty bum told him some shit about you? Please!"

"I agree with Alf," she said, smiling at me. "I doubt Dan would believe that story."

"Yeah, I guess," I said. "Maybe."

"To be safe, maybe we should get rid of the food we took, take it over to Sarah's house or something," Alfonso said. "Get rid of the evidence and all." We all looked at each other and with a nod of our heads, confirmed that plan. It seemed like the right thing to do at the time. "We'll reconvene in the morning but for now..." He put his hand on Laura Ann's shoulder. "You should go talk to your friend. She's crying."

"What?!" she said, stunned.

"Your roommate. She's out front crying."

"Oh my god! OK, I'll go check on her." She quickly left to find her roommate Con.

"Want a beer?" Alfonso said.

"Duh."

We approached one of the kegs and as the surrounding people saw us come close, they slowly eased away, like the sea of nerds in the movie *Sixteen Candles* parting for their young, cool messiah. The sight of Alfonso pummeling a dude as massive as Levonne must have made an impression on these people. The last thing anyone wants to go through at a party is an ass-whooping. It seemed Alfonso now had VIP status to the beer keg. Some meek dude handed him two plastic cups and Alfonso poured us two, cold beers.

"So, why was Laura Ann's roommate crying?" I said, sipping some beer.

"Man, I don't even know where to start."

"Oh, this sounds good!"

"Nah, it's not like that. We just started talking and we sat down out front then she started telling me about her boyfriend, what happened between them, and that they broke up earlier today. She just kept going on and on about it. I figured if I was nice and offered a strong shoulder for her to cry on that maybe, just maybe, I might get laid. But she was really hung up on this dude. She started crying and telling me she wanted to go home and call him so she asked me to find Laura Ann. I didn't expect to save your ass from an angry cook, though!" We both laughed. It sounded funnier than it really was. "So, that's what happened."

"That's not as fun as I was hoping it would be."

"True. True."

My nose finally stopped dripping blood and I sipped some more beer, stunned at the events that just happened, when Laura Ann appeared in front of us, a small box under her arm. It was a box I had seen before. It was mine. She handed it to me.

"I just wanted to give this back to you before I took my roommate home. I read it."

"All of it?" I said, confused, taking the box containing my book from her.

"Yep, all of it. It's good, I think. Literature was not my best subject in school but I liked it. That must mean something."

"It does," I said.

She placed her hands on my shoulders and planted a kiss on my cheek then left just as quickly as she came. I looked at Alfonso and he looked at me and we knew it was time to go. We left the party-goers behind, walked through the kitchen, past Warren and Paul and Fred who were playing another furious game of Quarters, the three arguing over the nuances of the game rules, past a couple making out on the sectional couch to the slinky sounds of Parliament-Funkadelic, out the front door then out into the street. We walked along the side of the street, hugging the curb, the small box tucked under my arm like a football. As we walked, searching for the place where I left my Civic, some headlights appeared in front of us down the street, the shape and color of an older model American car. We didn't think much of it until its engine roared and the car began approaching us. As it came close, it turned toward us and wobbled on its tires, rubber screeching across the asphalt. A husky arm extended out the side window, as if it was going to grab us, but it swatted at the box under my arm, sending it tumbling through the air and down in front of the car. And in a split second, the car ran over the box, the ream of paper inside exploding into hundreds of flipping sheets and cardboard shrapnel and dust. Some of the papers scattered in Warren's yard but the majority swirled in the car's smoky wake, following the car in a desperate attempt to coalesce before breaking my heart. I stood there in the middle of the street, watching what I only imagined was Levonne's car vanish into the darkness as months and months of my hard work floated and darted and tumbled into oblivion. I was flabbergasted.

"Oh shit!" Alfonso said.

Yep. Shit.

15. A Life Changer

On the counter in my kitchen, Mr. Whiskers inspected the frozen trays of Italian food, sniffing their frosty sides, then sliding the moisture off his nose with his paw. We had collected quite a bit of food from the P.W. and now it was time to get rid of it--the existence of this damning evidence would be lethal to our state of employment, for sure. Alfonso sat on the couch, talking on the phone to Sarah--the big dufus twirling the phone cord around his forefinger like a 16 year old girl preening on her bed--explaining to her that we had a surprise and that we wanted to stop by and bring her and Arthur some lunch. From what I could tell from Alfonso's demeanor and by what he was saying to her, it seemed she was pleased about that proposition.

But in the midst of what I was doing in the kitchen, all I could think about was my novel, blown to smithereens under the wheel of Levonne's car the night before. I imagined the papers scattered across the Hill Country on the outskirts of Warren's property, squirrels making nests with pages of my literature, birds shredding the soliloquies of my characters and stuffing them between twigs and leaves, and other various forest creatures whizzing and shitting on the rest of the loose pages of my literary dreams. It was pretty goddamn depressing, if you asked me. I started to realize that if I was going to follow my dream of becoming a writer, then I was going to have to be a little more protective of my dream and not do stupid things like give the entire first draft to a girl I was crushing on, in an ill-advised attempt to impress her. I didn't imagine Kurt Vonnegut ever doing such a thing to impress a girl (not that I know of, but who knows).

Fortunately, I had the first draft stored electronically on floppy disks, saved in pieces on various, 3 1/2-inch colored ones of the Memorex variety, labeled in pen or pencil or even crayon. The problem was, I was terrible at organizing all the various pieces of my novel; the compilation of the printed pages was my only organizational method. I knew there was going to be a few weeks' worth of sleuthing to restore a printed copy of my novel. I wasn't looking forward to that bullshit.

After a few more minutes of chit-chatting on the phone, Alfonso hung up then stood up from the couch and lurched over next to the bar in front of the kitchen. He inspected the food on the counter, his chin propped up by his arm, then said, "Sarah is cool with us stopping by for lunch."

"Yeah?" I said, closing the refrigerator after pulling out the last tray of food. The fridge was empty except for a 16oz can of Lone Star beer and a bottle of generic ketchup, both in the door next to each other like two strangers waiting for a commuter train at a deserted station. "We have a lot of food. Is it weird that we're taking them all this food?"

"Nah, they'll love it. It's the charitable thing to do."

"You think so?"

"Fuck yeah! Who wouldn't want a ton of free food?"

"I guess so." I was worried that it would seem very suspicious but maybe Alfonso was right, maybe it was the nice thing to do. Before I could ponder it too long, we heard the toilet flush in the bathroom and beautiful Laura Ann came into the kitchen, wearing a rumpled sweat shirt with holes in it and ragged jeans, a look of curiosity on her face.

"Did I miss something?" she said.

"Nah," I said. "Let's load up the car."

The three of us loaded up the trunk of my Civic with fifteen trays of food and, after petting Mr. Whiskers and locking the door to my apartment, we were off to Sarah's house. On the ride there, we listened to Ice-T's *6 in the Mornin'*. Alfonso and I knew all of the words: *6 in the mornin' police at my door / Fresh Adidas squeak across the bathroom floor*. It was a song about a street hustler who narrowly escapes being arrested by the police and I couldn't help but see the irony in it. Were we criminals, too? Or were we like Robin Hood, just assisting in the redistribution of things? I didn't know. But, for the first time in my young life, I felt a rush of adrenaline I had never felt before and I liked it. It felt like anything could happen. Laura Ann got a kick out of the fact that a small white guy and a big Mexican guy in a beat-up Honda Civic were rapping along to a gangster rap song. She eventually joined in, rapping 'Word!' in unison with us and Ice-T when he was ready to continue his story after the break from the DJ.

It didn't take long to get to Sarah's house and we found a place to park out front. The three of us unloaded the trunk, carrying a few trays each but leaving some behind, and we made our way to the door. Sarah must have been on the lookout cause she opened it before we could ring the doorbell.

"Well, well, if it isn't a welcome sight for my sore, little, old eyes. What do you have there?" she said, opening the door wider and motioning for us to come in. "And who is this pretty, young thing?"

"Hi Sarah!" I said, leaning over so she could kiss my cheek. "This is Laura Ann. She works with us at Pasta Warehouse." After kissing my cheek then motioning to do the same for Alfonso, she opened her arms wide and embraced Laura Ann, hugging her tightly.

"A friend of these boys' is a friend of mine," Sarah said, placing her hand on Sarah's cheek. "My, you are a *pretty* girl."

"Thanks!" Laura Ann said, blushing. "That's very sweet of you to say. We brought you some food."

"I see that. Come, please, to the kitchen." We followed little old Sarah into the kitchen and we placed some trays on the counter, some in the oven. Alfonso turned it on then bolted out of the kitchen back to my Civic for more. I followed him, leaving Laura Ann there for Sarah to fawn over.

Outside, Alfonso was leaning on my car, smoking a cigarette, looking proud. I stood next to him, bumming a smoke. He lit one and handed it to me, then said, "Fuck Levonne!"

"Yeah, fuck Levonne. What a jerk."

"He's Dan's little *bitch*."

"Those two are prolly jerking each other off right now."

"Or giving the good ol' reach-around!" We both got a good laugh out of that one. Alfonso nudged me with his elbow and motioned for us to continue. "Come on, let's take in the rest."

"Yeah."

We each picked up three trays and waddled to the front door. Before stepping inside, I spit my cigarette on the ground and crushed it with my foot. Alfonso, lazy and carefree, spit his cigarette into some bushes to the side of the front porch.

"Hey, man! Be nice," I said, entering the house carefully.

"What did I do?" he said, following me inside, pleading mock innocence.

"The last thing we need is for your dumb ass to burn the house down."

"The house isn't going to *burn down*," he said, sarcastically. He pronounced that with such sass that I could practically hear his eyes rolling into the back of his head.

Back in the kitchen, Sarah marveled at her unexpected fortune. She seemed genuinely surprised and a little flustered at the sheer amount of food being delivered to her kitchen. Alfonso and I moved things around in her freezer and refrigerator to make room for the extra trays that we obviously couldn't eat at that moment for lunch. It was kind of difficult to do; her refrigerator was already pretty full. One thing was for certain--despite our charitable donation, Sarah wasn't in need of anything. Laura Ann was sitting at the table with Arthur, who magically appeared while we were out front unloading the car. He was fawning over her beauty too, something that Laura Ann didn't seem to mind at all--a serene smile perched on her face like I had never seen before.

Sarah patted me and Alfonso on our backs, as if others doing things in her kitchen made her uncomfortable, and she said, "Please, please have a seat. Relax. Pour yourself a drink."

Alfonso and I agreed and sat down. The familiar setup of a bottle of rum and small glasses sat configured in an inviting pattern in the middle of the table, the glasses sparkling in the sunlight like a constellation of stars. The only thing absent this time was the ashtray and the one-hitter. Nonetheless, Arthur had already poured himself and Laura Ann each a glass of rum as he gently grilled her about where she was from, how she found herself in Austin, what she was doing working at a shitty place like Pasta Warehouse when she could be a fashion model, and so on and so forth. When we interrupted his interrogation by extending our hands for a shake, it was like he snapped out of a trance. He was mesmerized by Laura Ann and I understood why. She was a knock-out.

"How are you, boys?" Arthur said, crushing our hands with his wrinkly yet meaty hand. We both said we were fine besides the crushed hands. "Did you two kidnap this beautiful, young lady? Surely, she didn't tag along with you two knuckleheads of her own free will."

"Arthur!" Sarah said, snapping at him. "Be nice to our guests." She poured us some rum while patting our shoulders, as if to soothe our souls.

"But *I am* being nice," he said, then winking at Laura Ann. She giggled.

Sarah took a seat with the rest of us then pulled a sixth chair up to the table, then said, "I'm so glad you stopped by. I hope you don't mind but Arthur and I were expecting another neighbor to visit with us. His name is Gene and he lives on the other side of my house."

"But I have the *nicer* lawn," Arthur said, winking at Laura Ann again. He was really laying it on thick now, as if there wasn't a 50 or 60 some-odd year age difference between he and Laura Ann. But for whatever reason, Laura Ann didn't seem too bothered by it.

"All of you have nice yards," Alfonso said, being diplomatic.

"Bullshit! Mine is much nicer. I pay good money to those Beaners to make my lawn look that nice. I should enter it into a competition, it's that nice."

"Anyway," Sarah said, dismissing Arthur's insistent tone. "Gene is an interesting fellow. He's a retired chiropractor originally from Dallas. He had a practice in downtown Dallas for 30 years. He was an acquaintance to Lee Harvey Oswald, if you can believe that, of all the people in the world. He has some crazy stories to tell."

"You mean, he's just *crazy*!" Arthur said, laughing.

"Oh, hush, you old fart. Sorry I keep getting rudely interrupted." She gave a look to Arthur that would have melted steel. He quickly stopped laughing. Sarah then smiled and said, "What's the special occasion? Why all the food?"

Me and Laura Ann and Alfonso looked at each other for a cue of some kind but Alfonso ran with it and said, "We just wanted to do something nice for you. We just wanted to make you feel special."

"I agree," I said. Laura Ann nodded too. "And to be honest, it's been nice getting to know you. None of us have family in town. I think I speak for me and Alfonso when I say that you're kind of like our new family now."

"Yup," said Alfonso, crossing his arms and easing into his chair, as if we were going to stay for a while.

"Well, how thoughtful," Sarah said, obviously taken by what we had to say. She seemed genuinely pleased and touched. "And you too, sweetheart," she said, touching Laura Ann's arm. "That was thoughtful of *all* of you. As soon as Gene gets here, then we can all have a nice meal together and--" The doorbell suddenly sang a reggae tune. "And that must be him now."

Sarah got up to answer the door and while she was gone, Alfonso filled all of our glasses with rum and setup a new one for Gene, someone I was sure was just as interesting and charismatic and friendly as Sarah and Arthur and who, I imagined, had some very interesting stories to tell. Arthur didn't seem to think so. His enthusiasm for Gene's arrival was less than Sarah's, his disappointment hung on his face like a kid staring at an elementary school lunch tray, hungry in the gut but not excited to eat the lukewarm green beans from a can. He was dubious about Gene's stories and he didn't hesitate to admit it while Sarah was out of the kitchen.

"Gene is full of shit!" he said, punctuated with a mighty harrumph. "He didn't know Lee Harvey Oswald. That's just horse shit." Alfonso, Laura Ann, and I looked at each other but didn't know how to respond. As old as Arthur was, his stocky build and burly hands still looked like they could pulverize boulders. He had an intimidating presence, even for an old dude. Who were we to disagree with him? We didn't say a goddamn thing.

Even though Sarah was only gone for a few minutes, I was beginning to miss her already. I could hear her voice from the front of the house, cheery and breezy, then I heard footsteps coming toward the kitchen. A lighter pair of steps--obviously hers--and a heavier pair, ones I assumed were Gene's. When she got to the entrance to the kitchen, she had a despondent look on her face like she had just heard something grim and unexpected. I wasn't quite sure what to think.

"Well, we have a visitor everyone," she said, looking back then stepping aside. "I think you three may already know him."

A man I knew appeared next to sweet, old Sarah, his hulking frame no different than the last time I saw him at the P.W., his short-sleeved, button-down shirt partly untucked at his hip, his dirty khaki slacks slung low under his protruding gut, ink stains on his pants and on the pocket of his shirt: Dan the G.M. Sometimes, just sometimes, things in life are revealed to you in such ways that are either beautifully poetic or strangely perverse or plainly banal or whatever. This instance was none of those; it was a curve ball. It was a sucker punch. It was--thinking back now--a life changer. It was a new sign post in the history of me. After that, my life as I knew it was over.

SALUD!

***

Dan the G.M. took a seat where Gene was expected to sit upon his arrival. Sarah kindly offered him a drink of rum but, of course, he turned it down. What else would a tight-ass, corporate lackey who obviously hadn't been laid in a *very* long time do but refuse a cordial beverage from a kind stranger? Sarah sat down at the table looking pensive and uncomfortable and not herself. Arthur looked thoroughly confused and expressed it appropriately.

"Who the hell is this numb nuts?" he said, then taking a swig from his glass.

"My name is Dan Smith and I'm the General Manager at the Pasta Warehouse downtown."

"The Pasta Warehouse? Sarah?" Arthur said, looking at her. "Don't we eat food from there?"

"Yes, Arthur," she said. "We order food from there quite a bit."

"Are they the ones with the tasty bread?"

"Yes."

"Is this guy bringing us more bread?"

"No, I don't think so. Why don't we let him tell us why he's here?"

"Thank you, ma'am," Dan said, a smug smile on his goddamn smug face. It was rather strange to see him there in Sarah's house but I knew why he was there. I just didn't know how he found out we were there. "I'd be glad to tell you why I'm here. These three, young people work for me or, rather, they used to work for me. I came here to tell them they are no longer wanted as employees at Pasta Warehouse. I brought them their final paychecks and I wanted to tell them--in person--to never set foot in my restaurant ever again."

He reached around to his back pocket and pulled out three crumpled envelopes and tossed them on the table. I assumed they were our paychecks--me, Alfonso, and Laura Ann's checks--and like a deck of cards tossed in the air, an assorted array of information related to upcoming bills and rent and groceries and gas and stuff fell through my mind. I immediately knew that the amount of that last paycheck sitting there on the table wasn't going to last very long. He also unceremoniously set a restaurant check presenter on the table, a black padded one made of shiny black vinyl with the words "Thank You" embossed on the front in gold, fancy, script lettering--just like the ones we presented to the customers of the P.W. A bill protruded from the top of it.

"I'm leaving this bill with you for the food you have stolen from my restaurant. I hope you enjoyed the tasty cuisine that my kitchen staff prepared over the last few weeks. I take cash, checks, credit cards, debit cards, gift cards, and--for one time only--paychecks."

"Stolen food?" Sarah said, gasping. "Why, I don't know what you mean. I've paid for every order I have ever placed with your restaurant."

"That is true, ma'am, except for the one in your kitchen right now, the one I can smell warming up in your oven and the rest--I'm assuming--is in your refrigerator or freezer. These thieves took quite a bit of food from my restaurant. You couldn't possibly eat it all in one sitting."

An awkward silence settled in the kitchen, one that was stupefying and uncomfortable, and it was intermingled with the delicious smell of some type of Italian tomato-sauce dish warming in the oven. It was a strange environment for the truth, two worlds colliding, our low-paying place of employment and Sarah's comfortable place of retirement. Dan sat there with a sadistic smile on his face, knowing full-well that he caught us red-handed, probably with the information Levonne told him as well as my inability to follow directions and fill out the paperwork while supposedly dumping the food in the dumpster. Or the fact--something that was only clear to me at that moment--that the restaurant had security cameras everywhere but, like a dumb ass, conveniently forgot about while I was loading my car with trays of food. I was such an idiot and I knew I was an idiot. The three of us young servers sat in our chairs, deflated of our self-esteem, knowing also that Sarah reserved the right to judge us by what our former boss was telling her. But, for whatever reason (and I'm still not clear to this day why), she was not going to follow the script he was following or play the game he was playing. She just didn't give a shit.

"Well, sir. Dan, is it?" she said, standing up. She placed a hand on his shoulder. He nodded. "Whatever fanciful world you are living in, that is not the reality here. There is no stolen food here, only leftovers from orders I have gladly paid for in recent memory."

Dan shifted in his seat as if ready to jump up and confront her. "I'd like to look in your refridge--" he said before Arthur abruptly landed one of his meaty hands on Dan's shoulder and pressed him back down in his seat. Dan looked like he pissed his pants.

"You do not have permission to look in my refrigerator or to look anywhere else in my house. From this moment forward, you are not welcome here. If you have a warrant from the police, then by all means, look around. Otherwise, I'd like for you to leave this instant and never come back. I will be looking for another Italian restaurant to patron."

"But--" Dan said abruptly then Arthur grabbed him by the shirt collar and the waist of his pants. With the swiftness of a professional football player, Arthur pulled him from his seat and pushed him out of the kitchen, through the parlor, and roughly pushed him out of the front door. It happened so fast I couldn't believe my eyes. Alfonso and I jumped up after him and stood behind him in the front door, looking out on the front yard, Dan laying face-down in the lawn.

"Have a nice day, numb nuts!" Arthur said, wiping imaginary dust from his hands then straightening his shirt. A few strands of silver hair popped out of his meticulous haircut, waving in the air like seaweed bending in an undercurrent. He wasn't breaking a sweat.

"Dude," Alfonso said. "You're awesome!"

"I still got it," Arthur said, proud.

"Shit, I wouldn't mess with you," I said.

"You better not." Arthur winked at me then headed back to the kitchen.

I took a peek through some curtains at a window next to the door. Dan the G.M. limped back to his car. I could see someone sitting in the car waiting for him, a black dude, Levonne I suspected. I couldn't tell for sure but I was certain it was him. Alfonso looked out the window too and confirmed my suspicion.

"If Levonne had come in too, this place would have been a cluster fuck."

"Yeah," I said, closing the curtain.

We went back to the kitchen and sat back down at the table. Laura Ann was still there though noticeably upset. Arthur and Sarah were there too. Sarah had a concerned look on her face, as if she knew exactly what the three of us would have to endure in the coming weeks or months. Little did I know that I would never see Sarah or Arthur again after that day. If you would have told me that at that very moment, I would not have believed it. I liked her very much and in a weird way, thought of her in a matronly, grandmother way. She didn't have to stick up for us at all but she did, like something a mother or grandmother would do. It was very sweet. She poured each of us a drink.

"Well, I'm not sure what really happened here just now but I certainly have built up quite an appetite. Who's hungry?"

We all acknowledged that, yes, we were all very hungry. Alfonso made a toast about friends and we ate a very nice lunch together.

SALUD!

After we were finished, Alfonso, Laura Ann, and me said our goodbyes. We hugged Sarah and carefully shook Arthur's hand, who was still beaming. When Alfonso and Laura Ann headed out of the kitchen for my car, I lingered back. I reached in my back pocket and pulled out my wallet. I opened it and shuffled some things around--a condom, some scraps of paper with phone numbers on them, business cards, and family photos--eventually pulling out a shriveled and ratty $100 bill. I looked at the bill for a second--knowing full-well that I sure could use $100 in my immediate future--then I unceremoniously handed it to Arthur.

"What's this for?" he said, surprised, taking the bill.

"I don't know," I said. "For helping us, I guess."

Sarah smiled at me then I waved goodbye and left.

16. The Cicada and Ruminations about Childhood Dreams

Absolutely everything Alfonso owned fit into one duffle bag and one trash bag. Everything. I walked him out to his car and watched him throw the bags into his trunk. That morning, he had cashed his last paycheck and used the money to have his tires rotated and aired up, got an oil change for $19.99 with a coupon I had been saving from my junk mail, and filled his car with gas. His Accord was still a piece of shit but it was in good enough shape to get him to his mother's house in Rosenberg, Texas--about a three hour drive away, outside of Houston. He didn't want to go to his mother's house but he didn't have a choice. He had no money, no prospects for making money in the immediate future, and he wasn't any help to me. He had decided on a whim to drive back home and start over. I was sad to see him go. He was like a brother to me: my big, Mexican brother.

"Call me when you get there," I said, extending my fist. He tapped it with his fist.

"Mos def," he said. "It was fun. Thanks for letting me stay at your pad."

"No problem."

"Sorry I can't help you with the rent."

"Don't worry about it."

"What are you going to do?" he said, twirling his car keys around his index finger.

"Look for a job I guess. I'm not going to my parents' house in San Antonio. My home is here in Austin."

"I bet you could get a job at that Greek place you used to work at if you went home."

"Nah. I don't know if I want to work in another restaurant."

"Oh yeah?" he said, curious. "Where are you going to work then? At a fancy corporation? Be a big wig? CEO?"

"Maybe," I said, a smirk on my face.

We both laughed.

"Later," he said. He sat in his junky Accord--covered in bird shit and dried leaves and pollen and tar--and started the engine. The car farted black smoke and water droplets out the tail pipe. He slammed the door closed, rolled down the window, cranked his stereo--the squeal and boom-bap of Ice Cube introducing NWA on *Straight Outta Compton* crackling the stereo speakers--and he tore off. His car rattled and creaked down the incline to the parking lot exit. He squealed the tires as he drove away on his desperate trip back to where he grew up, his arm extending out the driver-side window, waving goodbye.

I stood in the parking lot for a few minutes after he was gone until I remembered that I might have left the door to my apartment open. I didn't want Mr. Whiskers to get out so I made my way back to my place. I didn't leave the door open.

When I went inside, Mr. Whiskers was waiting for me on the couch. Alfonso's stuff was gone and my small apartment was a little roomier without him there. I sat on the couch and my cat jumped into my lap, demanding I scratch his head. So I did. I debated putting my Christmas tree up but I wasn't in the mood.

BAH, HUMBUG!

***

Instead of look for a new job, I decided to go over to Laura Ann's place to see how she was doing and to see if she wanted to hang out with me sometime. I called her but when her roommate Constance answered the phone, she said Laura Ann was out running errands and to call back later. When I asked her for directions to her apartment, she reluctantly gave them to me.

"She's kinda upset right now," she said, in a tone of voice that was both concerned and whimsical. "If you do come by, please be supportive."

"OK. Thanks. "

I felt that even though her roommate was being kind of nosey, that was some pretty solid advice she gave me. I drove to the nearest grocery store to cash my last paycheck and to buy some flowers and maybe some other gift to give to Laura Ann when I finally saw her. I felt really, really bad about the three of us losing our jobs like that. It was shitty. But for reasons unknown, I wasn't too worried about it, or what was going to happen to me, or what may happen to Laura Ann, or if Alfonso would even make the trek home. I think, in the far recesses of my mind, I could have theoretically gone home if I needed to, just like Alfonso did. San Antonio wasn't too far away (only an hour and a half) and my parents would allow me to crash on the couch for a short while (my old bedroom was now a guest room and it felt weird to be in there) if I begged enough. But I had no idea what Laura Ann would do. In fact, I didn't really know her very well, at all, actually. I just hoped she was doing OK.

At the grocery store, I bought some yellow and white daisies, a humongous Hershey milk chocolate candy bar, and stuffed the rest of the cash from my paycheck in my pocket. Oh yeah, I also bought a travel-sized bottle of mouthwash cause you can't go visiting a girl to ask her to hang out if you have bad breath. As I followed the directions to her apartment that her roommate gave me, I poured the mouthwash into my mouth, swished it around, then spit it out my window while I drove. The green liquid splattered across the side of my Honda Civic.

When I arrived at her apartment complex and found her place, I was surprised when she answered the door.

"You're here?" I said. "Your roommate said you were out on errands."

"She always says that. Do you want to come in?"

"Yes," I said, handing her the daisies. She smiled then smelled them. I followed her into the apartment.

Their place was way bigger and nicer than mine with a living room and a dining room and a large kitchen with two separate hallways leading to other places, probably bedrooms. Con was sitting on a large couch watching soap operas. She waved to me when we came in. Laura Ann placed the daisies in a vase on the bar next to the kitchen then turned to me.

"She and her boyfriend got back together," she said, looking at the chocolate bar in my hand.

"It's for you," I said. She smiled.

"Want to sit with me on the balcony?"

I nodded and I followed her outside.

Their balcony looked over a massive swimming pool that was completely empty. Still, it was an impressive view. There were two patio chairs with a small glass-top table in-between them on the balcony. We sat down and I handed the chocolate bar to Laura Ann. She indicated to me that she wanted a cigarette so I fished in my pocket for my pack. We each lit up, smoked, and ate the chocolate bar.

"When you were little," she said, nibbling on a piece of chocolate then taking a drag from her cigarette. "What did you want to be when you grew up?"

"I don't know. I liked to draw, tell stories, read about space missions, and the ancient Egyptians. I don't remember anything that stood out as something I wanted to do when I grew up."

"I wanted to be a ballerina," she said, standing up from her chair, holding the metal railing at the edge of the balcony, and assuming a stance that only a trained ballerina could make. She lifted herself up on her toes quickly then her feet went flat again. "It's difficult to pointe without the right shoes."

"I bet."

"It's not good to smoke either if you want to do ballet," she said. We both laughed then smoked some more. She sat down next to me, extended her hand, and I held it gently.

"Are you going to look for another restaurant gig?"

She took a deep drag from her cigarette and shook her head, then said, "No, I called my sister. She lives out by the lake with her husband and baby. They said I could stay there rent-free if I would be their nanny for a while til I figure things out. They'll let me eat whatever I want and pay me a small salary. My niece is super cute. Seems like a good idea right now."

"Yeah," I said, taking a drag then looking at the cement floor of the balcony. A cicada exoskeleton was lying down on the cement, its lifeless shell split open at the top and missing a couple of legs, the shell left behind by the adult cicada looking to start a new life. "Sounds like a good gig."

"It's not fair for me to stay here with Con without helping pay for rent and bills."

"I understand. Alfonso went home to Rosenberg to his mom's."

"No shit?"

"Yeah, he left this morning."

"Are you going to be all right?" she said. "Do you have another job lined up?"

"No. I don't know what I'm going to do yet."

"You're still going to write, aren't you?"

"Yeah."

"Good," she said, squeezing my hand. "Don't give up on your dream."

"I won't. Laura Ann?" I said, looking at the cicada exoskeleton, its shape turning to a blur the longer I stared at it. "Do you want to hang out with me sometime? After we get things figured out?" I turned to look at her. Her eyes looked like they welled up with tears but I couldn't really tell cause she looked away so fast.

"Maybe. We'll see. I don't know what's going to happen."

"OK," I said, still holding her hand.

We looked out across the sparkling pool, still empty except for a lone figure on the other side of it, a lanky employee wearing a bright blue shirt, baggy khaki shorts, and white sneakers with a pool skimmer in his hands. He approached the pool and dipped the skimmer in the water, removing a single, brown leaf. He tossed the leaf into a grassy area beyond the cement walkway and then disappeared back into the club house. Laura Ann turned to me.

"Want to go swimming?" she said, a mischievous smile on her beautiful face.

"I don't have a bathing suit," I said, sheepishly.

"I have something you can wear and some beer in the fridge. Want to?"

"Fuck yes!"

Inside her apartment, she gave me some trunks to put on and I quickly did, right in front of her. She did the same, putting on a red, one-piece bathing suit, one like lifeguards wear at community swimming pools. The quick flashes of our naked bodies not impeding our wardrobe change. She grabbed four beers from the refrigerator and we made our way down to the pool. With the beers in her hand, she immediately jumped in the pool, submerged quickly then popping up and trudging through the water. I followed her in and we swam across to some steps on the other side. We sat there, in the water on the steps, drinking beer, talking, laughing, and telling stories well into the night.

***

It had been a few days since being "let go" from the P.W. and I hadn't once picked up a classified section of the newspaper or made any effort at all to look for a job or ask around to see if any of my friends had any leads or tips for finding a new job. Except for saying goodbye to Alfonso and visiting Laura Ann, I mostly just stayed in my apartment with Mr. Whiskers. I tried to write some stories but the loss of the only printed copy of my manuscript as well as the absence of my roommate and the lack of prospects for Laura Ann to be my girlfriend left me feeling blue and unmotivated. I just didn't know what to do with myself. I laid on the couch, one leg on and one leg bent over the side, with Mr. Whiskers laying on my stomach, his puss face looking content and mellow from my constant petting. He didn't seem worried at all that his master was unemployed. But rather than have him worry, I didn't talk to him about my sudden state of unemployment at all. It was for the best. I had a large cache of ramen noodles in a variety of flavors for myself as well as jumbo-sized bag of generic, crunchy cat food for my sole companion. As far as I was concerned, we were set--for a little while. I kissed him on his forehead then tossed him to the floor. I got up and shuffled to the kitchen. Inside the fridge was the last can of beer, a Lone Star 16oz tall boy. I pulled it away from its strange companion, the bottle of generic ketchup, popped the top, and took a swig.

Then my phone rang. I was expecting a call from my parents and I hoped it was them. I sat back on the couch--placing my beer can on a paper coaster and propping my feet up on the coffee table--and answered the phone.

"Hello?" I said, trying to sound tired and worn out but not sick. I didn't want to blow it.

"Seff? Are you OK? I got your message," said my mother. She sounded genuinely concerned. "You *sound* horrible. Are you eating good food?"

"I'm fine and yes I'm eating."

"You're not eating that crap from the Pasta Warehouse, are you? That food is filled with carbohydrates and fat and cholesterol and who knows what else. Preservatives!"

"I haven't been eating it lately, mom," I said. I lied.

"Good. You need to eat healthy. Are you still smoking?"

"No, I quit," I said. I lied again.

"Good. You don't need cancer sticks in your life."

"Yeah."

"Do you want to speak to your father?" she said. I could hear her place her hand over the phone handset and call for my dad but he didn't respond. "I can get him if you want?"

"No, that's OK, mom. Listen, I'm in a little bit of a jam. Can I borrow a few hundred dollars?"

"A few hundred dollars? For heaven's sake. What happened, Seff?"

"I lost my job. I need money for rent."

"You lost your job? Have you been looking for another job?"

"Yes, mother. I have some good leads." I continued to lie.

"Maybe you should find a normal job, an office job. Have you tried a temp agency?"

"Yes. They're looking for me." Nobody was looking for jobs for me.

"How about a headhunter?"

"What's a headhunter?"

"That's an agency that looks for jobs for people. You're smart. They could find you a job."

"I'll look into it."

"Seff, my dear?"

"Yes, mom?"

"Your father would be very upset if he knew you were calling and asking us for money. We did help you for a few months after you graduated from college by paying your rent and bills and buying you some groceries."

"I know and I appreciated it very much. I promise this will be the last time I call you about borrowing money." Another bald-faced lie. I was on a roll.

"You promise?"

"Yes, mommy." I knew if I called her *mommy* that it would work and it did. I still had it.

"OK. Do you want me to mail you a check? Or deposit it in your bank account?"

"Depositing it is good."

"And when will you pay me back?"

"ASAP!"

"Sounds good, dear. I'll go to the bank first thing in the morning. OK?"

"Thanks, mom."

"Oh, and Seff?"

"Yes?"

"Be good. I love you."

"I love you, too."

She hung up the phone and I held the phone handset for a good 20 seconds, the sound of the disconnect signal putting me into a trance. I knew I was fortunate to be able to make a phone call like that and I felt any last bits of stress in me dissipate into thin air. I put the handset on the phone cradle and took another swig from my beer. I thought about walking over to the GODDAMN, buying a newspaper, and looking for a new job. But, instead, I found a VHS copy of Eddie Murphy's *Delirious* and watched it, drank the last of my beer, pet Mr. Whiskers some more, then fell asleep on my couch--a finer evening I couldn't have asked for.

SALUD!

About the Author

Scott Semegran lives in Austin, Texas with his wife, four kids, two cats, and a dog. He graduated from the University of Texas at Austin with a degree in English. He is a writer and a cartoonist. He can also bend metal with his mind and run really fast, if chased by a pack of wolves. His comic strips have appeared in the following newspapers: The Austin Student, The Funny Times, The Austin American-Statesman, Rocky Mountain Bullhorn, Seven Days, The University of Texas at Dallas Mercury, and The North Austin Bee. Books by Scott Semegran include Sammie & Budgie, Boys, The Meteoric Rise of Simon Burchwood, The Spectacular Simon Burchwood, Modicum, Mr. Grieves and more. He is a Kindle bestselling author.

Books by Scott Semegran

If you enjoyed this book then check out the novel **The Meteoric Rise of Simon Burchwood** by Scott Semegran. On his way to New York to celebrate his impending literary success, Simon Burchwood is the prototypical American careerist. But a quick detour to Montgomery, Alabama to visit a childhood friend sends Simon on a bizarre journey, challenging his hopes and dreams of becoming a famous writer. **The Meteoric Rise of Simon Burchwood** is a character study that delves into the psyche of a man who desperately tries to redefine himself.

Is Simon pompous? Yes. A jerk? Yes. Will you like him? Absolutely! "The book is told entirely from Simon's viewpoint. Simon is not a very likeable guy; as a matter of fact, he is a self-centered, pompous jerk. But for some reason, it's pretty fun to be inside his head, mainly because he is an inadvertent, oblivious jerk... you will learn Simon's views on smoking, cleanliness and going to the bathroom, just to name a few. There were times that I laughed out loud... A very good novel that was humorous throughout." -- 4 1/2 Stars / *Red Adept Reviews*

The Meteoric Rise of Simon Burchwood was selected as one of the "5 Best Summer Indie Beach Reads" by the editors of *IndieReader*. Their verdict: "An ambitious, enjoyable read with a superb ending that changed my interpretation of the entire text."

"A clever and surprising twist… cutting observations of the writerly demeanor." -- *Kirkus Reviews*

Buy it today!

***

Want more Simon Burchwood? Then get the next novel **The Spectacular Simon Burchwood**. Recently divorced and his writing career in shambles, Simon Burchwood's life is a complete disaster. He reluctantly finds work as a computer support technician and resigns that his career as the next great American novelist will never come to fruition. When he learns that his ex-wife abruptly moves to Dallas with his children, he embarks on a crazy road trip with a nerdy coworker and a hitchhiking punk rock girl and discovers the inspiration he desperately needs for his new literary masterpiece. Take another trip with the one and only Simon Burchwood.

Praise for **The Spectacular Simon Burchwood**:

"The author is quite funny and some of the quips are great. Simon can be hilarious and great to read about in his recaps and memories." -- 3 Stars / *So Many Books, So Little Time*

"Simon is starting to understand something, and his luck literally changes. Semegran handles this quite deftly; even though Simon keeps warbling his "It's true!" declarations at a great rate, the reader does not tire of them, because, well, some of them ARE true, and we see the progress he is making in getting a grasp of what life is about, albeit in his own ham-fisted way." -- 4 Stars / *The New Podler Review of Books*

Buy it today!

***

If you enjoyed this book then check out **MODICUM**, a collection of short stories, musings, and cartoons by writer / cartoonist Scott Semegran. The book explores such themes as suicide, parenting, religion, masculinity, the apocalypse, and, most importantly, erections. It's guaranteed to make you laugh, cry, and pee your pants (hopefully, not at the same time).

Praise for **MODICUM**:

"Funny, sweet, dark, and sad, Scott Semegran's comics and short stories create a wholly convincing world of love, loss, and fear. His light touch with heavy subjects is a gift, and his forays into silliness are a delight. I can't tell if his kids should read it as soon as possible, or never." - Emily Flake, cartoonist and author of *LuLu Eightball*

"Hilarious, poignant, twisted... and those are just the stories. Scott Semegran's cartoons bring an added one-two visceral punch to a powerful collection of work." - Davy Rothbart, author of *The Lone Surfer of Montana, Kansas* and publisher of *FOUND Magazine*

Get it today!

***

Mr. Grieves started as a poke at human nature through the use of talking, narcissistic animals. It has evolved into a full-on assault to your funny bone. Where else will you find rats fighting over cubicles, camels worrying about aging, a parrot talking to aliens, and a lonely water snail longing for a friend? Welcome to the world of **Mr. Grieves**!

Praise for **Mr. Grieves**:

"An animal or plant — or maybe even an ovum — talks. Sometimes to itself, but more often to another of its kind. The idea is simple, but the execution is smart and almost always funny in Scott Semegran's collection of 140 four-panel comics drawn between 2004 and 2008, **Mr. Grieves**." -- Reviewed for *IndieReader* by Andrew Stout

Get it today!

***

From Kindle bestselling writer and cartoonist Scott Semegran, **Sammie & Budgie** is a quirky, mystical tale of a self-doubting IT nerd and his young son, who possesses the gift of foresight. The boy's special ability propels his family on a road trip to visit his ailing grandfather, a prickly man who left an indelible stamp on the father and son. The three are connected through more than genetics, their lives intertwined through dreams, imagination, and longing.

Simon works as a network administrator for a state government agency, a consolation after a promising career as a novelist flounders. He finds himself a single parent of two small children following the mysterious death of his adulterous wife. From the ashes of his failed marriage emerges a tight-knit family of three: a creative, special needs son, a hyperactive, butt-kicking daughter, and the caring, sensitive father. But when his son's special ability reveals itself, Simon struggles to keep his little family together in the face of adversity and uncertainty.

Sammie is a creative third-grader that draws adventures in his sketchbook with his imaginary friend, Budgie, a parakeet that protects him from the monsters inhabiting his dreams. Sammie is also a special needs child but is special in more ways than one. He can see the future. Sammie seemingly can predict events both mundane and catastrophic in equal measure. But when he envisions the suffering of his grandfather, the family embarks on a road trip to San Antonio with the nanny to visit the ailing patriarch.

Sammie & Budgie is an illustrated novel brought to you from the quirky mind of writer and cartoonist Scott Semegran. The novel explores the bond between a caring father and his children, one affected by his own thorny relationship with his surly father, and the connection he has with his sweet son is thicker than blood, going to the place where dreams are conceived and realized.

Praise for **Sammie & Budgie**:

"A quirky, mystical tale of a self-doubting IT nerd and his young son, who possesses the gift of foresight. Engaging and fun, with wonderfully crafted characters." –Derf Backderf, bestselling creator of the graphic novel *My Friend Dahmer*

"**Sammie & Budgie** is instantly absorbing, its affable narrator hooking you with wit and whimsy, then reeling you into the boat, where larger revelations await. Scott Semegran is a lively, vivid storyteller, and this book will delight readers of all ages, while leaving them with plenty to ponder about their own lives. I loved this book!" -Davy Rothbart, author of *My Heart is an Idiot*, creator of *Found Magazine*, and contributor to public radio's *This American Life*

"Scott Semegran's loose charm and conversational style brings his shaggy narrator to vivid life in this story of a loving, if imperfect father and his maybe-psychic son. A sweet story about an extraordinary everyday family, **Sammie & Budgie** will find its way into your heart, and stay there." -Emily Flake, *New Yorker* cartoonist, author of *Mama Tried: Dispatches from the Seamy Underbelly of Modern Parenting*, and creator of *Lulu Eightball*

***

Find Scott Semegran Online:
https://www.scottsemegran.com
https://www.goodreads.com/scottsemegran
https://www.twitter.com/scottsemegran
https://www.facebook.com/scottsemegran.writer
https://www.instagram.com/scott_semegran

Mutt Press:
http://www.muttpress.com

Made in the USA
San Bernardino, CA
12 September 2017